# SEVENS & SIXES

## THE CORRIDOR OF DOORS TRILOGY - BOOK TWO

B & T PECILE

Suite 300 - 990 Fort St
Victoria, BC, V8V 3K2
Canada

www.friesenpress.com


First Edition — 2016



ISBN
978-1-4602-8809-2 (Hardcover)
978-1-4602-8810-8 (Paperback)
978-1-4602-8811-5 (eBook)

*1. FICTION, FANTASY*

Distributed to the trade by The Ingram Book Company

# Table of Contents

IMAGINE THIS SCENE:

*"You can't give Frank a copy of the draft... not yet, it's too early. We need to work on The Book some more."*

*Bruno didn't listen.* Frank Sinko, thank you for reading an early draft and for our eclectic conversations. A definite pleasure.

†

And can you imagine this?

*You're in Rome, the Eternal City, where there are so many beautiful and amazing places to see, and Tina wants to walk around the outside of the Vatican (the entire circumference) on a hot and sweltering day.*

Filomena D'Andrea, thank you for walking around the Vatican Walls with me, and thank you for so many other things that cannot be counted… O (not oh but the Italian O) like 464 steps, 39 degrees Celsius, and 2,000+ kilometers in a white Fiat.

For-thy tak herte, and thenk, right as a knight,
Thourgh love is broken alday every lawe.
Kyth now sumwhat thy corage and thy might,
Have mercy on thy-self, for any awe.
Lat not this wrecched wo thin herte gnawe,
But manly set the world on sixe and sevene;

~ 617- 622, Book IV *Troilus and Criseyde*
Geoffrey Chaucer (1343-1400)

# Prologue

In the Sahara Desert, a lone Bedouin stood silent and still. His senses alert, he sensed something had changed, but his eyes noted nothing unusual. He tilted his chin curiously to the side and took a deep breath through his nose. The wind picked up and he watched the sand swirl at his feet.

Perplexed, he watched everything still. Granules of sand, picked up by the wind, remained suspended in the air, and then—as if time caught up with itself—dropped back to the earth. And the ground started to shake.

Earthquake, one would assume, but the cause of the tremors had nothing to do with two plates colliding. Perhaps it would be easier to believe so, for the alternative cannot in fact be explained by modern geo-sciences or physics. Scientists, as of yet, have no conclusive theories of how multidimensional layers of space and time are woven like a fabric or how it can be read, manipulated, and influenced—written, erased, and changed as easily as tearing a page from a book.

The air screamed in adamant protest, as if a heavy bomber had broken the sound barrier. The little moisture drawn from the arid air condensed into a white rotating cloud.

Had the Bedouin been closer to its epicenter, he surely would have been cast from his feet. Had it occurred several thousand years before, he may have bowed down in prayer believing that some kind of deity, a Jinn, was making its presence known. Would he have cowered or would he have been brave and turned his eyes to see?

A vague outline like a shadow appeared. It became denser and took form. The door, which was suspended in the air, opened. From the other side of time and place, flashes of light flooded the desert landscape... of a bridge and the red and yellows of a raging fire.

A figure landed on the sand and rolled down the steep embankment, coming to rest lying face up and staring at the sky. His sword, having been rent from his hand, stuck in the sand a few yards away.

Not too many seconds after his most timely arrival, the door imploded. The only testament that it had ever been was the crash of thunder that echoed.

He groaned.

Traveling through portals was never an easy feat, no matter how skilled one was. He had been to many worlds. His breath hard and quick, he struggled first to his knees and then lifted himself to his feet. He pulled his sword from the sand.

He started to climb. Reaching the crest of a dune, he looked out in all directions. To the west he saw darkness; to the east he saw the light of the approaching sunrise, giving the great sea of sand a surreal, all-alone feeling.

Crouching on his haunches, he grasped a fistful of sand and brought it to his face. Every world had its own unique qualities and aromas—volatile organic compounds that were unique to it. He knew he was where he needed to be. Sand trickled from his fingers like the sands of time.

He set his feet towards the north. An interesting smile played on his determined face.

"Khia," he said aloud, and wrapped the dark cloth around his head.

Soon their paths would cross again. Soon.

CHAPTER 1

# Vatican Walls

Khia Aleyne Ashworth went on the offensive. Gripping her kendo stick firmly with both hands, she attacked the four closing in. Twisting in the air, she kicked one in the ribs, knocking him to the ground, and then struck the second with such force and fury that the stick snapped in two.

Gasping for air, she could feel her blood flowing through her veins, her heart pounding hard, but she willed herself on. Launching herself forward, she rammed the third opponent with such vigor that he jerked backwards. His weapon clattered to the ground. Suddenly, strong arms wrapped themselves around her and she was dragged to the floor, kicking and screaming.

"Enough," shouted her martial arts instructor.

Khia lay on the floor, staring up at the ceiling. She had been so immersed in the fight, it took her a few seconds before she knew where she was.

"Well done!" The face of her Tibetan instructor hovered over her. Reaching out his hand, he pulled her effortlessly to her feet. "You most gifted student." The diminutive man's gentleness and light smile were at odds with the ferocity of his teaching methods.

"Khia," his voice echoed in the gymnasium, "you smart, always thinking." He tapped his forefinger to his temple. "You fast, must be faster. Need patience. Wait for right time to strike, and remember," he looked deep into her eyes, "it is in weakness you will find your strength."

"Yes Master Tsering." Khia bowed respectfully.

When she looked up, she was alone in the gymnasium.

†

Sister Clair guided Khia down the long corridor to the last door on the left. Her nun's habit flowing, she strode into the room and threw aside the curtains, bringing light. The room, painted in soft gray, was simple—a single bed, a worn Bible on the small bedside table, and an old crucifix nailed to the wall. The sparseness of the room was a harsh contrast to the beauty and grand architectural splendor of the Vatican, with its fine art and sculptures.

Darting across the room, Khia went over to Catherine and gave her a hug. "Do you feel well enough to go out today?" she asked.

For months Catherine had been convalescing. Hit by a high velocity bullet, she had come close to death's door—so close in fact that she had been given her Last Rites. Remarkably, she had pulled through, not only because of her strong will to survive, and the exceptional care that the doctors had provided, but perhaps assisted by some kind of divine intervention.

Sister Clair nodded in agreement with the question. "Yes." She turned towards them and smiled radiantly as the light from the window cast her in a halo of light. "Time in the garden will do you good. Get some color in your cheeks."

"Ma-mar-marvelous i-i-idea," said Brother Peccavi, as he appeared with the wheelchair.

In contrast to Sister Clair, Brother Peccavi was dark—dark hair, dark eyes, and olive skin—and his gait was awkward and clumsy, whereas Sister Clair glided into a room.

"Can I take her?" asked Khia, avoiding Brother Peccavi's eyes, so unlike Sister Clair's whose were a blue so light they were almost crystal clear.

Sister Clair nodded to Khia and said to Catherine, "Let's get you ready for your little outing."

"No need." Catherine slowly smiled at Sister Clair, but it wasn't a smile that reached her eyes until she looked at Brother Peccavi. "I'm ready."

Khia cringed as she watched Brother Peccavi reach over and help Catherine into her wheelchair.

Through a maze of paths, they reached an intricate wrought iron gate that led them to a garden. It was a peaceful place, an enclave within the Vatican walls.

Near a stone fountain, Khia caught her reflection in the water. It was like a silver mirror in the sunlight, and for a split second, she had the sense that she was in another world. She became aware of the fragrance of exotic flowers, the sounds of birds chirping, animals scurrying, and leaves falling—tumbling from the lightest touch of a breeze.

"Did you need something Brother Peccavi?" Catherine's voice was kind and patient.

Shuffling his feet, it seemed as if Brother Peccavi wanted to say something. "N-n-no," he stuttered. Not able to meet Catherine's gaze, he looked at his feet and walked away.

"Finally. I thought he'd never leave," sighed Khia. "He's so creepy."

"He's not so bad." Catherine looked at Khia and gently added, "Try to see what's on the inside."

"Yeah, I guess," replied Khia.

"Any news on McBride?" asked Catherine. She stepped out of her wheelchair and walked about, shaking off the stiffness that had settled into her legs.

Khia shook her head.

"We have to find him," said Catherine.

"I know. We will."

"We have to." Catherine's voice was strained. "I can't keep this going much longer. The doctors are suspicious."

Hearing footsteps on the path, Catherine quickly returned to her wheelchair.

"It's only Harold," said Khia.

"Harold," said Catherine, standing up again when she saw him, "have you found McBride?"

"And Norbert," added Khia.

"Mon, I'm starting to think they don't want to be found," said Harold. "You know how many people be locked up in here? So far I've found one mad monk, a rogue bishop, and two wannabe prophets. I tell you, the dregs of Christendom." A soft bird whistle alerted Harold. "Better get back in yo wheelchair… later ladies." He winked and disappeared just as quickly as he had arrived.

Concealed by a cluster of bushes, Catherine and Khia caught sight of two priests strolling through the garden—two black robed men absorbed in conversation. One was tall and the other was short and stout. They spoke in Italian and Khia listened carefully.

"You haven't heard?" said the tall one incredulously. "The princes of the Church have called a secret synod."

"There hasn't been one in ages," commented the other. "Will this decide the fate of our guests?"

"Most assuredly," the tall one said, nodding. "They say near the end that the pure and the fallen will create unholy alliances."

"Mother of God," responded the short one, making the sign of the cross. "So, you say they have called upon the Cardinal? The Nigerian Cardinal?"

*"Sì, sì,* he's been ordered to Rome."

"Because of the two in the Sanctuary?"

"Without doubt," affirmed the tall one.

"Do you know what this means?" asked the other, as their voices faded away.

Catherine smiled. She didn't care what it meant. She knew where they'd find McBride.

CHAPTER 2

# The Not-So-Swiss Swiss Guard

*I swear I will faithfully, loyally, and honourably serve the Supreme Pontiff and his legitimate successors, and also dedicate myself to them with all my strength, sacrificing if necessary also my life to defend them. I assume this same commitment with regard to the Sacred College of Cardinals whenever the See is vacant.*

~ Swiss Guard oath, read on May 6th of every year.

Khia ran across the square towards a young man in a Swiss Guard uniform. "Hi Jordan," she said, a little out of breath.

He had blond hair, an incredible smile, and she remembered everything about their first meeting.

"Hullo," he had said, in his Australian accent, "I'm your instructor against the Dark Arts." And then he had laughed, showing his perfect teeth. "Just kidding, but I can teach you a thing or two about how to swing a sharp weapon without inadvertently chopping your own head off."

"Hi Khia… Harold," said Jordan, bringing Khia back into the present moment.

*Harold!* Khia whirled around, having forgotten that he was there.

"I'm off to the mess. You two coming with me?" asked Jordan cheerfully.

"Yes," Khia replied quickly, and the three of them fell into step.

"Hey mon," Harold said to Jordan, "Been meaning to ask, what's an Aussie doing so far from home? An Australian Swiss Guard." Harold shook his head. "It don't make no sense."

"Blame me mum" said Jordan, his youthful smile contagious.

"Yo mum?" asked Harold disbelievingly.

"Yes, me mum. She's Australian. Her great great... great," Jordan stopped to count, "great granddad was an original convict." Jordan laughed and returned to his story. "Being a good Catholic girl, me mum goes on a pilgrimage to Rome. Then doesn't she meet a dashing Swiss Guard and falls in love." Jordan winked at Khia. "Can you believe that?"

"Yes." Khia sighed wistfully.

"I didn't ask for yo life story, mon," said Harold.

"Let him finish," said Khia.

"They got married and nine months later, to the day, I pop out in Switzerland." Jordan's tone shifted and became more serious, "But mate, life's no fairy tale. They never got their happy ever after. To make a long story short, me pop died, and me mum whisked me off to Australia. And that, me friend, is how I got my Australian accent," said Jordan.

"Now, how I got to be a Swiss Guard?" he continued. "Well, I'm glad you asked. A most interesting story, if I may say so me'self. When I turned sixteen, me mum drops this bomb and tells me she made a promise to God. Being her first born an' only son, she wanted me to become a priest."

Khia's eyes widened, she couldn't image Jordan as a priest.

"Didn't want to disappoint, but I couldn't be a priest... too much prayer for me taste. Mind you, I think I would've had a flare for the confessional. You have to have the right knack for handing out penance—just the right number of Hail Marys and Our Fathers—but the key," he emphasized playfully, "is to live in a really sinful city like Rio de Janeiro, right around the time of Carnival and just before Lent starts. Eh! Can you imagine that?"

"No," said Harold, unimpressed, looking around as they approached the mess hall.

"Mate," he said, turning to look directly at Harold, "knowing I had no vocation for the priesthood, I tried to be a Brother, but that didn't work out either—too much meditation. Couldn't take the vow of silence. Mind you, I did learn how to make some very good beer." He nudged Harold lightly with his elbow. "But one day it came to me. I was Swiss, single, and nineteen. It was like someone whispered in me ear—the Swiss Vatican Guard. So here I am, at your service." He bowed gallantly before Khia.

"I'll find us a table," said Harold.

"Give me a second," said Jordan, "I want to change into me civvies."

†

Shifting in the uncomfortable cafeteria chair, Khia checked the time again. What was taking Jordan so long? If he didn't get here soon, her lunch break would be over.

"Tonight," said Harold, "we gonna rendezvous. Catherine's anxious to find the Sanctuary..."

Khia had spotted Jordan, dressed in blue jeans and a pale yellow t-shirt, making his way towards their table. He looked like he should be heading to the beach.

"Khia?"

"Sorry Harold, did you say something?"

"Nah, nothing," muttered Harold, smiling inwardly.

"Hey Jordan, what took you so long?" asked Khia.

"I-I-I," he stuttered.

"Jordan, you okay?" asked Harold. "You look like you seen a ghost."

"I-I-I..."

"You, mon, are starting to sound like Brother Peccavi," said Harold.

"I s-s-saw..." Jordan stopped, swallowed hard, and leaned towards them. "I saw Dodger and Goula."

"Dodger and Goula!" exclaimed Khia at the mention of their old allies, whom they hadn't heard from since New York.

"Shhh, not so loud!" Jordan placed his hand on her arm and whispered, "They left you a message: 'You can't leave without The Book.'"

"What book?" asked Harold.

"They said Norbert and McBride would know."

Harold opened his mouth to say something, but Jordan raised his hand, "Wait, there's more." His whisper was barely audible. "*The Abraxis*—"

"The Abraxis?" repeated Harold. "How you spell that?"

"How should I know?" asked Jordan. "Like it sounds. Let me finish. The Abraxis will take you to the straits and narrows."

"You talk in mysteries," Harold said, with a hint of irritation. "Abraxis. What kind of name is that?"

"Could it be the name of The Book?" asked Khia.

Jordan shook his head. "No, I don't think so. Norbert and McBride will know."

"Yeah, but we haven't been able to find Norbert and McBride," she said.

"The straits and narrows?" Harold repeated. "Do you mean strait, as in s-t-r-a-i-t, or straight as in—"

"They didn't say," Jordan said, now sounding a little irritated himself.

"What's it mean?" asked Harold.

"Hey mate, how should I know? I'm a messenger, not a bloody walking encyclopedia."

†

That evening, long after prayers and the haunting echoes of chanting had faded away, Khia slowly opened the door to peek out. The coast was clear. Stepping out, she quietly made her way down the corridor, passing a dozen or so closed doors before reaching the end of the hallway, where Catherine and Harold waited.

"Yo late," said Harold.

"What took you so long?" asked Catherine.

"Brother Peccavi was prowling at my door again," Khia replied, exasperated.

"Don't that Brother ever sleep?" muttered Harold.

"Forget Brother Peccavi. Are you sure of the location of the Sanctuary?" Catherine asked urgently.

"Yes," replied Harold.

After walking up more stairs, around several corners, along another long dark hallway, and yet another set of stairs, they at last arrived at their destination.

Khia, Catherine, and Harold, three heads aligned like a totem pole, peeked around the corner. Two Vatican guards stood before a door. But it wasn't just any average door; it was made of metal, with spikes sticking out of it, and stood fifteen feet high.

"We have to get inside that room. What's the plan?" asked Harold. "Catherine? You do have a plan?"

Khia looked at Catherine. "The guards don't look like they can be distracted."

"That was yo plan?" asked Harold, his voice rising.

Catherine shrugged. "It's never failed before."

"We're in the Vatican!"

"And your point?"

Harold shook his head. "You do have a backup plan?"

"Uh," Khia interrupted, "someone's coming."

Jordan and Father Tobias appeared from the stairway.

"Jeez, this is like a pot luck party in spring," Harold said, through the side of his mouth.

"Hi Jordan," Khia smiled shyly.

"Father Tobias," said Catherine, making no attempt to hide her annoyance. "What an unexpected surprise!"

"Caught us in the act." Harold laughed, looking guilty. He figured there was absolutely no point in denying the obvious.

"We thought you might need our assistance." Father Tobias smiled kindly. "Wait here."

As they waited around the corner, Father Tobias, followed by Jordan, approached the guards. "I am here to see my clients," he said firmly. "Due to the delicate nature of this situation, I have brought my own guard."

The guards saluted and left their posts, leaving Jordan to stand watch.

Father Tobias motioned to Khia, Catherine, and Harold. "You have a few minutes of grace," he said, as the large door squeaked open. "The guards will check with their superiors. They will be back."

"Thank you, Father," said Catherine, as she entered the room.

"Well it's about time," said Norbert, looking up from the book he was reading. "Thought you guys might have gone on vacation or something."

McBride lay in bed, barely able to lift his hand in greeting. "S-s-Ca..." McBride tried to speak, but only unrecognizable sounds rolled off his tongue.

"He says, 'Catherine, you look nice as a nun,'" Norbert said, interpreting McBride's mumblings.

"What have they done to you?" Catherine asked, as she wiped the sweat from McBride's face with as much compassion as Veronica at the sixth station of the cross.

"Let's just say the place doesn't agree with him. I keep telling him it's all in his head," Norbert said matter-of-factly.

"Is it?" interjected Khia, herself stunned by the transformation that had taken place in a man she remembered as being playful, with boundless energy, now a shriveled shell.

"He's dying," uttered Catherine, horrified.

"Don't be so melodramatic. Consecrated ground goes against his constitution," said Norbert. "Enough about McBride; he gets enough attention. He'll be just fine once we get him out of this golden cage."

Catherine glared at Norbert.

"Don't you worry, missy," Norbert added, "McBride's been in worse places."

"Don't you missy me," said Catherine, who went from kneeling before McBride to standing up to Norbert.

Norbert laughed.

Before Catherine could say another word, Khia interjected, "Jordan saw Dodger and Goula. They sent a message. *The Abraxis will take us to the straits and narrows.*"

"Good plan," said Norbert.

"Good plan?" Harold shook his head, not getting it.

"But we can't leave without the book," said Khia.

"The Book?" asked Norbert. "Are you sure that's what they said?"

"Yup," said Jordan poking his head in the room, "that's what they said."

"Damn, that's going to take time," grumbled Norbert.

"And would you by chance know the name of this book?" asked Catherine.

Norbert nodded.

Catherine gritted her teeth when he didn't elaborate. "Well could you perhaps tell us the name, so we know what we're supposed to be looking for?"

"No."

"No!" Catherine wanted to scream, but she barely whispered the word.

"No, but I can write it down," said Norbert, as he picked up a pen and started to write. "Do not utter these words aloud."

"Yeah whatever," said Catherine dismissively.

Grabbing Catherine roughly, Norbert brought her closer to him, "*Never* utter these words aloud. *Ever.*"

Catherine nodded; she got the message, loud and very clear.

He handed the note to Catherine, who glanced at it. What he had written meant nothing to her. It seemed to be in Latin. "Thank you, Norbert," she said, folding and placing the piece of paper between her ample bosoms. Changing her tone, she added coquettishly, "The safest place in the Vatican."

Norbert made no comment. Turning his attention to Father Tobias, he asked, "Has the inquisition date been set?"

Father Tobias cleared his throat.

"Well?" said Norbert.

"The charges against you and McBride are heresy and abandonment of your oaths. I have to tell you, as your lawyer and official liaison between you and the Church..." he paused.

"Say it," said Norbert, impatiently.

"You don't stand a chance," said Father Tobias.

"Father, those oaths were sworn more than three hundred years ago," muttered Norbert. "Things have changed since then."

Father Tobias simply nodded, but Khia's eyes betrayed her surprise. *Three hundred years!*

Father Tobias continued. "They cannot condemn you to death, but they can and will hold you indefinitely."

"Could you define indefinitely?" asked Norbert.

"Forever."

"Damn. Forever is a long time." Norbert wasn't being funny; he was rarely, if ever, funny. "Any chance at parole?"

Father Tobias spoke somberly. "The oath is the excuse. If it wasn't the oath, they would have found something else to condemn you with. They do not want you anywhere near Khia."

Khia ears pricked up.

"There must be something you can do," Norbert said.

"I'm doing everything in my power."

"You're a lawyer, find a loop hole!"

"I've got Sister Ashema researching old texts and legal documents. But there is more: Within a fortnight, they plan to deport Catherine and Harold."

"Oh mon, I'll be deported back to the Bahamas," muttered Harold, "I'll never get back into the States.

"Clever," said Catherine. "They know that if we uttered a single word of what we know, we'd be considered certifiable."

"Yeah, and I don't want to spend the rest of my life in a mad house," said Harold.

"As for Khia," said Father Tobias, avoiding her gaze, "it is undecided. She's a thorn in their side. They won't harm her, but if the Secretary General has his way, she'll disappear somewhere in the Catholic world, hidden in some obscure monastery."

Khia looked at Norbert with wide eyes.

"They can't do that," said Catherine. "That's medieval."

"The Church *is* medieval," Harold laughed.

"After Christmas," Father Tobias continued, "a secret synod of the most powerful princes of the Church will gather and—"

"Time to go mates," Jordan said, poking his head into the room.

It was close to midnight when Khia, returning to her room, was intercepted by Brother Peccavi.

"Wh-wh-what a-a-are y-y-you d-doing ou-ou-out o-o-of y-y-your r-room a-a-at s-such a-a-an h-h-hour?" His stutter was even worse than usual.

Khia gave him a lame excuse about needing to go for a walk and closed the door.

## CHAPTER 3

# Sister Clair

Khia was feeling stifled and needed space. Ever since Brother Peccavi had caught her out of her room the other night, things had changed. Punishment, she supposed, for getting caught. Dragging her feet, she tried to widen the gap between herself and Brother Peccavi, but was unsuccessful.

Without asking permission, Khia switched course. She needed to do some research and headed towards the library. Brother Peccavi simply followed her like her silent shadow.

In the library, Khia pretended to do her homework, but it was hard to concentrate. She needed to find out more about the *Vigilanza*—the elite Vatican guards who watched Norbert and McBride. Spotting Brother Peccavi in her peripheral vision, Khia knew she had to be careful.

Eventually, Khia learned that the *Vigilanza* reported directly to the Vatican General Secretary, who held the second most important job in the Vatican. When she took into account the whispers she'd heard within the Vatican's corridors, that the Pope was ill and growing weaker, she knew it meant that the General Secretary's powers were growing.

Seeing Brother Peccavi approach, she casually closed her books, but had a shiver of warning… as if a spirit had walked through her.

"Si-si-si-si-sister Cl-Clair wa-wa-wants t-to s-s-s-see y-you."

*Uh oh*, thought Khia.

†

Having escorted her to Sister Clair's office, Brother Peccavi tried to speak, "S-S-S-Sister Cl-Cl-Cl—"

"Brother Peccavi!" Sister Clair was usually patient with him, but this time she didn't wait for him to finish, interrupting rather roughly. "Just go!" Then she took a breath and softened her tone with a smile. "You may leave us, Brother."

Hesitating, Brother Peccavi bit his nails and looked at Khia. His dark eyes wandered over and around her, but he didn't say anything. He just shuffled his feet and left.

Silence prevailed. Khia was waiting for Sister Clair to say something when two men of the cloth entered the room from another door—a door Khia hadn't even noticed was there.

"Your new tutors," announced Sister Clair with enthusiasm. "Jesuit Arctium Minus and Franciscan Xanthium Strumarioum."

"I'm sorry, I didn't quite catch those names," said Khia, hiding the uncertainty in her voice. Their religious vestments couldn't conceal their bulk; they were both tall and very muscular, and so similar to each other that they could have been brothers.

"Jesuit Arctium Minus and Franciscan Xanthium Strumarioum," repeated Sister Clair.

Khia still didn't catch their full names, but wasn't going to ask Sister Clair to repeat it a third time.

"I have heard a lot about you," said the Jesuit, extending his gloved hand. "Sister Clair tells me you are an adept student."

An image started to form in Khia's mind as she touched his white gloved hand, but he withdrew it too quickly. His cold eyes made contact with hers; she had to look away.

The Franciscan stepped forward and he too extended his hand, but remained silent, which made Khia wonder if he had taken the vow of silence. She didn't think that was common in the Franciscan order though (living at the Vatican, you learned those sorts of things).

He looked tired. In fact, both of them did. For two strong-looking men, they looked really pale—like they hadn't seen the light of day in quite some time.

"Jet lag," answered the Franciscan, breaking his silence.

Khia startled—not only because it was like he had read her mind but also because she had heard his voice before. She'd never seen his face, but she would never ever forget that voice. It belonged to the man who had chased them, and who Norbert had fought, in the tunnels of New York City.

"We arrived early this morning from the other side of the world," said the Jesuit, showing her his perfect teeth.

For the first time within the protective walls of the Vatican, Khia felt palpable fear. The two men closed in on her from either side. It was as if the space between them was shrinking and the way out was getting farther and farther away.

*Knock. Knock. Knock.*

The door opened and Jordan poked his head in. "Sorry for the interruption, Sister." He looked at Khia. "And you, young lady, are late for your class."

†

*Knock. Knock.*

Five a.m. sharp, like a fine precision Swiss clock. Khia knew by the sound that it was Sister Clair and not Brother Peccavi. Although both knocked twice, Sister Clair's knock was short and sharp, while Brother Peccavi's was soft and hesitant.

The nun smiled sweetly and almost sang out, "Good morning Khia, time for morning prayers."

"Yes, Sister Clair," Khia answered politely, groaning inwardly. She would have done almost anything to sleep a little longer.

During morning prayers, Khia almost nodded off a few times. Her day continued with her studies: classes in languages, mathematics, history, and the sciences. Khia was starting to feel like she was being suffocated by the nun and her all-encompassing watchfulness and constant care—smothered by kindness—but there was nothing she could do about it.

In the afternoon, it was Brother Peccavi's turn. It seemed as if he took a perverse pleasure in not letting her out of his sight. Escorting her to her classes, he waited in the hall. In the library, he sat in the next cubicle. And when she excused herself to go to the WC, he waited for her outside the door. She'd had enough.

Exasperated, Khia claimed illness and retired to her room early. After thirty-five minutes of restlessly pacing the floor in her small room, she decided she'd try to find Harold. She opened her door ever so slightly, to make sure Brother Peccavi was gone.

Stealthily, she crept from her room. She'd have to be careful; she could not get caught.

†

"Hey you snuck past the bro!" Harold was surprised to see her.

"I have to talk to Norbert and McBride," Khia said urgently. She had to tell them about her two new tutors: the Jesuit and the Franciscan.

"Not gonna happen," said Harold. "Not today."

"But—"

"I'm going on a fishing trip," he said. "Wanna come?"

She nodded.

Making their way around the labyrinth, they found a path that led towards the Academy of Sciences buildings. From beyond a closed door, they heard shouting.

"Norbert and McBride in there?" asked Khia.

Harold nodded. When the door burst open, he grabbed Khia's arm and they skirted away. Peeking around the corner, Khia watched as six guards roughly constrained a bound figure.

"Norbert," Khia whispered.

Harold put his finger to his lips.

It was hard to remain silent. Khia recognized the Monsignor. How could she forget that day in St. Patrick's Cathedral in New York City, when he had ordered them all (including Catherine and Harold) to Rome?

She saw father Tobias standing nearby, looking as though he wished he were anywhere else, as the Monsignor, his face as red as his vestment, approached Norbert and struck him hard across the cheek. "Such… such blasphemy should never be spoken," he sputtered, "least of all here, and by you."

Khia wanted to rush to Norbert's side, but Harold held her back.

The Monsignor turned to the guards. Pointing to McBride (who was slumped in a wheelchair with his head lolling to one side), he said with disgust, "Take that accursed thing from my sight."

"Yes Monsignor," said one of the ashen-faced guards.

"Tobias," the Monsignor said, "a word of caution. Do not be tempted by their words." The Monsignor turned and flew back into the chamber, slamming the door behind him.

Father Tobias looked grim.

"We better go," whispered Harold. "There's nothing we can do here." Khia had to warn Norbert about her two new tutors. "Yeah, but—"

"This is not a good time." Harold looked at his watch. "Catherine's in the library searching for The Book." With the millions of books it contained, it was the obvious place to start.

He thought that would get her attention—and it did. She quickly started off.

"Whoa girl!" Harold placed his hand on her shoulder, stopping her. "Where do you think yo going?"

"The library."

"I don't think so. Back to yo cell."

"But you said—"

"No way," said Harold firmly.

"Please."

"It should be enough that I let you come fishing with me. And don't pout."

†

"But what if it's not here?" asked Harold a few hours later, sounding defeated.

"It's *got* to be here," said Catherine intently.

Jordan popped his head in through a rack of books. "You didn't think it would be easy to find, did you?"

CHAPTER 4

# The Confessional

In the name of the Father, Son, and Holy Spirit

She traced her fingers along the finely crafted mahogany. Patterns carved in the wood felt smooth and warm to her touch. Quietly, she entered the small cubical and knelt on the wooden platform. Separated from the priest by a fine mesh screen, she bowed her head in prayer, "Bless me Father, for I have sinned."

"Hello Khia," said Father Tobias.

"Father," she leaned closer to the screen and whispered, "I… I don't know who to trust." In truth, she didn't know if she could trust him either… but who else could she turn to? She would have preferred to talk to Catherine, Harold, or even Jordan, but she hadn't been able to see them. There was no way she was going to confide in Brother Peccavi... and as for Sister Clair, she *had* been about to talk to her, but there was something in the nun's clear crystal eyes that had made her stop, which had left Father Tobias.

Sometimes one had to take a leap of faith. She knew it was no coincidence that Father Tobias had been there at St. Anne's Church—close to where she was living when this whole ordeal had begun—then at St. Patrick's Cathedral in New York City, and now here in Rome acting as Norbert and McBride's legal counsel. She could only hope that that was a good thing and not a bad thing.

Once she started talking, her words came out like a torrent of water breaking free from the ice. "I'm being watched. I'm no longer free to move around. It's either Brother Peccavi or Sister Clair. I can't even go to my classes on my own anymore. I'm not a kid. I don't need someone holding my hand all of the time. And what's really upsetting is that they won't let me see my friends." Khia gulped some air into her lungs. "I need to see Norbert and McBride. I've got to warn them about Franciscan Minus and… and Jesuit Strum… Strumor… something or other…"

Father Tobias closed his eyes. It seemed so long ago, almost an eternity, when he had stood with Khia on the steps of the 19th century church in the little town of Woburn—the day Hell had erupted.

If only he'd had more time. If only after mass he had spent less time with the congregation. If only… Father Tobias had been chastising himself over and over and over again ever since that day.

His heart had gone out to Khia, and her brother Devon. Shifted from one foster home to another, they were finally going to go to their grandmother's… but they had miscalculated. No one had anticipated the blatant attack on the church. Without time to explain, Khia and Devon had been whisked away by Ms Percival, Norbert, and McBride. It surely must have seemed like an abduction, not a rescue.

When Khia and Devon had been on the run with Norbert and McBride, he could not get any information on their whereabouts. It was like they had disappeared from the planet. He had appeased himself by saying that no news was good news… but that, he knew, was not necessarily so. What if they had been captured never to be heard from again? He had started to believe just that when the story had hit the news. He was shocked at how it had been spun. Not only were Norbert and McBride 'armed and dangerous', suspected of murdering two agents, they were also pedophiles, accused of abducting Khia and Devon. Atrocious lies.

Father Tobias, because of his position at Vatican Intelligence, had spent months gathering information. The more he learned the more he feared. He knew there were powerful forces at work (even within the Vatican) that desired Khia. For what, he didn't know. There were so many missing pieces to the puzzle. So he had kept digging.

When he had obtained camera surveillance tapes from Grand Central Station, he was hopeful, but it had only left him with more questions. The tapes revealed little except for the time-line of events: Catherine standing before the main entrance, Khia, Devon, Norbert, and McBride arriving like the four horsemen bringing chaos and destruction. Amidst explosions, they had slipped through the net that had been cast. Inside Grand Central Station, mercenaries waited for them. No one could possibly escape—and yet they had. How?

Interestingly, in that critical moment, all the cameras panning the area malfunctioned. A glitch? Not likely, but who could have orchestrated such a thing? Timed to perfection, they had disappeared. *Poof.* Like a magician's disappearing act. Almost an hour later, with the station still in chaos, the cameras malfunctioned once again and in those few critical seconds, a barely discernible amount of time, *poof*… Khia, Catherine, and McBride, looking a bedraggled motley crew, bloodied and hurt—reappeared on the screen.

It was seared into his memory. Khia walking beside a grim-faced McBride, who carried a seriously injured Catherine. The next occurrence was most fascinating. Rock debris exploded from everywhere and out of nowhere, and Norbert flew backwards across the screen. And as for Devon, there was absolutely no sign of him. It was as if he had vanished into thin air.

St. Patrick's Cathedral was a place of last resorts. Not sure if they would show up there, he had waited. Khia, Norbert, McBride, and another man—whom he later learned was Harold, the New York taxi driver who had picked them up at Grand Central Station—carrying a dying Catherine in his arms, entered the church looking for sanctuary. That's when the Sylph, the monstrous creature resurrected from fire, attacked. Vatican guards shot the creature with special bullets, and were thus able to subdue and cage the creature. Immediately thereafter, Monsignor Scarlatti ordered everyone back to Rome.

Keeping them at the Vatican had seemed like the right thing to do at the time. But with the Pope's failing health, things were at a tipping point. Opinions of those closest to the pontiff had started to diverge. Yet each, in their own way, believed what they were doing was right. To some, like Monsignor Scarlatti (who received his directions from the General Secretary), their interest was in keeping things quiet at all costs… to protect the Church. Was that not a noble cause? For others, it was time to tie up loose ends. Harold and Catherine should never have been kept at the Vatican this long.

"It is forbidden for anyone to see Norbert and McBride," said Father Tobias, trying to relay the bad news gently.

"No! You don't understand, I have to—"

"Khia, listen to me," said the priest. "I will find a way to inform them of the Jesuit and the Franciscan Monk. I promise. We are doing everything in our power to keep them away from you, but it is very important for you to follow your routine. No night excursions, okay?"

"Okay," Khia agreed, crossing her fingers behind her back.

After all was said and done, he knew Khia was a very special girl. She was clever, intuitive, and very much like her mother. His guilt resurfaced. He should have done more to help Valerie, but at the time had believed she suffered from a form of mental illness and needed psychiatric treatment rather than a priest. He did not want to make the same mistake with Khia.

Father Tobias was conflicted. It was such a delicate matter, and since he had never found the right time to talk to Khia… perhaps the words were meant to remain unsaid. In any case, what Khia's mother had told him in the confessional was confidential. As for the pieces he had uncovered… without doubt, these mysteries went beyond the Catholic teachings—perhaps even beyond Heaven and Hell.

Before he could say more, he heard a soft beeping noise; he looked at his watch.

"That's okay Father, I understand," said Khia. "Time has run out."

Kneeling in prayer nearby, Sister Clair raised her head. Khia avoided the nun's gaze.

## CHAPTER 5

# Shady's Day

One, two, three, four, count them off and search some more

The week before Christmas turned out to be both a good thing and a bad thing. Good because the Holy City was a beehive of activity (making it a lot easier for Khia to sneak around without getting caught) and bad because if they didn't find The Book soon their Christmas Eve escape could get kiboshed.

In their quest to find The Book, Harold had disguised himself as a custodian and lifted a couple of security passes, which had allowed them to expand their search into places they did not belong. In so doing, they had become more and more, shall we say, *creative* in not getting caught. Like the time they had found themselves in an isolated section of the Ethiopian College and Catherine had to distract a young priest by pretending she had gotten lost. Luckily, she could be very distracting when she wanted to be. He never even questioned why she was there, almost falling into her breasts in his willingness to show her the way. This had given Harold and Khia ample time to look around.

Even Father Tobias had helped… or perhaps it would be more accurate to say that he came to their rescue yet again. Khia, Catherine, and Harold had been in the back of the medieval section of the museum—a place prohibited to all but an elite few. With divine timing, he had appeared when they needed him most. Deftly, he had intercepted the curator and guided him away to discuss medieval art, thus allowing them to depart undetected. If they had been caught? Well… a moot point really.

Suffice it to say that they had had a number of close calls and Catherine (although she didn't show it) was worried. What if they didn't find The Book? Her primary concern was getting McBride out—no matter what. She didn't know why they needed The Book, but it was obviously important or why were they taking all these risks and going through so much trouble trying to find it? They had combed the Vatican, but The Book continued to elude them.

Catherine started to think they were looking at this all wrong. Perhaps they had to look outside the box. Having looked within the walls, her thoughts turned to what lay beyond. There was one glaring possibility... maybe, just maybe, The Book wasn't in the Vatican at all, but in this old bookstore in Rome that she'd heard about. It had been around forever, and people said you could find almost anything there.

When she broached the idea of checking it out, Khia had wanted to go on her own, but Catherine and Harold would only agree if someone went with her.

That's when Catherine had called a friend—and Shady got her trip to Italy.

†

On the day when Catherine and Harold were at their hearing, and Norbert and McBride were still locked up in the Sanctuary, Jordan accompanied Khia to the Vatican wall to an almost forgotten door.

The moment Khia stepped onto unconsecrated ground, she felt the subtle difference. It was like the air was different on the other side of the wall.

*"Ciao bella,"* said a female voice with the distinctive twang of the American south.

"Shady!" said Khia, springing forward. She'd only met her once (the night when she and her brother Devon had run away from Norbert and McBride, not yet trusting them, and found themselves at a storefront with Catherine and Shady), but she felt a connection to her that she couldn't quite explain. She knew what Shady did for a living, working late into the night from outside that storefront (she wasn't that naïve), but she also knew that Shady had a heart of gold.

As for Jordan, he was caught a little off guard.

Shady looked at Jordan and purred, "I do love a man in uniform." She was wearing a large brimmed hat and dressed in a flowing floral dress that accentuated her voluptuous shape.

"Shady is it?" said Jordan. "Unusual name."

She raised an eyebrow and smiled wickedly, "Why, it's because I do my best work out of the sun, darling."

Jordan blushed.

Having gotten the reaction she had intended, Shady turned to Khia. "And my my... haven't you become the prettiest young thing. Turn around, let's have a look at you," she said, looking at her approvingly as they started walking away.

"Remember," Jordan called after them, "you have to be back before sunset."

Shady flashed him a seductive wink and a coquettish seductive smile. "I'll have Cinderella back on time, don't you worry sweet cheeks."

"Sunset, not midnight," muttered Jordan under his breath, as he closed and locked the door.

†

The seven hills, the Tiber River, the Coliseum, the Pantheon... It was so exciting to get the chance to see Rome—the Eternal City.

"Taxi!" shouted Shady, bouncing Khia out of her reverie.

A taxi screeched to a stop.

"Do you speak English?" asked Shady.

He had eyes only for Shady, "*Sì, sì.* Yes."

Although the bookstore was no more than six or seven kilometers, it took ages to get there. Located on the other side of the Tiber River, they drove passed Ponte Sant'Angelo and crossed at the next bridge. Rome's traffic was a frenzy at the best of times, but Khia was enthralled. In the backseat of the taxi, she had her nose pressed against the window as she looked at Rome's busy streets, fascinated by the horns blaring and Fiats and scooters shooting in all directions.

Finally, the taxi turned onto a short, narrow, and twisted cobblestone street and maneuvered the car into the tiniest of spots. Cast in shadow was an old stone building.

"Are you sure this is the right place?" questioned Shady.

Khia nodded.

Shady passed some Euros to the taxi driver.

"I wait," said the taxi driver. "I wait… I pick you up."

†

The old wooden door squeaked open and Khia and Shady entered a very strange world indeed. Dimly lit, it smelled musty. Stacks of books on old wooden racks lined the aisles, sagging from the weight of too many pages. There were books from all over the world, many of them hundreds of years old—books that had been lost, found, borrowed, and a few (undoubtedly) stolen.

*"Posso aiutarla?"* asked the proprietor, an old Italian man.

"I'm sorry, I don't understand. Do you speak English?" asked Shady

*"Un po'.* A little," he replied. "How I help you?"

"We're looking for a particular book. An old book." Shady used the most polite drawl in her repertoire.

Knowing that the title of The Book should not be spoken aloud, Khia stepped up, unfolded the piece of paper and handed it to the old man.

The moment the old man read the title written in Norbert's bold script, he turned a pasty shade of gray. *"Dio,"* he swore, in the name of God. He made his way to the front door and turned the key in the lock.

A deathly silence descended upon them.

CHAPTER 6

# Pietro, Pietro

Ask, and it shall be given you; seek, and you shall find; knock, and it shall be opened unto you.

~ Matthew 7:7

"Pietro!" the old man shouted, breaking the silence. "Pietro!" he called again, impatiently.

A young man appeared from behind a stack of books.

*"Veni,"* spoke the man, waving his hand for them to follow him to the back room.

Shady glanced at Khia, unsure whether to follow or high-tail it out of there, but Khia took the lead and followed the old man into a small room. There was a wooden table with four chairs, and on the table, a half-empty bottle, three glasses, and an ashtray. With thick stone walls and no windows, the room was dark and appeared smaller than it actually was.

Pietro followed two steps behind.

*"Sedersi,"* said the old proprietor.

"Please for you to sit down," said Pietro.

With unsteady hands, the old man poured himself a shot of grappa and slid the bottle across the table to Shady. She declined.

*"Salute."* He knocked the alcohol back in one swift motion. Shady slid the bottle back across the table. The old proprietor promptly poured himself another drink. *"Una sigaretta?"* he offered Shady.

"I don't smoke," said Shady, but she took the cigarette anyway.

The old man lit his cigarette, inhaled deeply, and exhaled slowly. The smoke from the cigarette clouded the small room.

And he began to speak in rapid Italian, too fast for Khia to understand.

"I translate for Nonno, my grandfather," said Pietro. "He say he wait very long time to tell his story."

"Nonno, uh, my grandfather… *scusa,* English is not so good," Pietro smiled uncomfortably.

"You're doing great," said Shady encouragingly. "Please continue."

"The year is 1944. Nonno is a little boy. Very very bad the times. Italia at war. *La poverta, la miseria, il…*" Pietro stopped to look at his grandfather.

"The Book?" asked Khia, eager to hurry him along; it could be a very long story if it started in 1944 during the Second World War.

"Er, let me explain a little bit more. *Primavera…* first green…" stumbled Pietro.

"Spring?" said Khia.

*"Sì. Sì.* Spring. Nonno's mama, she die and they visit… *come si dice tomba…"*

"Grave?"

*"Sì, sì* grave. *Il padre di* Nonno bring the flowers to the grave… he kneel down and he cry much in the grief and the despair. *Piccolo* Nonno," he paused seeing their confusion. "*Piccolo...*" he thought for a moment, searching for the word. "Ah... *little…* little grandfather… he hear something in the dark. The voice like an angel call to him. He think it is the Archangel Michael or maybe it is Gabriel. Piccolo Nonno, he follow the voice to the old part of the *cimitero.* It be like the mistake to the eye, because the door he see is the door no should be there. It half open. Nonno see a little boy, maybe six or seven years, sleeping on the stone floor holding tight to The Book."

With hands that shook, Nonno lit himself another cigarette. He offered Shady another one, but she was still twirling the unlit cigarette in her hand.

"The little boy no sleeping," Pietro continued. "He dead. The voice of the angel, no angel. *Diavolo.*" Pietro looked at Nonno. "The Diavolo rise up and point the crooked finger at Piccolo Nonno and he say, '*No steal from the dead.*' Making joke, it laugh at Nonno, but it no funny because he say to Nonno to take The Book, and it point to the dead little boy."

Pietro cleared his throat. "The Book is red from the blood of the many it kill. The Book, it need the blood. Nonno, he say The Book take his blood."

The old man held out his hand, as proof that the story told was true. A faded white scar crisscrossed his palm. It looked like an "X", but when he turned his hand, it looked more like a cross.

*"Come si dice…* how you say, like in game of chess… *pedone?"*

"Pawn," replied Khia.

*"Sì, sì,* pawn. Nonno live, because he the pawn. It is very very bad this book. It no can be copied, no can burn, no can die."

"The Diavolo say to Nonno to take The Book and to hide it. One day, when he old, he to pass it on to someone else. Piccolo Nonno did not know who he must give Book to and ask the Diavolo, 'Who?'

"'You will know,' he say. Nonno never talk to no one. Many many years they pass. He old, no have much time on the earth, and he not know what to do."

"So he has The Book?" asked Khia.

Nonno sounded agitated.

Pietro listened to his grandfather for a moment, looking stricken by what he was hearing. "One week before, he give it, The Book, to the re-representa…" Pietro stumbled, took a breath, and then tried again, "the representative of the Pope. *Una sorella…* a nun. He say when you ask for The Book," he looked at Khia, "he know he make it the mistake."

"You," the old man pointed his arthritic finger at Khia.

Khia was a little startled by this.

"Can you describe the nun?" asked Shady.

Pietro conversed with his grandfather.

At last he turned to them. "My grandfather, he say the nun old and wrinkly, maybe *ottanta…* eighty. *Piccolissima…* very little," said Pietro, holding his hand out to chest level.

A small smile appeared on Khia's face. It had to be Sister Ashema.

The old man looked at Khia. *"Mi dispiace.* I sorry."

†

"This doesn't look right," said Shady. The space around Khia and Shady got very quiet.

A strong hot wind rolled in from North Africa, bringing with it a reddish orange mist of fine sand. Lightning slashed and thick black clouds darkened the sky. It quickly became quite dark, and the lights from the lampposts turned on.

Jordan should have been here by now. Where was he?

Alone on a dark deserted street, Khia thought she saw something in the gloom.

"What the hell?" said Shady, slipping into a New York accent.

Seven black vultures materialized… and waited.

"Shady," spoke Khia quietly, "get behind me."

Refusing, Shady resolutely stood by Khia's side.

Khia waited and watched, not sure what to do.

A few seconds passed before one of the birds stretched its wings and took flight, flying straight at them. Khia pushed Shady away. Avoiding the attack, Khia bent backwards, twisted in the air, and struck it hard, sending it to the ground. About to crush it with her foot, its coarse body dissolved into black mist.

The mist floated towards the six waiting birds and reformed into a vulture, but bigger and more menacing than before. Its red eyes looked eager to feast on fresh flesh. And then all seven vultures attacked in a mad scramble, trying to sink their sharp beaks and talons into Khia.

Khia fought like she'd never fought before. No matter what she did, there were always seven vultures, their red piercing eyes focused on her. As they clawed at her heels, she struck them down; as they flew at her face, she swerved; as they slashed at her throat, she weaved in and out. They were relentless.

"Shady, run!" cried Khia.

Shady tried to protect Khia, but it was more the other way around, and she knew it. Shady tried again to intervene, but this time she was roughly sent head over heels into a heap. The vultures could have easily killed Shady, but they left her alone. Just then, the heavens opened up and the rain started to fall.

Driven back until she bumped against the Vatican wall, Khia inched her way to the door. "Jordan, where are you? Please, Jordan!"

En mass they lunged for Khia. Slipping sideways, she felt a knife-sharp talon cut her arm. She screamed when a hand grabbed her other arm… and yanked her to safety.

"Jordan!" she hugged him.

The vultures tried to follow Khia, but it was like they struck something solid. They fell at the threshold to the door, one on top of the other. An instant later, they dissolved into a swirling heap of black smoke and were gone.

In the pouring rain, Shady stood alone in the middle of the street.

"Come with us!" called Khia.

Shady shook her head.

"You're hurt," Jordan looked at Khia,

"I'm okay. Only a graze."

"What was out there?"

"Nothing," she answered.

"Nothing!" repeated Jordan incredulously. Khia failed to tell him that, in the final moment, just before Jordan had pulled her through the door, she thought she had seen her mother.

CHAPTER 7

# The Librarian

In all of the Holy City, the Vatican Archivist's domain was the most difficult place to gain access to. She jealously guarded her treasures like a dragon. Respected and feared, she was a forceful woman, and no one was immune to her acidic tongue when her priceless books and documents from antiquity were threatened—not even the princes of the Church.

Sister Ashema, the Vatican-Archivist, an octogenarian standing barely 4'11", was originally from Palestine—born in the old Christian quarter. For more than fifty years she had resided in Rome and had become irreplaceable, watching over the vast stock of extremely rare and priceless books and documents within the racks and vaults of the Vatican Library.

Her abilities were legendary, her skills invaluable, and her reputation was known throughout the religious centers and theological universities of the world. She had an eidetic mind and could sort through a vast amount of information with ease. She could speak six or seven languages, including Latin, Greek, and Aramaic. It was even rumored that she had been instrumental in avoiding two schisms. Had she been the right gender, she could have been Pope.

With the advent of computers, she had risen to the challenge, and (as her blessed superiors had not expected) had set order where there had previously been chaos, creating a database system so impressive that absolutely everything within the Holy City's libraries was cross referenced and archived. She had molded the system—her system—like clay. It was she who weeded out viruses, worms, and Trojans, creating impenetrable firewalls. In other words, without the password, her system was impossible to hack.

Catherine entered the Archivist's domain.

"Hello Catherine," said Sister Ashema, who was hunched over a computer.

The library was empty. It was Christmas Eve.

A few seconds later, Khia joined them. It felt to her as if Sister Ashema had been waiting for them.

"Sister Ashema, I was wondering if you could help us; we we're looking for a book..." Catherine paused, "a children's book."

Sister Ashema's eyes seemed to sparkle at the suggestion. Without logging off the computer, she motioned for them to follow her into the least requested (but not restricted) section of the library.

"Many don't know it," she told them, shuffling stiffly down a narrow aisle, "but the Vatican has a significant children's book collection. Some go back many centuries..." Her voice trailed off.

As soon as they were out of sight, Father Tobias, Jordan, and Harold entered the library. Jordan, positioning himself as if he was browsing the bookshelves, stood guard.

Father Tobias, a computer expert in his own right, was familiar with the Vatican's system. He sat at the computer and within moments was navigating its labyrinth. But even so, the wily octogenarian had set numerous road blocks and safe-guards.

"Paranoid is she? Must be how she survived for so long," commented Jordan.

"I still don't know why you just didn't ask the old woman for The Book," said Harold, nervously playing with his dreadlocks.

Father Tobias, totally focused on finding his way, followed an obscure coded path that led him into a secret section—to a catalog of rare books and documents, purposefully buried and sealed away to be... almost forgotten. Only a few had heard the vaguest of whispered rumors of their existence.

"Oh my God," Father Tobias gasped. It was like he had suddenly found the Holy Grail, his eyes ablaze at the letters on the screen. He'd found The Index! Thought abolished decades before, it was a secret list of forbidden books.

"Father," Harold's whispered voice pierced the silence. "Father, The Book! You gotta do that stuff on yo own time, mon."

"Ahh yes," said Father Tobias, but he was visibly distracted. A few more clicks of the mouse and he was jotting down the location of The Book—Section Rev 12.1141—and returned the screen to how he had found it. Reluctantly he tore himself from the computer in a kind of hypnotic daze, never pausing to wonder why Sister Ashema had never logged off.

†

Seeing that Father Tobias had completed his search, thanks to a subtle signal from Jordan, Catherine and Khia delayed Sister Ashema no longer and the old nun made her way back to her station. Fortunately, Catherine and Khia had lagged behind. Movement caught their eyes—black, brown, and white. Hiding behind the racks of books, they spotted the Jesuit, the monk, and Sister Clair.

Catherine looked at Khia with concern.

While Catherine remained hidden, Khia stealthily made her way through the aisles. Reaching the top of the stairs, Khia heard Sister Clair's soft voice floating up towards her, "Good day, Sister Ashema."

"The library closes in few minutes," Sister Ashema declared.

"Oh, this won't take long," the Jesuit said icily.

"A simple search," said the monk.

"You have the title of what you are searching for?" asked Sister Ashema.

The Jesuit handed Sister Ashema a folded piece of paper.

Unfolding it Sister Ashema read the script: *Ab Comissio Occauss Aborior.* "A rare book indeed."

"The Book," said Jesuit Arctium.

"Why would you think it could possibly be here?" responded Sister Ashema, meeting his piercing gaze.

The monk leaned forward. "Where else would it be, Sister?"

Sister Ashema complied, going to her computer. The search took a few moments. "There is no match."

The monk smiled sinisterly as he reached within the folds of his garment and withdrew an envelope, tossing it onto Sister Ashema's desk. It slid towards her.

She slowly picked up and opened the envelope. Inside was a piece of white parchment paper. Even more slowly, Sister Ashema read its contents. "An edict... an edict signed by the General Secretary himself."

"Yes. The General Secretary has instructed you to assist us in procuring what we seek," said the Jesuit.

"Of course," said Sister Ashema. She had little choice but to comply.

Between the rows of books, the old Librarian spotted Catherine. Sister Ashema was no longer undecided, and for Catherine's eyes only, pointed at the desk drawer. Sister Ashema's arthritic fingers crept along the keyboard initiating another search.

A few moments later, the computer bleeped.

Sister Ashema, the 213th Vatican librarian, slowly led them to the elevator. "I can't take the stairs anymore," she explained.

†

Father Tobias, Harold, and Jordan lightly sprinted up the stairs. Passing rows of books, they reached the inner sanctum—the area where highly sensitive material was located, the section of the library that held ancient scriptures and priceless documents.

"Don't we need a key or something for this area?" asked Harold skeptically.

"No worries mate, I've got this one covered," answered Jordan, not sounding very convincing. The truth was that they were having a little trouble getting the door open when Khia burst in upon them.

"Trouble," said Harold, as if he had expected it all along.

She nodded. "Guess who just walked in the library." And then, with a look of disbelief, Khia said, "You guys haven't gotten in yet?"

"Almost there," said Jordan.

*Click.* The door popped open.

They entered a perfectly controlled environment.

"The security cameras?" asked Harold.

"Took care of that," said Father Tobias.

Khia and Harold waited at the door. "Mon, we gotta leave," said Harold.

Father Tobias and Jordan raced down the vault's corridor, lined with a matrix of metal safety-deposit boxes. They scanned left and right, up and down. EZK, GJHS, KGT, MASS, NSA, NSF, QTT, REV.

"REV," declared Jordan, at the far end of the room. "Here it is."

Father Tobias sprinted over and inputted a six digit code onto the panel.

*Beep.*

Red light. Wrong code.

Flummoxed, Father Tobias moaned. "I thought that would surely be the code." And then his face lit up and he tried ASH213.

*Beep.*

Green light. Right code.

The small door opened. It was a dark compartment that was… empty.

"Oh for the love of God," Father Tobias said dejectedly, as he closed the vault.

They raced out, scurrying down the corridor to where Harold and Khia waited.

*Bing.*

They heard the sound of the elevator.

Quickly, they dived behind a rack of books, but Father Tobias (who had been the last one out) was a little too slow. The librarian (the first to exit) spotted him and their eyes met.

It was then that the librarian did an unexpected thing. She turned the other way, to straighten one of her books, commenting to her followers (who couldn't care less) how careless her young apprentices were. Sister Ashema was well aware that her comments fell on deaf ears and would most likely be interpreted as the ramblings of a senile nun. She smiled a little. She'd often been underestimated.

Impatient for her to lead them to their prize, Sister Ashema finally arrived at the door. She fumbled with her keys, which dropped to the floor. Painfully stooping down to pick up her key chain, which held a silver cross and ten gold keys, she straightened and smiled ever so slightly... for she saw four figures swiftly making their way down the stairs.

†

"You didn't get The Book," said Catherine.

Khia shook her head. "Someone must have got there first. We found the location, but the box was empty."

"How'd you know that the combination was ASH213, mate?" asked Jordan amazed. "The little bitty nun getting old?"

"No," said Father Tobias, "it was a hunch."

"And I have one too," Catherine smiled, as she walked towards Sister Ashema's desk, and opened the drawer.

"What are you doing?" asked Khia.

Catherine reached in and removed a velvet bag.

"We got to go," said Khia urgently.

Catherine opened the velvet bag and there it was: The Book—*Ab Comissio Occauss Aborior.*

She had been careful… but not careful enough.

CHAPTER 8

# Brother Peccavi

'Twas the night before Christmas...
and a creature was stirring.

Eyes closed, feigning sleep, Khia went over the plan again in her mind. It was as if she were right there, with Catherine, Harold, and Jordan, making their way to the Sanctuary to free Norbert and McBride.

She could visualize Harold splitting from the group and making his way to her cell. Then they would make their great escape. She expected to hear the knock at her door any moment.

What if something went wrong? What if they weren't able to get Norbert and McBride? What if they got caught? Various scenarios played out in Khia's mind. She took a slow deep breath. If Harold didn't show, she knew what she was supposed to do. She was to wait twenty minutes, and when she thought it was safe, make her way to their rendezvous point. Failing that, she was to find Father Tobias.

Eighteen minutes passed... and Khia was getting more anxious. What had happened?

†

Things had started going awry practically from the beginning. Harold and Jordan arrived at Catherine's room without incident, but no one, not even Catherine, had expected the doctor's late night call. Harold and Jordan quickly snuck under Catherine's bed, while the good doctor, who was slightly inebriated, pondered over her slow recovery.

Finally, after what seemed like an awfully long time, Catherine gently said to the doctor, "Don't worry about me doctor; I'm sure I'll be out and about real soon. You, however, look tired." Concern sounded in her voice. "Take a few aspirins and get some rest." She smiled.

"Yes dear," said the doctor, thinking, *she truly is a beautiful woman.*

"Merry Christmas, Doctor Lawrence," said Catherine.

"Merry Christmas, Catherine." He left the room.

"I thought he'd never leave," said Jordan, sliding from under her bed and throwing his knapsack over his shoulder.

"Do you think he suspects?" asked Harold.

"Most likely," said Catherine, jumping out of bed.

"I do believe the good doctor is smitten by the beautiful Catherine," laughed Harold.

"Who wouldn't be?" said Jordan and then clamped his mouth shut. Making himself useful, he walked over to the door and checked the hallway. It was empty.

A few seconds later, Jordan in his Swiss Guard colors, Catherine in her nun's habit, and Harold in Jesuit black raced through the Vatican halls.

When they got near the Sanctuary, Catherine whispered, "Something's not right."

"This night, of all blessed nights, is jinxed," muttered Harold.

"Crikey, something's up," said Jordan. "The guards would never abandon their post."

Edging closer, Jordan approached the open doors and peeked in. He saw six Papal guards strewn across the floor and Norbert inspecting various weapons, including several P220 pistols.

Jordan laughed at the sight.

Harold's expression turned from doom and gloom to faint hope. "Norbert, you good, mon."

"You're late," said Norbert.

Catherine went straight to McBride and whispered, "Hang on."

Only a barely discernible sound escaped McBride's lips.

"What did he say?" asked Catherine, forced to acknowledge Norbert.

"He's happy to see you," answered Norbert, lifting McBride—who hardly weighed anything at all—into a wheelchair.

"Father Tobias instructed me to give you these," Jordan said to Norbert, handing him a head set with an ear-piece and microphone. "We're all wearing one. Father T is viewing the security cameras and will be our eyes."

They heard Father Tobias' deep Italian voice testing the equipment, as Norbert silently handed out weapons that were easily concealed under their religious garments. Catherine placed her leg on the bed, lifting up her habit, revealing her slender leg. She placed the weapon securely in the well-positioned holster on her thigh.

Everything turned quiet.

"What?" she asked coyly. "A nun must protect her virtue."

Caught staring, Jordan and Harold quickly busied themselves. Catherine noticed the slight flush on Jordan's cheeks. She smiled. He was a young one.

"Guards approaching," the voice of Father Tobias came over their ear-pieces. "Get out of there now. No, no... go right and take the next left. I'll direct you to the square. You won't have much time before the corridors are swarming with guards."

"Okay Father, lead us," said Norbert.

They followed Father Tobias' instructions. "Take the next right and the stairs down. Thankfully, Midnight Mass will be starting shortly. The crowds will afford you some measure of safety and obscurity, but need I remind you, there are security cameras everywhere and there will be extra eyes scanning for any hint of danger? Take the door on your left, quickly." No sooner had they closed the door behind them than they heard voices in the corridor.

"Feels good to be out," said Norbert, stretching his back.

"Harold," said Father Tobias.

"Yes, Father?"

"It's time for you to get Khia."

"Yes Father, of course," said Harold, leaving the group.

"I'll be watching all the monitors and will keep you abreast of happenings. Proceed to the rendezvous point."

"Best way to escape is through the *Passetto di Borgo*," Jordan suggested.

"Exactly," agreed Father Tobias.

†

Harold was approaching Khia's room when he abruptly changed direction. Hiding in the shadows of a doorway, he softly spoke into his microphone, "Oh for the love of the islands, we have a problem. Sister Clair just entered Khia's room."

"Are you sure it's Sister Clair?" asked Father Tobias.

"Yes."

"Patience, Harold," said Father Tobias, but Harold detected a note of concern in his voice.

Harold had a bad feeling about this. Faint hope had flipped back to doom and gloom. Their well-laid plans were fraying. They were already behind schedule. Mass provided but an hour of grace.

†

Khia heard the door open and softly close. She didn't stir. Deepening her breathing, she pretended to be asleep. Everything was quiet; perhaps whoever it was had left.

Then she heard the sound of footsteps nearing her bed. She had hoped it would be Harold, but knew it wasn't him. The footsteps were different.

She quickly rolled out of bed, trying to surprise the intruder, but she hadn't been quick enough. She felt a clammy hand clamp tightly over her mouth.

She tried to strike out, but she was overpowered.

"Sh-sh-shh!" Brother Peccavi hissed like a stuttering snake.

Khia felt herself quiver fearfully under the Brother's touch. He was a lot stronger and a lot more coordinated than she would have ever believed. Mistake. Big mistake. She'd underestimated him.

"D-d-do wh-wh-what I-I s-s-say," he whispered into her ear. She felt the moist heat from his breath. "U-u-understand?"

Seeing a glint of steel rise up to her throat, and feeling its cold sharp edge touch her hot skin, Khia nodded. She was quiet and did not resist his advance.

*Please don't hurt me,* prayed Khia silently, looking for a way out. Anger started to boil from deep within her.

He forced her to kneel beside the bed. His body pressed hard against her, making escape impossible. In the dim light, with one of his hands pressed against her mouth, Khia watched as his other hand slipped over her. He repositioned the pillows on her bed and pulled the blanket over them, so that it looked like a figure slept.

He pulled her closer. It seemed to Khia as if Brother Peccavi, who had taken vows of service to God, was crying in anguish, as if he were fighting his inner demons. Perhaps she could use this to her advantage, she thought. Being forced to her feet, Khia pretended to stumble, hoping to get him off balanced. It didn't work. It was like he had become taller and stronger.

Her senses heightened, Khia heard something… but so had Brother Peccavi.

*Harold? Please be Harold,* prayed Khia.

Brother Peccavi pulled her into the small confining closet. There was nothing she could do. She couldn't lash out, kick, or scream. He was wrapped around her like a second skin, preventing her from moving, and he had one hand tightening around her mouth, preventing her from screaming.

Khia's heart raced; *please,* she prayed, *let it be Harold.*

Khia heard the door to her room squeak open.

Quieter than she thought possible, she heard (or maybe just imagined she heard) the Brother's softly whispered words, pleading with her to listen, "Pl-pl-please." She felt his hot tears fall onto her neck, burning her skin. Grief seemed to envelop him. "K-K-Khiaaa."

Something in the way he'd softly stuttered her name, something in the tone of his voice touched her… and Khia stopped struggling. Through the crack in the door, Khia watched wide-eyed as Sister Clair entered the room. Nearing Khia's bed, Sister Clair rolled up the sleeve of her garment, revealing a glint of something metal and a flash of something sharp.

Sister Clair raised her arm. Her lips moved, but no sounds came out; it was like she was reciting a prayer (or a curse), and she struck down hard with the knife.

Khia watched in horror. Her bed had become some kind of an unholy altar that the Brother had prepared for Sister Clair.

"No!" cried out Sister Clair, ripping the blankets off the bed and (in frustration) viciously plunging the knife deep into the pillow and right through the mattress, causing feathers to fly everywhere.

For a moment, Sister Clair looked in disbelief. She touched the sheets and realized they were still warm. She looked around the small room, perhaps sensing that Khia was near.

Sounds in the hallway (a group of joyous priests and nuns making their way to Midnight Mass) prompted Sister Clair to leave Khia's room. Hiding the knife beneath her vestments, she smoothed the fabric of her habit, unaware of the two white feathers that had clung to her back. She appeared relaxed and serene, but her clear crystal eyes could not hide the seething rage within. Her head bent, as if in prayer, she left the room and the two feathers floated to the ground.

CHAPTER 9

# The German Graveyard

This time it was Khia who followed Brother Peccavi like a shadow. Walking silently down the corridor, they quickly met up with Harold, who had been anxiously waiting. He didn't ask, they didn't tell, and without further mishap, they reached their rendezvous point.

Greeted by her worried friends, Khia realized she'd grown to love them: Norbert, McBride, Catherine, Harold, and Jordan. They were like family… and Brother Peccavi? Wow, had she ever misjudged him!

Inserting her ear-piece, Khia heard Father Tobias. "Ciao Khia, I trust Brother Peccavi protected you." Father Tobias was about to say more but the calmness in his voice changed to urgency. "I have company." They heard a commotion, sounds of what might have been a door bursting open, a struggle, and then nothing as their communication with him was cut off.

Khia looked at Norbert.

"He'll have to handle it himself," stated Norbert.

Jordan took the lead. "This way mates."

It wasn't long before they were forced to take evasive action. The group of seven hid behind a corner. Vatican guards blocked their path.

"What do we do now?" asked Harold. Their escape had relied on the element of surprise. But, it appeared that their disappearance had not gone unnoticed.

"There's always another way," declared Norbert.

Backtracking, they managed to slip by the Vatican guards and found their way to another door, which took them out onto Saint Peter's Square, where thousands upon thousands of the faithful had come to celebrate Midnight Mass.

Abandoning the wheelchair, Harold took McBride in his arms so as to better manage their way through the throngs of worshipers.

"We're on the wrong side," Jordan said. "We have to make it through to the other side of the square."

"Norbert! NORBERT!" an old man called out madly, waving his arms and attracting a lot of attention.

It couldn't have been any worse if Norbert and his crew were on a stage with a spotlight aimed right at them. Abruptly, Norbert stopped and the rest of the group skidded to a halt behind him. "I'll deal with this," said Norbert. "Go on."

But no one made a move.

Norbert skirted towards the crippled old man, who was being pushed in a wheelchair by a deacon. "Father Romano! I didn't expect to see you here," said Norbert, as he knelt down on one knee.

Father Romano smiled reminiscently. "Look at me. I'm an old man and you... you haven't aged a day, except for that scar on your face." Father Romano took in the scene around him and his eyes twinkled, "You're on one of your adventures again, aren't you?"

"I see you still have mischievousness in you. Age hasn't worn it off," stated Norbert.

The toothless old priest grinned. "I knew I'd see you again before I died. I *prayed* I'd see you again. The best times of my life were our adventures." His old eyes did not miss a thing. "McBride doesn't look good. What possessed you to bring him here?"

"Didn't have much choice," answered Norbert.

Suddenly Father Tobias' voice came over their ear-pieces. "Back in business. I have relocated to a more secure site. Listen up my little lost lambs; the wolves are on to you, and are starting to circle."

"We read you," whispered Khia. "I can see guards, in groups of sixes, quartering off and moving in towards us."

"The square is swarming with uniforms. You're going to have to find another way. It is Midnight Mass; *per favore*, please," begged Father Tobias, "try to be subtle."

"Let me be of assistance," said Father Romano, placing his arthritic hand on Norbert's large muscular arm.

Norbert smiled at the opportunity that had presented itself. "You're an answer to my prayers Father Romano."

"No, *you* are an answer to *my* prayers," said the old priest. "I told him," tilting his head towards the young deacon, whose mouth hung open in absolute wonder, "about our adventures, but until this moment," he laughed lightly, "he believed that it was the ramblings of a demented old fool."

Norbert looked beyond the priest to a group of Vatican guards that was converging on them, the crowd oblivious to the drama and danger unfolding around them. As a collective whole the faithful bowed their heads in prayer. Mass had begun and the chanting voices of thousands floated up to the sky.

*"Campo Santo Teutonico,"* Norbert said to Jordan, in tempo with the prayer.

*"Campo Santo Teutonico?* The German Graveyard," clarified Jordan.

Norbert nodded.

"Okay," said Jordan, shrugging his shoulders. He was a little baffled.

"Father Romano, thank you," Norbert bowed respectfully.

"My pleasure," cackled the old man. "My pleasure."

From four sides, Swiss Guards were closing in.

Playing his last act, Father Romano created a small kerfuffle, enough for Norbert and his followers to disappear into the crowd: Just as the Vatican guards were heading towards them, Father Romano maneuvered his wheelchair with a quickness and dexterity that belied his frailty. Grabbing his cane, he thrust it between moving feet, causing the young deacon to overreact. A heap of Vatican guards were strewn on the ground, arms and limbs tangled together like a game of pick-up sticks.

†

Barricaded in the surveillance room, the satellite imagery Father Tobias was accessing switched to infra-red camera mode.

He saw his group of seven: Khia, Catherine, Jordan, Norbert, and Harold (carrying McBride) and Brother Peccavi. They were in the German Graveyard. Why? That wasn't part of their plan. Norbert must have had to improvise.

On the periphery of his screen, he identified a new threat. A dozen white wraith-like shapes were moving towards his lost lambs. He yelled into his microphone to warn them. No one answered.

Feeling helpless, and unable to do anything more, Father Tobias stared tensely at the screen. With the help of Father Romano, they had succeeded in giving the Vatican guards the slip, but now twelve mercenaries employed by Blackwood moved in. How had they known? It was like playing chess with a better player—they always knew what move was to be played next.

Father Tobias easily identified Norbert—his signature very different from the others. Norbert dropped back, and one by one, took each mercenary down. *Miraculous,* thought Father Tobias, but his joy was short lived, for more soldiers of fortune followed in their wake.

Khia reached the mausoleum first. The moment she placed her hand on its cold surface, the door creaked open, despite the fact that the entrance had not been opened for a century or so. She didn't have time to think about that and dove in, avoiding a spray of bullets.

Right on her heels, the rest stumbled inside.

"Now what do we do?" cried Harold, who positioned McBride at the foot of a stone sarcophagus in the middle of the room.

"We wait," declared Khia, "for Norbert."

Scanning the enclosure with their flashlights, their eyes were drawn to the walls. An ancient Renaissance master had painted them with stories found in the Old Testament: images of Adam and Eve cast from Eden and of Abraham's hand being held back by an angel. But the most disturbing image was of the beasts rising up, heralding the end of the world… Judgment Day, as found in the New Testament in the Book of Revelations.

McBride mumbled.

Catherine, who stood close to McBride, leaned in closer. "What is it?" With a catch in her throat, she continued, "I don't understand what you're trying to say."

With great effort, McBride moved his hand slightly, but to the human eye, it looked like he hadn't moved at all; he looked immobile. Catherine's eyes filled with tears. It was like looking at a dead body that had already gone cold.

They needed Norbert, but he was a little busy.

Bullets, fired from high-powered rifles with silencers, whizzed by… and speak of the devil, Norbert dove into the chamber. Rolling onto his side, he fired into the night.

Jordan kicked the door, shutting them in.

"There are more… coming for you," announced Father Tobias. "You have to get out of there. They're all around you. Get out of there now."

"Too late Father. We're trapped," said Khia. All she heard was static, as their communication with Father Tobias failed.

CHAPTER 10

# Sinistra

Mortui vivos docent—The dead teach the living

"Brother Peccavi, Harold, on your knees," ordered Norbert, waving his gun about.

"Mon, this is no time to pray," quipped Harold, but one look at Norbert and he joined Brother Peccavi on his knees. He remembered all too well the day he had met Norbert and the gang in New York. He'd picked them up in his taxi outside Grand Central Station. Catherine was bleeding to death and Norbert had insisted on going to the Cathedral. Harold had argued that the woman needed a doctor, not a priest, but Norbert could be very persuasive… especially with a gun.

"Look for a hidden entrance," explained Norbert, pressing his ear against the mausoleum door, listening.

"In the floor?" asked Harold.

"Between the stone slabs!" Norbert said, exasperated.

"M-m-m-m..." stuttered brother Peccavi, looking scared.

"What?" asked Harold, impatiently.

"M-M-M-M-M—" repeated Brother Peccavi, his eyes growing wider by the second.

"What the hell you trying to say?" asked Harold, shaking his head.

*"M-M-M-Malacchio!"* he finally got out, pointing over Harold's shoulder.

Harold looked where he was pointing and screamed. On the wall behind them, in the dark crypt, the red eyes of a beast were glowing. Its shadow cast a ghoulish shape that was getting larger and larger.

Frantically, Harold scraped the space between two stones with his sharp knife, in a desperate attempt to escape the Evil Eye.

The shadow on the wall grew more threatening… and then it spoke. "Hello," it said to Catherine, as it stepped out of the shadows. Its voice wasn't deep or threatening. It was high pitched… like that of a boy whose voice hadn't yet broken. And its form, although transparent, wasn't big and scary like its ghoulish shadow, but that of a little ghost—merely a small boy wearing a dirty white shirt, short pants, and laced up shoes. His eyes were red and glistened from the tears he had shed in his last few moments of life. "At last." It heaved a tiny sigh. "You have come."

Khia thought the little ghost to be about seven years old, maybe eight at the most—the same age as her little brother—and he looked so scared.

Loud noises penetrated the crypt. Those who were outside were trying to get in.

Harold rose to his feet in wonder as the stone started to glow. At first it was dull and barely noticeable, and then it brightened into a cold blue light. With help from Brother Peccavi, they were able to lift and slide the stone slab to the side… revealing a dark passage beneath.

Jordan dug into his knapsack and handed out flashlights.

The little ghost smiled, but even when he smiled he looked sad. "I can lead you," he offered.

"You?" said Norbert. "I don't think so."

"You have but two choices. Follow me or wait for those who come for you," said the little ghost.

"Good point. Down the hatch, now," ordered Norbert.

Last to descend was Norbert, complaining bitterly. "I hate underground places. How come it always has to be underground places? Why can't it be bridges, or tall buildings; I love tall buildings."

Straining, his arms overhead, Norbert slid the heavy stone slab back into place just as the thick mausoleum doors blew apart. Bullets blasted the empty room, riddling the frescoed walls with holes. Heavy footsteps were heard above.

Deep in the cavern, the ghost's shimmering form guided them like a beacon in the night.

One after another they followed. The passageway hadn't been used in a long time. It was weird, but each step seemed to take them back in time, into the heart of the renaissance, into the depths of the dark ages, and to the very foundations of ancient Rome.

Khia's curiosity conquered her trepidation. "What's your name?" she asked the little ghost.

It took so long for the little ghost to reply that Khia thought he might have forgotten.

"Bastone. Bastone is my name."

"Bastone," repeated Khia. "Did The Book take your life?"

Bastone nodded.

"I'm so sorry," said Khia

The ghost boy looked at her and Catherine. "Do not feel sad for me. It is I who should feel sad for you. My liberation is at hand, while yours… your journey is just beginning."

Khia startled at the words.

The little ghost stopped. They had reached a fork in the path.

"Which way?" asked Norbert, who had joined them at the front. "Right or left."

"*A sinistra*," the little ghost spoke.

"Left?" queried Khia.

*"Sì,"* said the little ghost.

They went left and hadn't gone more than fifty feet when their path was blocked by a bricked-up door.

Norbert glared at the little ghost.

"It is the way," said the little ghost, going through the door.

"Easy for you," grumbled Norbert. Norbert threw himself at the door. On the first blow, visible cracks appeared; on the second blow, bricks fell away revealing yet another passageway.

"Jordan, stick your head in there and have a look," said Norbert.

"Me! You stick your head in there," countered Jordan.

"We're beneath the Vatican. What could possibly happen?" asked Catherine.

Norbert shot back, "That's what I'm afraid of."

"Fine. Get out of my way." Norbert nudged Jordan aside. Light from their flashlights revealed another passageway and steps that led deeper into the catacombs. Without preamble, Norbert disappeared. Moments later the lights came on.

"Electricity! Thank you Lord," said Harold.

Conduits and old rusted wires, laid decades before, lined the wall. It was damp and moldy. Water dripped from the ceiling.

"Are you guys coming?" shouted Norbert.

Mutely they followed, going deeper underground.

"I-it's g-g-g-getting h-h-hot d-down h-h-here," said Brother Peccavi, breaking the silence.

"Must have been how Dante got his ideas," commented Harold.

"Y-you sh-sh-shouldn't s-s-say su-su-such th-th-things," said Brother Peccavi, using his sleeve to wipe the sweat from his brow.

"I know where we are," announced Norbert.

"Glad to hear that," said Catherine, sarcastically.

"I know a shortcut." Norbert grinned. "Follow me."

The little ghost hovered over Norbert's left shoulder. "No, you must not go that way," he said, as he floated in front of Norbert, trying to block his way. "You must not go there; it is forbidden."

"Will you shut up? I have to concentrate. Where is it? Where is it?" muttered Norbert pacing back and forth. He suddenly stopped and felt the wall with his hands.

"What are you doing?" asked Khia.

"Trying to get us out of here. What does it look like I'm doing?" snapped Norbert.

"Norbert, who is after us?" asked Khia.

"Do you have to ask me right this minute?" asked Norbert, tapping the wall with his knuckles. "I'm busy."

It was taking too long. They could hear voices getting nearer... the drum of pounding boots.

"Hurry," said Catherine. Although everyone was thinking the same thing, she was the only one to say the word aloud.

They all held their breath, even the little ghost.

"They're really close," whispered Jordan, as he checked his gun.

"They look for *you,*" said the little ghost, his red eyes staring at Khia. "They want *you.*"

"Here it is," Norbert declared triumphantly.

"Do not go there. I beg you," said the little ghost; his high-pitched voice quivered in fear. "There is evil... older than the stone foundation we stand on. I have heard whispers; spirits in the graveyard talk."

"Jeez, there's gossip everywhere," said Norbert.

"Stories have been passed down over the centuries; the ones that persist have some truth to them," answered the little ghost.

"I don't listen to gossip," interrupted Norbert.

"Many ills have been done on this Earth, angel," the little ghost said to Norbert. "Evils have been buried in the catacombs waiting for the day they will be released."

"Be gone," said Norbert.

The little ghost shook his head. "You are vexing, aren't you?"

"I've been around a lot longer than you."

"I've been here for more than seventy years—"

"Yeah, as I said, I've been here a lot longer than you," shot back Norbert.

"My... you look good for your age," said the little ghost.

"Well you still look like a little kid," said Norbert.

"I am not a child. Had I lived I would be an old man. I have touched The Book. I hear its thoughts. I remain in this realm. Neither here nor there—between and betwixt. I hear whispers from other worlds. It would be best if you heed my words."

"Mon, if we don't get a move on," urged Harold, "McBride will be in the hereafter and so will we."

Striking the wall with his fist, Norbert released a cloud of dust that skidded down the face of the wall, causing Khia to sneeze.

"Bless you," said the little ghost and Catherine at the same time.

Norbert pressed one of the perfectly fitted stone, and it moved.

*Clunk.*

They heard the sounds of rattling chains. As designed by a master craftsman, several tons of rock moved. Stone sliding on stone, counterweighted for centuries, grated across the floor revealing an entrance of blackness.

"Our path of escape. Just like we planned, eh McBride?" said Norbert, but McBride lay motionless in Harold's arms.

Their LED flashlights pierced the black hole. Below was a corridor that ran straight and true, wide enough for them to proceed single file.

They needed no encouragement.

"After you," grumbled Norbert sarcastically, as everyone passed by him.

Not a hundred feet behind, and rapidly gaining ground, were the mercenaries who had chased them into the catacombs. Red lasers from their weapons danced on the walls.

Norbert pulled the trigger of his revolver three times.

*Bang. Bang. Bang.*

Everyone froze in mid-stride.

"What! We're in a hurry," said Norbert.

It took three blasts to break the weakest link. The chains flew in opposite directions and the door slid shut.

"Ar-ar-are w-w-we s-s-s-afe?" asked Brother Peccavi, sounding worried.

"Mon, you trying to be funny?" asked Harold.

*Plop.*

No one heard.

CHAPTER 11

# Twists and Turns

Having taken so many twists and turns, Khia had lost her sense of direction. She hoped Norbert knew where he was going. On the next turn, she heard snippets of sound coming from above. Even though the music was faint and far away, it lightened her spirit—until she had the thought that they might have been going around in circles.

Another turn and they found themselves in yet another dark corridor. She couldn't hear the music anymore; it was like it had stopped, but in the silence, in between their steps, she heard something else.

*Plop.*

What was that? She tried to identify the sound. A match being lit? No, that would have been more like a hiss and it wasn't a hiss, a scratch, or a scrape. "That's it," she said aloud, and snapped her fingers. It sounded like a small stone falling into a pool of water.

Norbert stopped so abruptly that the little ghost went right through him. Brother Peccavi (clumsy at the best of times) almost stepped on Khia's foot, sidestepped, and bumped into Harold, who almost dropped McBride.

"Easy bro," said Harold, who was breathing hard from the brisk pace.

*Plop.*

"Did you hear that?" asked Khia, her eyes wide.

"Hear what?" Jordan spun around. Beams from his flashlight scanned the dark eerie corridor. It was as if the light was trying to catch the source of the sound, but only found dust particles lingering in the air.

"What is it?" asked Khia, feeling the hair on the back of her neck rising.

"You don't want to know," announced Norbert.

"Know what?" asked Catherine.

"Run!" Norbert shouted.

Lights bobbing up and down, they ran. The light from their flashlights caught the fissures in the rock and made it look like the expanding lines were chasing them along the length of the dark corridor.

"The tunnel collapsing?" questioned Harold.

"Let's hope not," said Jordan.

Reaching a fork in their path, Norbert slowed. A decision had to be made and quick. About to turn right, the little ghost, anxiously floating up, down, and around, and shouted frantically, *"Sinistra. Sinistra. Sinistra!"*

"Speak English," demanded Norbert.

"Left. Go left," answered the little ghost.

Shrugging, Norbert went left.

This path opened into a surprisingly large chamber—not what one would expect to find in the depths of the catacombs.

Norbert looked accusingly at the little ghost, "You betrayed us."

"It was not my intent." He looked nervously about. "The other way was a false path."

"Harold. Put McBride down. Quick, form a circle. Now," demanded Norbert.

Standing shoulder to shoulder, Norbert, Khia, Jordan, Brother Peccavi, and Catherine, on the other side of Norbert, tightened their protective circle around McBride like a golden ring.

"Facing outwards, Brother Peccavi," groaned Norbert.

"S-s-s-s-sorry," he stuttered in reply, but closed his mouth when he saw Norbert's face.

The good news was that they had lost the mercenaries; the bad news was that they were about to face something far far worse. They stood in their circle, shoulder to shoulder, and waited.

The beams of light from their flashlights caught the fissures circling the chamber. Seeds, pebble-sized, burst from the crumbling rock, and when they landed on the ground, cracked and transformed into grotesque beings right before their very eyes.

Someone or something had released them from their tomb-less sleep. For millennia, the seeds had lain dormant in the foundations waiting for this day. The handiwork perhaps of some mad scientist—a creator who had spliced DNA of divergent species with that of tormented human souls. The creatures, deformed, demented, and newly born, acted like restless children. Gleefully, they gathered around craving the sweet taste of flesh—of blood—to sate their overriding hunger and quench their insatiable thirst.

Norbert was the first to react. Pulling out his revolver, he shot at a creature but the bullet went through black mist and struck the wall, releasing more seeds.

"Uh oh," said Norbert.

The little ghost floated chaotically around, not knowing which way to turn.

One creature, which might have been a Roman centurion in life, was bolder than the rest and stepped towards them, laughing. "Come my brothers and sisters… supper… at last."

Its brethren needed little encouragement, and they moved in.

One creature punched Norbert with such force that it caused his head to move a few inches back.

Massaging his jaw, Norbert retaliated, but before making contact the creature transformed into eddies of black swirling mist.

"Strike them when they're solid," shouted Khia, thinking of the black vultures that had attacked her outside the Vatican, and how they had turned into black mist and reformed. Concentrating on one of the creatures, she patiently waited for the right time to strike, applying the martial arts skills she'd learned from her Tibetan instructor.

Norbert broke their living circle. There were too many of them and he needed more freedom to move.

"B-b-behind y-y-you!" Brother Peccavi shouted to Jordan, but the warning came a stutter too late. The blow slammed Jordan into the wall, causing parts of the wall to crumble and more seeds to escape.

Stepping in to protect Jordan, Catherine slashed her nails across a creature's face. Black mist swirled around her, but she'd made contact—dark blood encrusted her finger nails.

Swirling above, around, and through them, the little ghost distracted the beasts. On the floor, in the center of the chamber, McBride lay helpless and unprotected, but none of the creatures bothered him. It was as if he were invisible to them.

But not so for Norbert; they were drawn to him. Norbert stepped forward and crashed his fist into a creature, breaking its nose. Swirling around, he attacked four more. Khia, at Norbert's side, was right there in the thick of things.

Inspired by Khia, Harold charged at a beast with renewed vigor, yelling, "If I can withstand the sight of the Vatican exercise room full of priests, sweating in the name of Christ, I can do this!" And at just the right moment, he shot a beast between the eyes; brain matter splattered the wall.

Surrounded by creatures, Norbert fought his way towards the Roman centurion. With lightning speed Norbert jumped and twirled in the air, knocking down creatures like pins at a bowling alley. Without stopping, Norbert moved onto the next, and the next, and the next... and with one magnificent blow after another, creatures wobbled and fell in heaps about him.

In the meantime, Brother Peccavi had found his weapon of choice by accidentally spilling a small vial of Holy Water, which inadvertently splashed a beast, which caused it to sizzle and scream in pain and to evaporate into black mist… never to reform.

"Have any more of that stuff?" questioned Jordon.

"N-n-n-not m-m-m-much," stuttered Brother Peccavi, trying but not succeeding in punching a creature with his fist.

"Can't you make some," retorted Jordan.

Brother Peccavi shook his head.

"You're a holy man! For God's sake, bless the water!"

Catherine, in between strikes, threw her bottle of water to Brother Peccavi, who caught it, narrowly avoiding a creature lunging at him.

More and more creatures materialized, growing in number and stature. Khia's heart was pounding, her breathing strained. She didn't know how much longer she could keep this going. She was tiring and she was losing hope. They weren't going to get out of this. Not this time.

And then she saw a glint of twinkling light moving towards them… and she smiled.

"It's about time," shouted Norbert, as he reached out for his great weapon, which flew towards him like a twirling star of light. His sword.

†

*Some months before…*

*In the dinginess of the damp underground tunnels of New York City, Cocklebur found Burdock impaled by Norbert's sword. Unable to control his emotions, tears blurred his vision. "Burdock, I am here," he called out in a fearsome voice that could have raised the dead.*

*There was no response.*

*Driven by blind fury, he found what he needed. Using his bulk and all of his immense strength, rusted metal bolts snapped and a makeshift platform was thrown down. He jumped onto the platform, and heedless of the consequences, grabbed the sword.*

*A great flash of light illuminated the tunnel. Cocklebur, flung backwards in the air, landed hard beside a teenage girl who was waiting in the wings.*

*Excruciating pain surged through Cocklebur. Roaring in agony, he plunged his hands into a small pool of muddy water. Hissing steam escaped and the acrid smell of his burnt flesh swirled through the dark passage.*

*"Girl, the Sword!" Cocklebur yelled.*

*Katrina did nothing.*

*Inhaling sharply, he glared at her. "The Sword will not let me touch it. Free my brother! Free Burdock!"*

*Katrina hesitated.*

*"Do it!" he demanded.*

*Glaring at him, Katrina climbed onto the makeshift platform. It tipped. She shifted her weight to steady herself. Inches from Burdock's impaled body, she felt as if she were in a house of horrors. He was waxy and limp. She held her breath. When his eyes slit open, she startled.*

*He was alive! That was… impossible.*

*"Now!" bellowed Cocklebur.*

*Wary that the sword would do to her what it had done to Cocklebur, she reached for the intricately carved hilt and tentatively wrapped her fingers around it.*

*No flash of light, no searing pain, she gripped the sword more firmly. The hilt molded itself to her hand and she felt its power. Her breath caught as an image flashed through her mind: an angel spreading out his wings to embrace her.*

*She drew the sword from stone and flesh; Burdock crashed to the ground; his body jerked, seizure-like, and stilled.*

*Enthralled by the sword, she didn't want to let it go… but the ancient weapon became heavy and she could no longer bear its weight. It crashed to the ground and she watched, in awe, as it transformed from solid steel to liquid. In the pool of silvery liquid, she saw her face reflected for a moment before it seeped between the cracks in the earth and was gone.*

*Ignoring the searing pain, Cocklebur drew his brother into his arms. "Norbert, I will find you! I will hunt you down!" he vowed. Struggling to his feet, Cocklebur carried Burdock out of the tunnels. Katrina followed silently behind.*

*Ezrulie, in her penthouse apartment, walked across the granite tiles out onto the enclosed glass balcony. A storm raged. Gusting winds and heavy rainfall lashed at the windows. It was the remnants of a hurricane that had started in the Atlantic Ocean and had grown into a CAT 4, making its way up the eastern coastline.*

*From her vantage point, Ezrulie watched the millions of city lights and thought they looked like a galaxy of stars… and then the lights flickered on and off. The city, left in darkness, was like a black hole, which only served to magnify the sound of the wind and the lashing rain. A few moments later, the lights flickered back on.*

*And then she felt their presence seventy-four floors below, in the underground parking. As they rode the private elevator to her suite, she was there waiting for them.*

*"You pathetic fool," Ezrulie did not mask her anger. "Show me! Show me your hands!" she screamed, as she struck Cocklebur.*

*Like an obedient dog returning to a brutal master, Cocklebur accepted his punishment. His legs buckled, and he fell to his knees. Gently, he lay his brother at her feet like an offering and opened his palms to her.*

*"You've been marked."*

*"And Burdock," Ezrulie hovered over his semiconscious form and sneered, "Crucified by the sword... by Norbert's sword."*

*Dead silence was broken by a nervous cough.*

*Ezrulie turned, "Ah, Mr. Elliot," her eyes narrowed, "I had almost forgotten."*

*He remained silent.*

*"Your organization has failed me," said Ezrulie, her voice syrupy sweet.*

*Mr. Elliot nodded stiffly. "I-I am fully aware of our recent setbacks—"*

*Ezrulie wouldn't let him finish. "I think not." She approached the man who seemed frozen to the spot. "You have not proved your worth, Mr. Elliot. I expected results."*

*More words would only fuel her anger. He knew he was damned no matter what he said. He handed her a hard copy of his last report.*

*"I have read your reports," said Ezrulie tossing the papers onto the coffee table. "Full of excuses. Justifications. Drivel. We had an agreement, Mr. Elliot. Did we not?"*

*"We have a contingency plan," sputtered Mr. Elliot.*

*"You misunderstand. I am no longer in need of your services."*

*She reached out her hand, as if to caress his cheek.*

*Mr. Elliot flinched. There was an audible crack and his eyes bulged. He staggered back a few paces; a look of pain and confusion crossed his face and then he fell… dead at her feet.*

*"Get rid of him," Ezrulie said to Cocklebur, as she walked out onto the balcony. Lightning flashed across the sky. Her hands squeezed the top of the railing with such force that deep fissures cracked across the pane.*

†

As Norbert tightened his grip on his sword, images flashed in his head. He knew Cocklebur had been branded by his sword and that a young woman had been the one to release Burdock from its hold… and the young woman... she reminded him of someone—someone he had known a very very long time ago.

Gregarious and giddy, the creatures hesitated upon seeing Norbert with his sword and were not quite as confident as they had been before.

The Roman centurion laughed a terrible laugh and recited his Latin malediction, "In death you shall await with us in the hereafter." Looking directly at Norbert he said, "Until the last day—"

"Your day! Not mine!" cried out Norbert, and engaged the Roman centurion in battle.

Blocks, parries, and blows... the centurion was pushed back, but he was not unskilled, nor hindered by the body he possessed. With his shorter sword, he quickly matched Norbert's rhythm blow for blow, even as Norbert's weapon flew almost too fast for the eye to see.

"I don't have time for this." Norbert changed his tempo and stabbed the centurion through the heart, killing him instantly. Even before he vanished into black mist, Norbert was swirling and moving at speed, killing more and more creatures.

Khia, Catherine, Jordan, Brother Peccavi, and the little ghost just stood there staring at Norbert and the flash of steel, which looked like a swirling ring of white gold.

"Don't just stand there gawking!" yelled Norbert.

Norbert launched his sword into the air. The blade rose up to the ceiling and pierced the rock above.

Music, like a choir of angels, wafted through.

The creatures' glee turned to screeches of agony, bewilderment, and pain. They covered their ears, fell to their knees, and started to dissolve before their very eyes.

Norbert glowed.

Khia looked in disbelief. It was over. Evil had not prevailed. But when she thought about it, this was no ordinary place and this (of all nights) was no ordinary night.

Harold bent down to McBride. "Oh mon... no... You still with us McBride?"

Catherine flew to his side. "McBride," she whispered. "Please… don't die." Her tears fell and rolled down his face as if they were his own. She shook him, but there was no response.

Cupping his mouth, she blew a deep breath into his lungs. His body convulsed once, and then his chest rose, fell… and then rose a second time as he grimaced in pain.

"Still here," he tried to speak.

"Stop horsing around McBride," said Norbert. "Can you see now why I hate underground places?" Then, returning to his gruff self, he barked, "Harold, make yourself useful. Pick him up."

At an almost leisurely pace, they made their way to a set of steps that would lead them out of the catacombs and onto the streets of Rome.

"This is where we part company," proclaimed Norbert.

"I cannot go," said the little ghost, hovering at the bottom of the stairs.

Catherine stopped and turned around.

"Be careful," said the little ghost. "It is a hungry thing." Then he was a little boy again, too tired to climb the stairs. He sank to the ground. "I'm scared," he said to Catherine.

Catherine sat on the first step. "Come here." She gently reached out to him. He curled up in her lap and he closed his eyes. "I'm here," she soothed. "Don't be scared. Everything is going to be okay." It didn't take long before he sighed and took his last ghostly breath.

†

Hours later, after a pint or two, Brother Peccavi and the Swiss Guard walked together arm in arm.

"I'll miss them," said Brother Peccavi.

"Me too," responded Jordan wistfully.

"I never had so much excitement in my entire life. Did you see how we got them?" Brother Peccavi cried out exuberantly, boxing the air with slow-moving fists, showing the young man yet again how he had fought off one of the creatures. "I had him by the scruff of the neck I tell you, the scuff of the neck!"

"Brother Peccavi," said Jordan, not wanting to bring the brother down from his high, "We have done what had to be done, but we can expect no reward and no one must know of our involvement."

"Come here boy, let me give you a hug" said Brother Peccavi, and before the young Swiss Guard could defend himself, the brother had taken him up in his arms and given him a great big hug... and because he was so happy, he swung him in a great circle as if he weighed nothing at all.

They had fought together, protected each other, but more than that, Jordan understood that they had seen what few people of faith, or the non-believers, had seen. It had reaffirmed his faith, but if he uttered one word of what they had experienced, people would think he was nuts.

Jordan heard the brother walking away, singing almost as loud as the whole Vatican choir. "Well I'll be," Jordan commented to himself, "he didn't stutter once."

CHAPTER 12

# The Watchers

Three figures spoke in low tones lest someone (by chance or by design) should overhear. God's representative on Earth rested in his bed. He was exhausted after midnight mass. It had taken superhuman strength. The Nigerian Cardinal, one of the princes of the Church, paced the floor and Sister Ashema stood so still she could have been a stone angel.

Well aware that the fugitives had escaped the confines of the Vatican, they were glad that they had (in a small way) helped make it possible.

"We can no longer protect them," said Sister Ashema.

"I pray we did the right thing." The Pope slurred his words, doubt clouding his fading judgment.

"We could no longer keep them here," said the prince. "Stretching their stay for as long as we did was a feat in itself. Let us hope that Khia's time spent at the Vatican has not been in vain. If they do not succeed, I fear for our world. A darkness, never seen before, is coming."

"Sister Clair?" asked the Pope, making a great effort to hold his head up.

"We have been unable to find her," replied the prince. "We suspect—"

"Rest now," said Sister Ashema to her Holy Father, cutting off the Cardinal's words. "You have done everything in your power. They are now in God's hands." She held the old man's hand and kissed his ring.

As the Nigerian prince and Sister Ashema walked out of his chamber, attendants rushed in to see to the earthly needs of the dying man. The disease was accelerating, taking a cruel hold on him. He would not be long for this world.

Just outside the Pope's chamber, the Cardinal said to Sister Ashema in a low voice, "I suspect that the General Secretary will set his misguided lap dog after them."

"Most likely," she agreed. "And if he learns of our involvement?"

"We have been careful."

"But have we been careful enough?" Sister Ashema sighed roughly. "Oh, it pains me so… how crassly he fights for position and power. As *il Papa* approaches death's door and his influence wanes, how he plots!" Sister Ashema sounded disgusted. "His strength grows with each passing day."

"His ambition to be Pope may yet be his downfall," said the Nigerian.

"Or ours," said Sister Ashema. "I pray that, after everything we have risked, they do not get caught."

"The odds are not good," he said frankly.

"I will light a candle and pray," she said.

The prince of the Church shook his head sadly. "Our salvation rests with a whore, a taxi driver, and a teenager."

"An angel," smiled Sister Ashema.

"And a demon," said the black prince, his voice deep with emotion.

†

In a deep section of the catacombs, where the greatest secrets lay, two figures emerged. One was dressed in Jesuit black, the other in a gray garment the color of stone. Silently they made their way through the poorly lit tunnels to a door, where the monk stood guard.

"Jesuit Arctium," the monk acknowledged his brother with a bit of a smirk. "My Lady."

The woman, with haunting hazel eyes, seemed to look through him. "Is she here?" Her voice was hoarse; she had strained her vocal chords.

The monk (aka Burdock) nodded and opened the door.

With an icy stare, the woman walked in the room.

Burdock scowled and whispered to his brother, "She's crazy, that one."

She entered a chamber that looked more like an operating theater. Strewn about the room were men and women of science, dead or unconscious, it didn't matter to her; she was only interested in one thing.

Flood lights illuminated a glass sarcophagus. Highly sophisticated medical equipment recorded the slow breaths and heartbeats of a creature held in stasis.

Sister Clair was standing next to a young woman, a little older than Khia, who never glanced up. She was well aware of who had entered the room, but she never took her eyes off the creature in the glass box.

The woman with the haunting hazel eyes ignored Sister Clair and went straight to the teenage girl.

"Isn't she beautiful?" sighed the teenage girl.

"Your idea of beauty is beyond me, Khia," the woman said coldly, astounded as always by her daughter's ideas.

"My name is Katrina," said the girl angrily.

The woman blinked and looked down into her niece's face. Her niece. Of course. *No matter,* she thought. Pretending not to have heard, the woman said in a scolding voice, "That creature before you is an instrument. Such infatuation is of no use to us. Is that clear?"

"You're starting to sound like great Aunt Ezrulie," said Katrina. "Why isn't she here?" she asked, but silently felt that Ezrulie would never dare step on consecrated ground. *She'd probably melt like the wicked witch that she is.*

The woman took the young girl's hand and bent it back in a painful unyielding grip. "Set it on its task."

"You're hurting me Auntie Val," said Katrina.

"Awaken our sleeping child."

Katrina looked up at her aunt, pretending not to understand.

"Do not be stupid," Valerie said. "The Sylph needs sustenance; there is a surplus in this room." She looked around, as if they were making the selection from an extensive wine menu. "It's better fresh, still warm." Valerie nodded to Sister Clair.

With the same sharp knife she would have used to kill Khia, Sister Clair slashed the neck of one of the unconscious victim's. Filling the cup with warm blood, she handed it to Katrina.

Gently lifting the Sylph's head, Katrina brought the cup to the creature's mouth.

Almost the moment the blood touched the creature's lips, its eyes fluttered opened. Stretching, as if waking from a night's sleep, her skin changed from a dull brown to saffron and brightened like a sunrise. Seeing the face of Katrina, its mother, it realized two things in that moment: love and failure. It loved its mother—not like most of us would love our mothers, but a love indeed—for Katrina had brought her to life, not once but twice. As its saffron skin glowed, it cowered before her in stigma and shame for having failed its mother—for having failed to kill Devon.

"Drink my darling," said Katrina in a soothing voice.

Greedily, the Sylph drank more of the blood. Licking and savoring every last drop.

"Do not fail me again," Katrina cooed.

The Sylph looked to its mother, shape shifting into Devon.

"No, no my darling," said Katrina in her soothing voice. "You won't find Devon here; he's gone."

"Tell it. Tell it to kill Khia," said Valerie.

Katrina stared at her aunt, then turned to the Sylph. "You must find and kill Khia," reaffirmed Katrina, as she handed it a piece of cloth. It was a torn piece of cloth from a baby blanket, once white but now yellowed with age. The letter "K" had been finely embroidered on it in silver and gold thread.

The Sylph breathed deeply and caught Khia's scent in the cloth.

It raced from the chamber, almost bowling over Burdock and Cocklebur, who stood guarding the door. It gained speed, remembering the feeling of freedom, movement, and life, and raced through the ancient corridors.

From its underground cavern, it dug itself out of the earth, exploding through the dirt and rock into the last vestiges of the night. It sniffed the air, catching the exhilarating sweet scents that were all around it.

"Khiaaa!" it screamed into the night.

CHAPTER 13

# Knock, Knock, Knock

How long will you vex my soul,
grind me down with words?

~Job 19:2

"How much longer do we have to stay here?" complained Catherine, about the rat hole she shared with Norbert, McBride, Harold, and Khia.

"We stay until it's safe for us to leave," snapped Norbert. "Don't interrupt me again."

Catherine wanted to hit something—hit Norbert. She had never felt like this before, she preferred more subtle approaches. What was happening to her? She sunk on the shabby sofa in the corner of the room and squeezed the pillow to her chest.

"As I was saying," said Norbert to Khia. "They weren't liberal with information."

"Noorberrt," said Khia, dragging out his name. "Tell me what you know."

"Okay, okay. We were hired by Ms. Percival. You remember Ms. Percival? Tall beautiful woman who pretended to be your social worker?"

"Yes, Norbert," said Khia, rolling her eyes. "I know."

Norbert cleared his throat. "As I was saying, Ms. Percival hired us."

"Gave us quite a bit of money at that. Remember that gold credit card," interjected McBride. "Gold is such a pretty color."

"McBride," said Norbert.

McBride clamped his mouth shut.

"It was a simple assignment. Get you and Devon to your grandmother's. Easy, right? Who knew you were Lady Tiamore's granddaughter? Ms. Percival didn't tell us that part. McBride and I worked that out later, at Nora's."

"Going to Nora's was a stroke of genius," added McBride.

"Yeah, we hadn't planned on that," responded Norbert.

"Do you think she's still alive?" asked Khia. It had suddenly become more important for her to ask about Nora than to find out about her grandmother.

"Hard to say," answered Norbert, skirting the question. Nora was a powerful shaman, but he didn't know if she could have survived the Sylph and the forest fire. "It was a major detour, took us way off course and complicated things. But we did get you to New York City. It's not easy going through portals these days, if you've noticed. Why *didn't* you go through the portal? You had plenty of time."

They both stopped and looked at Khia.

How could she explain her decision? She still questioned it herself. "Norbert, it was my choice to make."

"Well, at least Devon got through the portal okay. Such a nice little tyke. I miss him," said Norbert.

"I miss him too," said Khia sadly. Would she ever see him again? There wasn't a day that went by that she didn't think of him. She had missed his eighth birthday. It wasn't like she could send him a birthday card or anything; there was no possible way of contacting him. He was in another world with their grandmother, and every time she stared into the night sky, she'd wonder what star he might be on. Oh jeez, Norbert had done it again. She shook her head, refusing to let him distract her. "Norbert, why did they lock you up in the Vatican?"

"We weren't really locked up… we could have escaped anytime."

"What?" She shook her head in disbelief. "Okay then, who is after me and why?"

"Well, that is not so easy to explain."

"Why don't you start with Burdock and Cocklebur," suggested McBride.

"Yeah, I could," replied Norbert.

"Or maybe you should start with Ezrulie," added McBride.

"Who's telling this story?" asked Norbert, getting a little irked.

"Norbert was never any good at telling a story," chirped McBride. "You should get me to tell the story."

"No comments from the gallery," grumbled Norbert. "As I was saying, it was at Nora's that we figured out you were Lady Tiamore's granddaughter."

Khia looked confused, weren't they just talking about Burdock and Cocklebur?

"And that, my young lady, is significant," said Norbert.

"What is?" asked Khia.

"That you are Lady Tiamore's granddaughter," said Norbert.

"How so?"

"Well," stumbled Norbert, not really sure how to answer that. "A lot of it is myth and hearsay. I'm not into gossip. It would impair the facts."

"Norbert!"

"Uh, McBride, you want to explain this part?" asked Norbert.

"What part?" asked McBride, "the part where she's coveted or the part where she's in danger?"

"You're not helping," said Norbert.

"We think you are Lady Tiamore's granddaughter," McBride said, as if that explained everything.

"Okay, but what does that mean?" asked Khia.

"You tell her," said Norbert nudging McBride.

"No you tell her," said McBride. "You're doing such a fine good job of it."

"Tell me what?" asked Khia.

"Your grandmother is one of the Guardians of the Corridor of Doors—"

Three sharp knocks at the door interrupted them.

"Expecting anyone?" asked Harold. Reaching the door, he cautiously opened it a crack.

"Let her in," Norbert ordered gruffly.

Shrugging, Harold let the door swing open.

A woman with big brown eyes, dressed in a dark blue burka, which enveloped her from head to toe, swept into the room. "I have a vehicle waiting. Let's go."

In about thirty seconds, they had vacated the room, leaving no trace that they had ever been there.

Cloaked in the Italian darkness, they jumped into the waiting cube-van. Their driver, who looked like a jihad terrorist on a mission, revved off as if he were driving a Ferrari—tail-gaiting cars, passing, swirling, and swearing at people as they sped through the narrow streets of Rome.

In the front seat, McBride stretched out his back before reclining, looking totally relaxed (except for every now and then when he'd scan their surroundings—what was ahead, what was behind, and what was up in the sky).

No one spoke. Before sunrise, their vehicle came to a final resounding stop.

The doors flew open and they jumped out.

Revving the engine, their driver rolled down the window and spoke to the burka-clad girl. The sweetness in his voice belied his intimidating look, "See? Apples and honey." He stopped to look at his watch. "I get you here. Record time." With that, he put the van in gear and squealed away, leaving them in a squalid Italian port.

Diesel oil and rotting fish overwhelmed Khia's senses. On the dock, they walked past hulking tankers loaded with cargo from around the world. Sandwiched between two behemoths, they came upon a relatively small (but only in comparison to the behemoths) rusted old freighter. It looked decrepit, and not in any way seaworthy. Eerily quiet, it seemed lifeless: no lights, no movement.

The burka-clad girl floated up the gangplank. On the side of the ship, written in bold letters, was the ship's name: ABRAXIS.

No sooner had her feet touched the deck when the woman abruptly flung off her burka. "Only for you," she said, looking at Norbert and McBride who were halfway up the gangplank, "would I wear that cloak of repression."

"Your father would be proud of you," McBride said teasingly.

"Tell me something I don't know," she laughed freely.

Harold caught his breath; she had the most incredible laugh. He couldn't stop staring at her. Before she had discarded the burka, he had been entranced by her eyes and her voice. She couldn't disguise her voice—melodic, with a hint of an accent he couldn't place. He wondered where she'd learn to speak English. But when she flung off her burka, he was transfixed; she was beautiful, absolutely beautiful—golden skin, dark hair, tight jeans. Harold was completely under her spell.

"You can close your mouth now, Harold," Catherine smiled.

"Please, welcome aboard the Abraxis," said the young woman. "I am the captain's daughter. My name is Melalaia, but my friends call me Mela."

For a moment, Harold thought she smiled right at him. He smiled, and before he knew it, she scampered away (light on her feet) to find her father.

"Poppy, I'm back!" she called. "I've brought Norbert and McBride."

Poppy, smoking a cigarette, appeared from above and waved, "*A hoi.* A nick in time saves nine lives." Wearing a black and white keffiyeh, he rested his hand on the corroded steel railings and leaned over. "Time cast!" he shouted.

Sea-salted and sun-drenched men, more pirate than sailor, sprang from the holds and hatchways. Khia felt the rumblings of the old freighter through her feet, the deep vibrations of the diesel engines chugging over, igniting and then turning into a thrumming beat. The dead ship came alive with activity and the rusted freighter slipped unnoticed from the old Italian port.

Weathered by the sea, the captain had deep lines on his face; nicotine and oil stained his fingers. "Norbert," he kissed Norbert three times on the cheeks.

"Good to see you, Salix. Thanks for helping us," said Norbert.

"UIO. Big debt of gratitude," replied Salix. "Welcome, welcome aboard Abraxis. Come, come see my ship. She good ship. New second-handed engines," he beamed.

"Engines?" said McBride, his interest peaked.

"I show you engine. Art of the states. Very good, very good."

Looking at McBride, Salix said to Norbert, "He look no so good."

"You should have seen him, Captain Salix," said Harold, trying to make friendly conversation, "when we were in the Vatican."

"Who is?" asked Salix.

"Harold," said Norbert, as a form of introduction. "And this is Catherine and Khia."

But Salix was more concerned with McBride. "McBride? Holy City? No surprise he look no so good."

"Consecrated ground does it to him every time," said Norbert nonchalantly.

"Sea air she be very good, no?" nodded Salix. "Me hire new chef. Honoré make food for McBride. Make no never mind."

Chef Honoré approached and clasped Norbert's hand. *"Bonjour.* Norbert, it is so good to see you again."

"What he do, fire you and hire you back?" asked Norbert.

*"Bien sûr,"* smiled the chef. He shook McBride's hand and said, "I will fatten you up. I have some goose liver."

Salix shook his head sadly, then cheered up. "You here is what counts." Reaching into his breast pocket, Salix took out another cigarette, lit it, and inhaled deeply. "Melalaia," he called, as he exhaled the smoke.

"Yes Poppy." Popping out of a nearby hatch, she glided towards her father.

"Mela—oh. There you be, miserable girl." In spite of his gruffness, everyone could tell that Salix, the captain of the Abraxis, loved his daughter as much if not more so than his ship. "You take to cabinets."

"Cabins," Melalaia corrected him.

"Go, go!" He waved them away so he was left alone with Norbert.

"Come, come my old friend," Salix put his arm around Norbert. "You fa coffee?"

Norbert nodded. "Sure, coffee sounds good."

"Norbert, Norbert," Salix said in a conspiring tone, "I have chess board, play chess—no!" Three things to know about Salix: First, there was absolutely no way of dissuading him once he'd made up his mind; second (and this is where it could get a little tricky), sometimes *no* meant no and sometimes *no* meant yes; and third, after you got to know him, it was easy to figure out which was which.

CHAPTER 14

# Practice, Practice, Practice

Fall seven times stand up eight

~ Japanese Proverb

"Come ladies. I've got all day," said Norbert. With a berserker's frenzy, he flung himself onto the deck.

It was hard enough for Khia and Catherine to keep their balance amidst the rage of the Mediterranean Sea and the gusting wind. They tried to work as one, slashing and pressing their attack on Norbert, but to no avail. Two against one. You'd think this would have them at some advantage, but he was too big, too strong, and too fast. Under a cold gray sky, with the bow of the ship rising and falling, Norbert pushed them… and when they had reached their limits, he pushed them beyond. Again, and again, and again. Going over the finer details of movement and sparring, and the proper way to use a sword, a knife, a gun…

"Catherine. Again," Norbert commanded.

Being a little too eager, she over extended. The moment she'd made the move, she knew it had been a mistake giving Norbert an opportunity. One thing you never wanted to give Norbert was an opportunity.

"Enough!" screamed Catherine. She fell to her knees; her sword slipped from her hand.

Norbert's hand tangled in her hair, forcing her head back, his knife at her throat. "Why did you invite yourself on our little sortie?" he yelled at

Catherine. "So that you could help us fail? You should have stayed home where at least you could have been some use to someone."

"I'm not a fighter!" she shot back.

"I know what you are," he said to her cruelly. "Never, ever get distracted in a fight."

Catherine turned away, her face flushed from exertion and embarrassment, quiet tears streaming down her face. She thought she could handle this; she had thick skin, but Norbert was peeling it away, layer by layer. More often than not, these sessions with Norbert ended with tears of frustration and seething rage.

Khia stood quietly. Her heart went out to Catherine, but she said nothing—did nothing.

Walking away in disgust, Norbert turned the corner and spied McBride. "Been watching the exchange?" asked Norbert tersely.

McBride didn't answer.

"What?" Norbert knew McBride had something to say.

"Cut her some slack," McBride said quietly.

"She's a liability."

"She can help," he responded firmly. "She *has* helped."

"Your infatuation with the whore has addled your brain," said Norbert, inches from McBride's face.

"Our priority is Khia," McBride said. "It has always been Khia, but she needs a friend and—"

"Khia's got us," snapped Norbert, turning away.

"We can't be all things to her," said McBride, as Norbert was walking away. "It's a girl thing. Whether you like it or not, Khia and Catherine have become friends. Khia confides in her."

McBride shrugged his shoulders and strolled back to his vantage point where he had watched the exchange. He'd seen the hurt expression on Catherine's face; he'd seen her tears and knew better than most how strong she was. He was about to go over and console Catherine when he saw that Khia was already there.

"You okay?" asked Khia.

"Sticks and stones," said Catherine.

McBride watched as Catherine picked up the sword and started sparring with Khia. Working together, helping each other. Step by step, like a dance, they practiced the moves, again and again.

†

"Are you coming Catherine?" asked Khia.

"No, I'm not hungry." Catherine forced a laugh. "I have bruises on my bruises. I'm going to rest awhile."

"Okay," said Khia, deciding that Catherine needed to be alone. She'd never seen her so discouraged.

The moment Khia left the cabin, Catherine waited just long enough for Khia to be out of reach before she bolted the door.

Rummaging through her knapsack, Catherine's fingers felt the velvet cloth. She dug out The Book and placed it gently on the desk. Slowly and carefully, like a special Christmas present, she unwrapped it. Seeing it, she had an even stronger urge to touch it—just one more time. What harm could it do? Her fingers inches away, she stopped.

Ever since she'd first touched The Book, its voice seductively called to her. She adjusted the lamp so the light shone on it. It glowed, coppery red. She sensed that this book possessed a power she should be wary of, but she couldn't resist its sweet sultry voice. The temptation was too great.

She ignored Norbert's warning, she ignored the little ghost's warning, and most disconcerting of all, she ignored the warning in the back of her own mind. And although she knew she was never to speak The Book's name, as she traced her fingers over the words on the cover, Catherine found herself saying them aloud: "*Ab... Comissio... Occauss... Aborior.*" An opiate thrill went through her as she unconsciously caressed its cover.

"Catherine," it whispered to her, like a long lost lover who wanted to look into her soul. She wasn't sure if the voice was real or inside her head.

An old rusted metal lock held the leather clasp shut. Her hands shook, like someone going through withdrawal, in her urgency to open The Book.

"Ouch." She looked at her finger. The wound, saw-toothed and jagged, was bleeding. She watched in disbelief as two drops of her blood fell onto The Book.

Suddenly, Catherine was afraid.

The room grew dark and Catherine started to whimper. All she could hear was the voice from The Book. It had lost all of its affection; now it screamed cruelly at her—words like a fist entangled in her mind—and an invisible force pushed her face toward The Book, pulling her head up and exposing her throat.

She was confused, trying to make out whether The Book was talking to her or if she was recalling buried memories. Cold fingers had wrapped themselves around her throat, tightening.

She couldn't breathe.

"I'll let you scream..." it whispered seductively in her ear, "... but not out loud."

†

"Oops," said Khia, quickly retreating from the galley.

Chef Honoré and Captain Salix were arguing… yet again. On the other side of the door, she heard the chef say, "I am not a happy camper. My galley is spit spot clean and you want a food contest! A food contest!" His voice rose. "Too many chefs, no little Indians!"

"*My* galley," Salix corrected. "Food contest. No."

*"Eh bien,"* the chef threw up his hands and conceded. Having known Salix a long time, he knew when *no* really meant *yes*. "I, however, put my foot down!" Honoré stomped his foot for show and protest. "Captain or not, I will roast you alive if you mess up my mess."

Khia felt like laughing, but the urge left her when the captain, like a wild-eyed Caliban character, called out to everyone. "Us begins!" He held eight straws in his fist.

The lots were drawn. Honoré and Harold; Melalaia and Khia; Salix and Norbert. Salix placed the last two straws on the counter, which he left for Catherine and McBride.

At random, Salix handed each pair a folded piece of paper. Harold's eyes lit up when he read the recipe. Immediately he started to dig into the cupboards, looking for the ingredients he would need.

*"Non. Mon Dieu."* The chef stopped Harold. *"Q'est que tu fais? Monsieur,* cooking is all in the preparation. We do not start until we toast." Rooting around, he emerged holding two bottles. "Rum or red?"

"Red," replied Harold.

"Red? A man after my own heart," he said, as he uncorked the wine and poured two glasses. *"Santé."* The Acadian chef from the east coast of Canada and the New York City taxi driver from the Bahamas leisurely sipped their wine.

"Now, my friend," smiled the Chef, "we can start."

In the meantime, Norbert and Salix were having a rather loud discussion over, of all things, a large sack of flour. It ended abruptly when Salix said, "Flour, *no!*"

"Fine," said Norbert, and conceded, handing the sack of flour to Salix. He also understood which *no* was which, having known the captain for years.

The large smile on Norbert's face surprised Khia; she had rarely seen him smile. Salix and Norbert had come to some sort of compromise, but would they come up with something edible? She'd tasted Norbert's cooking once before at Nora's. It was no wonder Nora had left McBride with cooking duty.

Where were McBride and Catherine? Khia hoped they wouldn't be too long. McBride loved this sort of thing.

Khia looked at her recipe. Goat Curry was scrawled across the page in bold letters. Khia made a face. "Ugh."

"Don't worry, we don't have to use goat," laughed Melalaia. "We'll use chicken."

"It's freight range," laughed the Chef, taking another sip of wine. "You gonna have to catch, kill, and pluck the chickens first."

Khia looked questionably at Melalaia.

"Don't listen to him," said Melalaia. "Already been done. Chickens are chilling in the refrigerator and we have some wonderful spices from India, or if you prefer, we can use Moroccan spices."

"India sounds good," said Khia, but she really didn't know.

"Indian spices it is," smiled Melalaia.

Khia noticed that Harold kept glancing over at Melalaia, and once or twice, she'd seen Melalaia glance back at him.

As the evening unfolded, someone outside the galley started to play the fiddle. Chef Honoré danced a little jig and grabbed a couple of spoons. Spontaneously, Harold twirled Khia in a quadrille.

†

"I wouldn't do that if I were you," said McBride.

If Catherine had been more lucid she would have wondered how McBride had gotten through a bolted door, but she was not lucid; she was in pain and almost delirious.

The creature, ever so slightly, loosened its death grip on Catherine. It wasn't much, but it was enough for Catherine to twist from its grasp and retreat to the corner of the room. Gasping for breath, she saw the horrific creature that had ensnared her. It was truly terrifying to behold: thin and sinewy muscles, bent and deformed. Strong and powerful, it could have easily snapped her neck.

It snarled at McBride, showing its fangs. "How is it you can see me?"

"I can see a lot of things," said McBride. "Quite the little creature we have here. A captive Rand. How fascinating!"

"Hrrggg, Human, how is it you know these things?"

"What makes you think I'm human?"

"Demon!" it shrieked.

Ignoring it, McBride continued, "And what's your story? A book always has a story."

"Life. Eternal life."

"Great reward! Eternal life trapped in a book," laughed McBride sarcastically. "Seems more like eternal damnation to me."

"You would know," sneered the Rand. "I get to play. Some things are fun to play with." It looked at Catherine cowering in the corner. "I shall enjoy driving her to madness. It won't take long. It will be short, but it will be so sweet. Would you like to watch? I can make her do some incredible things. She's done some interesting things already… without my influence." The Rand laughed, "I know everything about her." The vile creature turned to Catherine and licked its lips suggestively. "Drive you insane with pleasure and pain. I bet you'd like that, and you... you can watch me bend her to my will." Suddenly, with incredible fury, it sprang at McBride—but McBride was ready.

McBride cuffed it. It recoiled, but its look was pure hatred.

"Don't forget I know what you are, Rand," warned McBride. He went towards it, but it dissipated into gray smoke and drifted back into The Book.

McBride went over to Catherine and held her close.

"What is a Rand?" asked Catherine.

"An ancient race that died out long ago. They don't age well, do they? But they're even uglier when they're young. You could say they're an endangered species."

"Where's it from?" asked Catherine.

"Its world doesn't exist anymore. A conundrum, it will search forever."

"I thought I was the *Book Bearer*," said Catherine, but she was confused.

"And so you may be." He looked at her gently, "But that doesn't mean you control The Book. The Book will test you and use you." What he left unsaid was that, in time, it may even try to kill her.

"It would have been nice if someone had bothered to explain that to me," said Catherine.

"I'm sorry Catherine. When you touched The Book, said the words aloud, and it tasted your blood, it… kind of took possession of you."

There was fear in her eyes. "How can I fight something like that?"

"You'll find a way." McBride cradled her in his arms.

She rested her head on his chest and started to cry.

"I'll always be here for you, I promise," he said gently.

"Come on." He knew she needed a distraction... to be around people. "We don't want to miss all the fun. You ever taste French pastry made by an Afghan and an Angel? It's a heavenly treat. And I'd say just about now… Chef Honoré may have been fired again."

McBride lightly kissed Catherine on the lips. Turning out the lights, he closed the door and slipped his hand into hers as they made their way down the corridor towards the galley to join the others.

## CHAPTER 15

# The Start of a Storm

Betwixt us and the sun

~ Samuel Taylor Coleridge, *The Rime of the Ancient Mariner*

Just as the sun burst from the horizon, ablaze in a stunning red display, Khia walked into the control room and stood beside Norbert. She looked up at him and wondered what he'd be teaching her today. You never knew with Norbert; every day was different.

"Good morning," smiled Khia.

"Sky red at night is sailor's light. Sky red at break of day is warning," Salix said solemnly, as he looked over the radar operator's shoulder.

"Weather's fine, Captain. Nothing on any of the screens," said the operator.

"No, cannot so be," said Salix, puzzled by the red sky.

"Uh!" Khia suddenly bent down and pressed her hands to her ears.

"What's wrong?" asked Norbert.

"I hear screeching sounds!" she said a little too loudly, as if she were wearing ear-buds and listening to blaring music.

"Sounds? What hear you?" asked Salix, concerned.

Could no one else hear it? "Voices. Voices in the wind," explained Khia.

"Sirens," Salix shuddered.

"Myth," snarled Norbert. The last thing he needed was for Salix and his crew to go all squirrelly superstitious on him. There were enough *real* things to be afraid of, and sirens weren't one of them. Sylphs and wizards, on the other hand, were something to be concerned about.

On the open sea, and with the swirling wind, the location of the source was difficult to pinpoint. Khia closed her eyes, trying to discern its direction. "Over there," she pointed.

"Where?" asked Norbert.

"There," she pointed more forcefully. It was like the sea and the clouds were merging together. Gray shapes were forming. Could no one else see them?

"How far?" asked Norbert.

"I don't know."

*"How far?"* Norbert demanded.

"I don't know! About—"

Suddenly the radar operator's voice broke through, "What the hell? Where did *that* come from?" The screen suddenly detected all sorts of atmospheric disturbances.

A jagged line of dark gray mist on the horizon was rapidly moving towards them, looking as threatening as an angry Poseidon rising out of the sea.

Salix hit the alarm. Bells screamed out their warning.

Khia found it hard to concentrate. The voices bombarded her head. High-pitched female voices chanted, their words bringing the wind and the sea together. Stratus fractious clouds formed in the sky and merged with the cold sea air. The sea began to bubble and boil. The Abraxis creaked and groaned, and the Liberian flag strained on its mooring, whipping in the wind.

Khia's head felt like it was ready to explode. Not able to take it any longer, she screamed at the voices in the wind. "What do you want? Tell me! TELL ME!"

"Khia stop!" Norbert yelled. "You're drawing them in!" He grabbed her and shook her, but he couldn't get through to her.

A black bird, with a massive wingspan, swooped down out of nowhere and clawed at the heavy glass window, screeching, "Khhhhiiiiiaaaaa. Khhhhiiiiiaaaaa."

It startled Salix and his radar operator and jolted Khia out of her trance. Khia touched the pendant that was glowing around her neck. It was not the first time that one of Timothea's totem animals had come to help her.

Norbert wrapped his great arms around her. "Do you know how stupid that was?"

Captain Salix steered the freighter sharply to the starboard side.

"Damn." Norbert's voice filled the Abraxis' bridge. "Damn!"

"Hurricane."

"No," said Norbert, "it's a lot worse than a hurricane."

Those aboard the Abraxis turned their eyes towards the ship's flag and watched as the fabric ripped from its flagstaff and was swallowed by the sea.

Gathering in a circular formation, the clouds closed in on them. "Down! Get her..." ordered Salix but Norbert was already hauling Khia out of the control room and skirting around the scrambling crew. Against the violent freak of nature that was heading towards them, Salix steeled himself to save his ship. The ship rose up on a swell and dipped dramatically. Then he saw a huge tsunami accelerating towards them.

Khia and Norbert ran through an open door as crew members spilled out. Running down the long corridor, Khia careened into the wall as the ship pitched from side to side. Righting herself, she clutched the railings, and followed Norbert down the metal staircase to the deepest part of the ship. Making their way to a door on the left, they saw McBride running towards them from the other side, carrying two rucksacks, one in each hand.

Entering the dark recess, McBride at their heels, the metal door closed with a clang as the huge wave struck.

Above, the crew of the Abraxis braced themselves against the turbulent sea. The first wave crashed over the ship with a jarring hammer strike, so strong that, had the men not been tethered, they would have been washed out to sea.

The alarm ceased its shrilling cry.

The Abraxis rose up from the sea as if gasping for air. There was barely time to take another breath before a second wave hit, bringing with it freezing mist. By the strike of the third wave, the ship was covered in hoar frost. Then all was eerily still.

From the fog, ghostly mist shapes danced on the deck and wrapped their forms around crew members, to gaze into their eyes and into their souls, to feed on their fears… while others, as if cloaked in gowns of white, descended into the holds looking for someone to dance with.

†

Pitch black. Khia couldn't see a thing, but she could hear the Abraxis creaking and groaning, feel her jolting movements. It was making her feel sick… and then, just when she didn't think she could handle the motion any longer, everything turned eerily still and silent.

"We're in the eye," said Norbert, as he lit a match. The match went out and he lit another.

"Here." McBride turned on a flashlight and handed it to Norbert.

Norbert blew out the match. The beam from the flashlight caught the gray smoke. It lingered as if looking for a way out to betray them.

With a quick swish of his hand, Norbert sliced through the smoke, so it lost whatever integrity it had and dispersed without form or purpose.

Khia shivered; she felt the cold. And as for the voices, they were getting louder inside her head.

Norbert pointed the flashlight up. Strange cold shadows moved across the ceiling like a bride's white train.

A moment later, the door latch shook… buckling... back and forth.

Khia looked at Norbert.

A silvery blue sliver of mist framed the door. Mist wraiths were trying to find a way in.

Slowly Khia let out her breath, while McBride rummaged through the rucksacks and tossed a butane torch at Norbert. Lighting the torches, the yellow sparks coalesced into hot flame.

Bony dead fingers of freezing mist seeped through cracks and rivets.

Norbert and McBride aimed their butane torches, transforming the icy mist into water droplets.

Liquid pooled at their feet. Khia felt dread as she watched the water rise.

*Bang. Bang. Bang.*

The sound broke the fog. The mist seemed to hesitate.

*BANG. BANG. BANG.*

The wraith-like figures started to thin and their voices became discordant. They lost their focus and could no longer hold their form.

Khia, Norbert, and McBride staggered onto the deck of the Abraxis. The sunlight, startlingly bright, hurt Khia's eyes.

Crazily, Chef Honoré was yelling and banging his metal spoon against a huge iron pot. The crew had taken up his theme, banging a loud discordant tune. The wraiths had fled, and the white blanket of frost started to melt off the Abraxis.

"What were they?" asked Khia.

"Fog pillars," said McBride.

"Mist wraiths," said Norbert.

"Same thing," said McBride.

"They feed on fear."

"What do you think they wanted?" asked Khia.

"You."

†

Khia walked around the ship, passed Salix speaking with a Persian crew member, and knew they were assessing the damage to the ship. She needed a distraction; she couldn't stop thinking that this was all her fault. She'd put everyone on the ship in danger.

She made her way to the crow's nest. Any free time that she had—that's where she liked to be. High up on the freighter, she'd look at the world, close her eyes, and feel the breeze on her face, smelling the salty air. In her mind's eye, she could imagine planet Earth as a big ball in the sky circling the sun. She could think up there, clear her mind.

"Hello Khia," said Melalaia, walking up beside her. "We haven't had this much excitement in a long time. Actually, probably not since Norbert and McBride were last here," she smiled.

"I put everyone in danger," said Khia, blaming herself.

"Stop," Melalaia grabbed both of Khia's arms and looked into her eyes. "Listen to me. We all accepted this challenge, knowing the risks."

"And the crew?"

"Yes, even the crew. Our business is risk."

Khia looked over and saw Salix in the distance, pensively taking a drag from his cigarette. As he exhaled, two gray smoke rings lingered in the air.

Khia shivered. "I heard he's in the import/export business, but he's a pirate, isn't he?" asked Khia.

"Yes, he is a pirate of sorts," smiled Melalaia.

"A drug smuggler."

"It is drugs and it is smuggling." Melalaia laughed. "Pharmaceuticals, actually. He gets medicines to poor and war-torn countries."

"Oh."

"If not for my father, the Abraxis would have been left abandoned on a Bangladeshi shore. There would have been no ship to protect a crew who themselves have been driven into exile, refugees no country would accept. My father has a heart of gold, and his men would go to the end of the world for him. He has skirted danger, severe weather, and the authorities—but he's getting older."

"Mela, how did you get out of Afghanistan?"

"My father says it was fate. One day, in the busy market place, a man my father once helped brushed his shoulder and secretly handed him a crumpled piece of paper. Scrawled, in a barely legible hand, was my father's name. It meant an order had been given. My father rushed to his home through treacherous mountain paths and mine-laden roads, his worst fear realized. Part of him died that day. His family, his home, his small plot of land, his livestock, crops, everything… everything destroyed, burnt to the ground.

"Then, unbelievably, he heard a small cry." Melalaia smiled. "He told me this story many times. It was a miracle; he said I must have been protected by angels.

"He found me in my cradle. The house burnt to nothing, yet I was unharmed. He carried me out of his cursed land that had been, at some point or another, controlled by the Russians, the Taliban, the warlords, and the drug lords, and he walked until he reached the sea. The first time he saw the sea, he said he understood why everything that had happened had happened. It was meant to be. We were to become seafarers. It took many years and many setbacks. My father has had a very difficult life, but he would say his life is blessed."

CHAPTER 16

# Milk Run

At the helm, Salix had chosen to take a south westerly course in a zigzag pattern in an attempt to avoid trouble… but trouble undoubtedly followed. There had been a few tension-filled encounters at sea, but nothing Salix couldn't handle with what he called *baksheesh*—or a 'not-so-small charitable donation'. Khia had actually witnessed an exchange at sea. Up in the crow's nest, she had seen fast boats approaching. Aligning themselves to the Abraxis, she had watched as goods and money had quickly changed hands. It had taken no more than six minutes.

As the freighter docked, Khia was making her way to the lower decks when she saw Salix walking off the gangplank. On the creaky wooden pier, he made his way to a group of local merchants who seemed to be growing in numbers, surrounding him. Animated voices and waving hands turned into angry diatribes and clenched fists. The art of haggling.

"Watch what he's going to do now," said Norbert, causing Khia to jump.

"How many times have I told you?" he reprimanded her. "Always be aware of your surroundings."

"Sorry."

Norbert said nothing.

"So, what's Salix up to?" she asked.

"You tell me."

"It looks like he's in trouble," said Khia a little anxiously, as the crowd of merchants pressed around Salix. "Aren't you going to do something?"

"It's a game," said Norbert. "Watch… and learn."

The captain, who could speak about sixteen languages (and none of them very well), protested as the group of merchants squeezed around him. To get the best price, Salix lamented his situation, his poverty, and the cruelties of fate.

Somehow Salix knew he was being observed; he turned, looked up at Khia and Norbert, and gave them a clandestine wink.

"It looks like Salix has made a deal," chuckled Norbert.

Price agreed upon, money changed hands and Khia had counted thirteen boxes unloaded from the freighter when a soft whistle blew. Without appearing to rush, Salix boarded the ship, and with stop-watch precision which belied the old ship, they quickly left the port.

†

Next morning, as Khia was making her way to the crow's nest, she saw a fast boat approaching. She knew something was up; she could feel the tension. That's when she noticed that the freighter carried a different flag. What she couldn't see (although she would find out shortly) was that the Abraxis had also undergone a name change, becoming the FAB XI. The paint had barely dried (but to the observant eye, there was a little too much space between its name and its number).

By the time she reached the crow's nest, the EU government powerboat was coasting alongside the freighter. A young custom's officer, with six armed soldiers, demanded to be let on board to see their papers.

Salix, the captain of the FAB XI, slowed the freighter. Always a most hospitable man, he generously welcomed the government official aboard as if he were a long lost second cousin, proudly showing him his ship. He offered the young man coffee and pastries, and told him stories.

Perplexed, the government official left. Everything had checked out; their paperwork was in order. He had thought for sure it was the Abraxis… but with no proof, there was nothing he could do.

†

Loud voices from the captain's quarters caused Khia, Harold, and Catherine to hesitate outside the closed door.

Inside the room, Norbert and Salix were engaged in a heated argument, while McBride didn't say a word, which was unusual; he just looked out the window at the unusually calm sea.

"What do you mean things are too hot? You easily manipulated the government official!"

"Ah, he be a happy puppy," replied Salix.

"You agreed to take us to the straits and narrows! We shook hands!" Norbert snarled, and then went to the door, opened it, and stuck his head out. "This is none of your concern!" He slammed the door.

Khia opened the door and entered.

"Get out!" he cried. "This is none of your business!"

"It is," said Khia, her anger making her bolder. "We're all involved."

"Norbert. You listen. It a 22 catch," said Salix.

In total frustration, Norbert ran his hand through his short-cropped hair and said, through clenched teeth, "It is not a catch 22."

"Actually, I would describe it as a 'damned if you do and damned if you don't' situation," said McBride, with a slight grin.

"You're not helping," said Norbert.

"You not listen to the babble on radio," said Salix.

"Chatter," corrected Norbert.

"You cat on hot roof. High price for your head; I can no haggle." Salix rubbed the stubble on his chin. "I can no get you through such a glove."

"You mean a gantlet," corrected Norbert.

"What is gantlet?" queried the Afghan, confused.

"A glove," said Norbert.

"Is that not what I said?" said Salix.

"What's your plan?" asked Norbert.

"Next clear coast, you leave Abraxis," said Salix, as Melalaia entered the room carrying a tray of coffee. McBride quietly looked at the map splayed out on the table.

"In one hundred and one days, on the crescent moon, the Abraxis," Melalaia smiled, "or should I say, the FAB XI, will be waiting for you in

Morocco. My father will get you to the straits and narrows, even if it's the last thing he does."

"That's cutting it close," said Norbert. "One hundred and one days... you think you need that long for things to cool?"

"No," said Salix (meaning yes). "Here be coordinates."

Norbert went over the details, possibilities, and contingencies in his mind, and finally conceded, "Okay, we'll meet you in Morocco."

"Casablanca was my favorite movie," said McBride. "Humphrey Bogart, Ingrid Bergman..."

†

The next clear coast turned out to be a small rundown port in North Africa. Once a buzzing place with lots of activity, now it was a mostly quiet, if not too peaceful, fishing village.

So she could look out one last time, Khia was making her way to the crow's nest. Norbert, McBride, Catherine, and Harold were on the pier having a discrete look around before setting off at dusk. In the meantime, cargo—lots of cargo—was being unloaded and transferred onto trucks, and (perhaps most importantly) the freighter was filling up on fuel.

A whistle of warning was heard. Suddenly, the quay was swarming with vehicles, blocking all exits. Those who tried to flee in fright, or in guilt, were quickly corralled. Soldiers and mercenaries, in strategic locations along the peer, pointed their guns at the crowd. On the upper deck, Khia ducked and peered over the railing. She spotted Harold slowly trying to make his way back to the freighter, his dark skin blending in with the local people. But there were too many soldiers; he placed his hood over his head and merged into the background without getting noticed.

Khia continued to scan the area. A flash of red caught her eye. In one vehicle, she saw the stern face of the Monsignor, and at his side, his guards and the colder, crueler faces of mercenaries.

Separated from Norbert, McBride, Harold, and Catherine, she watched them vanish into the crowd.

"That too hot to handle situation has caught up with us," said Melalaia. "They seem to know our next move. But my father always has a backup plan."

As the first of the mercenaries made their way up the gangplank, Salix walked towards them. To greet (and to stall), Salix spoke in his best mix of Arabic English.

Ruthless, and without hesitation, a guard rifle-butted Salix in his mid-section. Khia watched in horror as Salix fell to his knees. Not interested in the papers, they forced their way past him.

No emotion showed on Melalaia's face. "Come on, I have to get you out of here." Taking Khia's hand, she gripped it far too tightly.

Racing below deck, they went deeper and deeper into the bowels of the ship.

"I hope you can swim," said Melalaia.

CHAPTER 17

# The Well of the Prophet

The setting sun cast growing shadows on the white-washed town. For hours, Harold had stood at the periphery, not drawing attention to himself.

From his vantage point, he had watched as the mercenaries had boarded the Abraxis. He had been there to see Monsignor Scarlatti get out of his vehicle and reach into the folds of his garment. Tensing, Harold had thought the worst, but the Monsignor had only pulled out his cell phone. The call had been brief, but something significant had been relayed, because the Monsignor's face had changed. As the Monsignor marched towards the Abraxis, he seemed to grow in stature with each step.

Salix stood at the top of the gangplank, papers clutched to his hands. An animated conversation between the two had ensued. A lot of hand gestures and body language was all that Harold could see. Papers scattered on the deck and then the Monsignor made the sign of the cross and stomped off the ship. His red robe flailing in the breeze, the Monsignor screamed out an order, his men got into their vehicles, and they roared off, leaving dust in their wake.

Salix remained on the bow of his ship and lit a cigarette with shaking hands. When Salix's cigarette was finished, Harold watched as the rusted freighter slipped out of the port. The Abraxis' horn reverberated mournfully.

No sign of Khia. He dejectedly slipped deeper into the shadows.

Walking through the narrow streets, Harold kept his head down. People had come out of their homes. His bleached white robe and dark skin allowed him the freedom to blend in, almost like he was invisible, but he avoided any encounter with the locals. He was careful too of obstacles in his way, of flea-infested dogs, goats that wandered about, and children playing soccer in the dusty streets.

The heaviness of the centuries of time had tied this place to its past. Harold thought of his own life. He could never have imagined this—ending up on the run in North Africa—and it made him question the path he was on. It had all started the day he had picked them up in his taxi. He could just walk away now and never look back... pretend it had never happened.

Despite his thoughts, he walked towards the Well of the Prophet, where he spied Catherine at the edge of the fountain, McBride at her side tapping his foot to his own beat, and Norbert pacing back and forth. They were talking in low tones.

"It's not as bad as it appears," Harold heard Catherine say.

Norbert stopped. "It's not as bad as it appears?" His voice rose. "Are you paying any attention to what's going on here or are you drifting into mindlessness? This is not some fairytale that's going to work out happily ever after just because you want it to. Let me tell you what we've lost. I'll use simple words so it won't tax your brain."

"I am fully aware of our current circumstances," she condescendingly replied. "We don't know where Khia is, the Abraxis has left, I don't have my book—"

"Oh, I see, it's *your* book now," said Norbert bitterly. Leaving The Book on the Abraxis was probably the only good thing to come out of this sorry mess. He hoped it would be safer there. He didn't know a lot about The Book, but he knew it protected itself. If it didn't want to be found, it wouldn't be found.

He didn't want to contemplate Burdock and Cocklebur getting their hands on it. He looked at Catherine. He knew, without McBride telling him, that Catherine had touched The Book. And it really pissed him off that his friend hadn't told him. And it hurt too (although he wouldn't admit that part even to himself) that McBride was keeping secrets from him now... after so many years.

Catherine blanched. Had she actually said that out loud? It's not what she had meant to say; she was thinking of their packed bags left on board the ship. She was relieved when Harold made his appearance.

"Any sign of Khia?" asked McBride.

Harold shook his head.

†

"Swimming, it's your only chance," said Melalaia.

What looked like a solid steel wall was in fact a camouflaged door. Melalaia opened it and handed Khia a mouth piece, "You should have enough oxygen in that container. The chamber will flood with water before the hatch opens. It will be very dark; use your hands and stay to the right. She handed her a sealed plastic bag. "The burka. Wear it and go to the Well of the Prophet." They heard the sounds of shouting men in the corridor, going from door to door. Unbeknownst to Khia and Melalaia, one burley fellow went to one particular door, and was about to kick it open, when he stopped. A deep-seated fear that he had not known existed rose up within him and he it passed by. He went to the next door and kicked it in with unusual zeal, not understanding why he was suddenly so angry.

"Khia," Melalaia hugged her hard. "Go! Remember, one hundred and one days. Morocco. The night of the crescent moon. My father is a man of his word. He will take you to the straits and narrows. I promise. I give you my word."

The steel door whooshed shut, leaving Khia utterly alone in a tight and enclosed space. Brackish water poured in, quickly covering her feet, and continued to rise. Then the light went out, leaving her in total darkness. The water rose quickly; she could feel it rise up to her knees, her waist, her neck... Khia's heart pounded, and she felt like she couldn't breathe. Khia forced herself to relax as she stuck the tube in her mouth. Water flooded over her head. With a loud clunking sound, the outer steel portal released and opened and Khia pushed herself into the abyss.

†

"All right, let's figure out what we have to do," said Norbert. "If Khia has been captured, let's hope it's the Vatican. She could be heading back to Rome."

"No mon," Harold shook his head. "The Monsignor definitely left without Khia."

"If Khia's been captured by Burdock and Cocklebur, we've got problems."

"I don't think they're here," said McBride. "I don't sense them."

"What if she's still aboard the Abraxis?" queried Catherine.

"Not likely," said Norbert.

"She could be," said Harold.

"No, there would have been a thorough search of the ship," stated Norbert.

"There are places to hide," said Catherine.

"We have to go back to the beginning and retrace our steps. If we look hard enough, we'll find all the clues we need." Norbert started to pace again.

"Yeah, Norbert is good at that," said McBride. "Unfortunately, so are Burdock and Cocklebur."

"But what's the other option" asked Catherine, not understanding.

"There are no other options. We have to find Khia."

"How about we go to Morocco?" said a voice from the deepening shadows in the square.

"I know that voice," smiled Catherine.

Harold jumped towards the figure that appeared in the dark burka. "Ah little lady, what took you so long?"

"It was awful," said Khia, revealing her face. She explained how Melalaia had helped her escape. "It felt like I was in the water for hours. It took me a while to find a safe place.

"I could have been here earlier, but I hid until I was sure that the Monsignor had left the port. After the Abraxis had sailed, I made my way here. Melalaia told me to find the Well of the Prophet, but it took me a while. It's not like I could ask for directions."

"You done good kid," said Norbert.

Khia smiled.

"Let's get out of here," urged McBride. "I found a great place we can stay tonight. Great view of the bay."

As they left the Well of the Prophet, McBride chattered away, "Tomorrow I'll take you to the medina. You're going to love the bazaar. We're going to need some new clothes. That burka does nothing for you."

Khia fell a few steps behind and turned around.

"What's wrong?" asked Harold.

"I'm not sure," said Khia. She didn't see anything, but she had the feeling that they were being followed. But if anyone was out there, surely Norbert and McBride would have sensed it, so she dismissed it as her own imagination.

But if she had trusted her instincts, and looked longer in the shadows, she might have noticed a figure in black pressed within them. Regardless, he was skilled… for he had eluded the considerable detection abilities of Norbert and McBride, as if he himself was cloaked by some kind of magic.

CHAPTER 18

# Aloysius

The smell of roasting coffee beans permeated the air of the small coffee shop.

"Take note," demanded the young Tunisian, who was impeccably dressed in a light-weight linen suit that suggested he would be at ease on the streets of any European city, instead of this North African backwater.

"I don't need to take notes," said Norbert, impatiently.

Smiling, the young man was not in the least put off; in fact he seemed to find the situation humorous. "You want me, a Carthaginian, to lend you, an American, my finest Arabian horses."

"My place of birth is irrelevant. You've heard my offer," retorted Norbert. "Give me an answer."

Placing his index finger on Norbert's chest, the young man scoffed. "And this is the best you can do?"

One look from Norbert and the young man quickly withdrew his hand.

"It's a fair offer," said Norbert, who was tempted to grab the arrogant young man's hand and twist his arm right out of its socket.

Why had McBride sent him on this fool's errand? Norbert knew he would get no horses from this Tunisian—at any price. He was wasting his time.

Sitting at a nearby table, a deeply tanned man dressed in black sipped his strong coffee. This did not go unnoticed; Norbert was always aware of his surroundings. What he hadn't expected, however, was that the man approached their table without being invited.

"You know this American tourist?" asked the young Tunisian disdainfully.

"No," the man in black smiled. "You and I both know he is no tourist."

Irritated, Norbert stood up to leave, but the man in black placed a hand on Norbert's shoulder. "A moment please."

At that moment, the young Tunisian's cell phone rang. The ring tone sounded suspiciously like "Take on Me" by A-Ha.

Norbert raised his eyebrows. He was out of here.

"Please let me introduce myself; my name is Aloysius. I see you have already met Sartouche. Young people with their gadgets." He laughed, showing the deep lines on his face. "Tell me my friend, what is your name?"

Without saying anything, Norbert peered into the stranger's eyes. A quick assessment confirmed his suspicions. This man (looking the part and speaking the language fluently) was not a North African. In other words, it took a tourist who wasn't a tourist to know another one.

Not bothered by Norbert's silence, Aloysius continued. "These days horses are an unusual request. Ah, but before the automobile…"

Norbert's eyes narrowed.

Aloysius smiled. "These people revere their horses. Although they may seem backward to your eyes, stuck somewhere between here and the Punic Wars—"

"Don't presume to know what I think," interrupted Norbert.

"Yes, yes, of course. My apologies. Do you know the desert my friend?" he asked, changing the conversation's tack.

"I have been through such places before," said Norbert, gnashing his teeth.

"Good. Good, you know the desert. The desert is very beautiful. And you must know she is merciless… the heat, the sun, and sandstorms that can bury the foolish six feet under."

"I cannot go," said Sartouche into his cell phone, as he raised his index finger… indicating to them that he would be only a moment.

Norbert pressed his demands. "Seven horses. Twenty percent down, the rest payable when we arrive." Norbert heard his words and didn't even believe them himself. He hated haggling.

"You bargain shrewdly, my friend," Aloysius lied easily. "Eighty percent and a guide for your excursion."

Through the darkly tinted coffee shop window, Norbert could see the crowded streets. Amidst the rug dealers and small shop owners calling out in rapid voices, vying for business, something looked amiss.

Out on the street, two darkly dressed guards carrying traditional sheathed scimitars, and automatic weapons slung over their shoulders, were talking to a group of merchants who were pointing to the coffee shop.

"We must leave. Your presence," said Aloysius, "has attracted attention."

With steely calm eyes, Norbert met Aloysius' eyes.

Aloysius turned to the young North African. "Enough." He grabbed Sartouche's arm, his long sinewy fingers pressing into his soft skin.

Norbert knew that he stuck out; it was true just about everywhere he went.

"My friend," said Aloysius diplomatically, "we must find a place where it is safer to talk and conclude our… negotiations."

Sartouche threw a few bills onto the table, more than adequately paying for their coffees. The proprietor quickly pocketed the money, his silence procured as he cleared up the table, thoroughly wiping away any trace that they had been there.

Exiting through the back alley, Norbert followed Sartouche and Aloysius, just as the scimitar-wielding men entered the front door of the coffee shop, setting the bell over top of the door to ringing.

Norbert, Sartouche and Aloysius made their way through a maze of streets that could easily make a tourist disorientated and hopelessly lost. The aromatic scents of cinnamon, tamarind, and cumin wafted through the narrow crooked streets. Overhead, laundry lines with bleached white cotton sheets swirled in the wind and satellite dishes pointed to the sky.

†

"Where's Norbert," asked Khia, parting the curtains a few inches and looking out onto the busy street below them. "He should have been back by now."

"Don't worry about him," responded Catherine. "He can take care of himself. I'm more concerned for McBr..." Her voice trailed off, as if she'd forgotten what she was going to say.

"Yeah, but Norbert should have been back by now."

Khia was on edge. She didn't like this place. She felt exposed, in spite of having been hidden all day. Early that morning, McBride and Norbert had split up to try to find some type of transportation to get them to Morocco. They had a desert to cross.

The sound of the cell phone made Khia jump. "Hello?" she answered quickly.

†

Khia checked her watch.

As instructed, Khia, Catherine, and Harold had made their way on foot to their rendezvous point: a deserted building on the outskirts of town.

"Sure this is where Norbert told us to wait?" asked Harold.

"Yes," answered Khia.

Looking through the gaps of the rusted metal cladding of the building, Khia signaled to Harold and Catherine. Two vehicles, creating great dust clouds, approached.

A shiny red Ferrari and an old Land Rover came to a skidding stop. Khia retreated into the shadows. Standing perfectly still, she watched as they turned their engines off. Silence reclaimed the deserted place.

Two men, their features indistinguishable from that distance, stepped out of their vehicles. But there was no sign of Norbert.

"My friend!" called out one of them. He was greeted with silence.

"My friend!" he called out again. "It is Aloysius. We have come as promised, to conclude our negotiations."

Like a phantom from the sand, Norbert was behind them, his revolver touching Aloysius' temple.

"Clear."

Weapons drawn, Khia, Harold, and Catherine ran out of their hiding place and stood near the vehicles.

"I understand precautions are necessary," protested Aloysius. "Please put away your weapons. We have made the arrangements. Sartouche's father has agreed to meet with you."

Catherine stepped closer to Sartouche.

"I am sure you are a reasonably man," said Aloysius, as Norbert cocked his weapon.

"Reason is not one of his character traits." Catherine laughed, whispering in Sartouche's ear. "Nor is it one of mine. What would be the fun in that?"

"Get into the vehicle," ordered Norbert, nudging Aloysius roughly into the Land Rover. "We're going to pay a visit to Sartouche's father."

Catherine promptly snatched the keys to the Ferrari. "I'll drive."

CHAPTER 19

# Salazar's House

The gate, reinforced with several thick bands of iron held together by giant bolts, swung open. Flood lights beamed down and cameras swiveled on their axis. It was a large sprawling complex with high, thick stone walls made centuries before. It was like an ancient Saracen stronghold but with the trappings of a modern-day fortress.

They slowly made their way down a long driveway lined with cypress trees. Khia was thankful for the protection the vehicle provided. Armed guards, dozens of them, stood in strategic positions—at least seven atop the wall—cradling automatic weapons.

At the wheel of the Land Rover, Harold slowly rolled down the window as a guard approached, calling out in rapid Arabic. One didn't need to know the language to surmise that tensions were high.

"This should come as no surprise," said Aloysius, to those in the vehicle with him. "Sartouche's father is not a man who can take his liberties lightly. Before entering his home, you will be searched for weapons. You are not armed besides these weapons?"

Khia and Harold's awkward smiles made Aloysius grimace, as if in pain. "It is a good thing I am here with you. Step out of the car... slowly." They did, raising their hands over their heads.

More Arabic. "You are to remove your weapons," translated Aloysius.

"Better do what he says," said Norbert, as he in turn handed over all sorts of weapons, hidden in all kinds of places. An arsenal of weapons—a Colt 45, revolvers, an AK47, knives, and ammunition—was heaped on the table… and with each additional weapon removed, the men around them grew more rigid and on edge.

"Is that it?" asked a female guard, likely of Eastern European origin, who spoke with accented English.

Harold pulled out his brass knuckles, "Do these count?"

"Anything else?" she asked.

Khia bent down and removed a knife from her boot.

Aloysius proceeded to the house but was immediately stopped by the butt of a rifle. "You too Aloysius."

"I am a guest. I have been invited," Aloysius insisted.

"And I am telling you to hand over your weapon," she looked at Aloysius with cold unyielding eyes.

"You embarrass me, Roo. I have no need of such things. Have I not proven this?" Aloysius sounding offended.

"Don't ask questions you don't want answers to," she responded. "I do what is necessary." Turning away from Aloysius she called out to one of her men. "Stiff, search them thoroughly. All of them."

Aloysius' eyes narrowed, but a moment later he smiled graciously. "But then, of course, how can I refuse my friend."

As they were being frisked, Sartouche and Catherine drove up in the red Ferrari. Waving off the guards, Sartouche gallantly ran over to open the door for Catherine, and arm and arm, they strolled up to the house.

"But what about the woman?" asked Aloysius.

Roo looked at Catherine. "Sartouche's friend? I think not."

Catherine turned and smiled brightly at Norbert and Aloysius.

Escorted by their armed entourage, they followed Catherine and Sartouche up the stairs, made their way through a large sky-blue door, and entered the home of the Carthaginian.

"Father!" shouted Sartouche. "I'm home!"

A muffled call was heard.

"He's in the garage," said Sartouche, as his cell phone rang. He didn't answer it—didn't even glance at the display to see who might be calling.

Aloysius walked ahead. "Follow me."

"Aloysius," reminded Roo, "do not overstep your bounds. Taking liberties places all of us in danger. That you would involve Sartouche would most surely not make the boss very happy." Roo called out to her second in command, "Stiff!" She nodded at Aloysius. "If our gifted colleague tries to take the lead, put a rope around his neck. That should slow him down. If he utters another word, gag him."

Stiff nodded, almost relishing such a development.

Aloysius bowed his head and retreated to the back of the group.

"Let me introduce myself. My name is Roo and I am head of security." As if she were leading a personal tour in a museum, she continued. "Please, follow me."

Aloysius sidled up to Norbert and whispered, "Allow me to negotiate."

"Aloysius," reprimanded Roo, "be silent you fool."

"Wow," said Harold. The garage looked like a vast hanger filled with a wide array of very expensive cars, SUVs, and motorcycles.

Navigating their way towards the one car with its hood up—a 1964 silver-gray Aston Martin with two pairs of legs sticking out from underneath it—they heard a familiar voice drift up towards them, "My favorite James Bond movie…"

"McBride," Norbert's voice echoed in the large garage, as he grabbed the skid and pulled it, rolling McBride from under the car.

"Hi guys. What took you so long?" asked McBride.

"McBride, you're a menace. Did I ever tell you that?" said Norbert.

"Yeah, a few times. A few too many," said McBride, sitting up, grabbing a cloth made of exquisite Egyptian cotton, and wiping the oil from his face and hands. A cherub-like face appeared, laughing heartily. "It is precisely as you said it would be McBride. Your big and strong friend is all business and no play… and none too pleased it should appear." This only infuriated Norbert even more.

Sartouche's father stood up. One of his servants promptly stood by his side with a glass bowl full of water and a white cloth, also made from the finest cotton. Once he had dried his hands, he took the hand of Norbert and shook it vigorously. "I am Salazar. I am so very happy to make your acquaintance. I have never… I have never…" He stumbled as if he were at a loss for words. Still holding onto Norbert's hand, he looked at Roo and said, "We are in the presence of greatness."

Norbert took his hand back.

"Thank you Roo," said Salazar, "for your most excellent protection. You and your men may leave. I am as safe here as in the Garden of Eden before the serpent marred its perfection."

Turning to his other guests, he said, "Ahhh, the most exquisite and beautiful Catherine!" He bowed before her, took her hand, and kissed it. Salazar then stepped back to admire her. "McBride did not exaggerate."

"The pleasure is all mine," smiled Catherine.

Salazar turned to Khia next. "And you must be Khia. McBride did not tell me how enchanting you are." He kissed both her cheeks.

"And Harold," Salazar shook his hand. "I hear that you drove a yellow taxi on the hazardous streets of New York City, where there are gangs and hoodlums."

He glanced around at the group, nodding at them. "I welcome you all with favor and affection, beloved and noble friends of McBride."

"I thought we were supposed to be getting horses," said Norbert to McBride. "We discussed the hazards of machines in the desert, engines getting clogged, running out of petrol..."

"We did," said McBride.

Harold was eyeing a 1500 horsepower motorcycle. That is, after he had eyed the 1966 Rolls Royce, 1942 Bentley, the Jaguar, and the old VW Beetle that was tucked in the corner.

A great smile came over Salazar's face. "We have ample opportunity to talk business, my most welcomed guests." He went over to Harold, "I see, like me, you appreciate beauty." He beamed. "Come, come let me show you. Dinner will taste much sweeter after a ride in the desert before the setting sun."

Harold and McBride needed no persuasion. Strapping on helmets and putting on leather gloves, Harold, McBride, and Salazar each straddled a motorcycle. Harold picked a heavenly white one. The machines thundered to life, their deep rhythms filling the garage with a deafening roar.

"Are you coming, Catherine?" shouted McBride, full of playfulness, avoiding the palpable glare of Norbert.

Catherine shook her head.

"Can I come?" asked Khia excitedly.

Harold nodded and Khia eagerly jumped on.

"Helmet!" yelled Norbert.

"Think quick," said McBride, as he threw a helmet towards Khia, which she easily caught.

As if by magic, the garage door opened and they zoomed out onto the estate towards the formidable main gate, which opened to reveal an eerie Mediterranean sandscape. With a burst from the throttle, Salazar flew across the desert. They seemed to effortlessly split the floating sea of sand.

"Sartouche, will you take me to see the horses?" Catherine suggested sweetly.

Sartouche took Catherine's arm and led her away, leaving Aloysius alone with Norbert.

Aloysius had been expecting a confrontation with Norbert but had not been prepared for the speed in which it happened, as he found himself slammed against the garage wall, dangling more than two feet from the floor. Norbert held him effortlessly around his neck. He couldn't breathe.

"Show me the mark," demanded Norbert. "Now."

Aloysius couldn't speak. He could feel his trachea being crushed; he'd soon lose consciousness. He drew his sleeve above his right elbow.

On his forearm, embedded in the skin between his wrist and his elbow, was the wizard's mark. A barely discernible white scar, for those who knew of its significance, it screamed of sorcery.

"I..." gritted Aloysius, "could… never be," he gasped, "a threat to you… or McBride. Never."

Norbert loosened his hold on him.

"Believe..." Aloysius gasped for more air, "me."

"Believe *you?*"

"You will need my help," said Aloysius, through gritted teeth.

Norbert released his grip and the wizard fell ignobly to the ground. On his hands and knees, he took deep gasping breaths.

"Why didn't you tell me before?" asked Norbert.

"You didn't… need… to know."

"I didn't need to know! You're wrong. I needed to know."

Now he had a wizard to worry about.

CHAPTER 20

# Learning to Ride

"Race you to the door!" McBride cried out, sprinting ahead of Norbert. Like two young colts jockeying for position, they ran the last one hundred meters up the magnificent white marble steps—with Norbert taking the steps three at a time and McBride every other—to the finish line.

It was a virtual tie. Their movements mirrored each other. At the exact same time, they turned and splayed their hands on the wrought iron railing, waiting for the others.

"Seems like you've made a full recovery," said Norbert.

"If I was fully recovered, it wouldn't have been a tie," laughed McBride. "I would have whipped ya!"

It was some time later that they saw Khia, Catherine, and Harold, slowly walking the long driveway.

"Look at the sorry lot," said Norbert, shaking his head.

"How are we going to..." Norbert paused, looking for the right words, "whip them into shape?"

"They're making progress," responded McBride.

"I'm afraid it's not enough."

"Afraid! You?"

Khia slowly climbed the stairs and finally set her foot on the landing beside them. Reaching for the blue door, she was relieved that training for the day was over; all she could think of was a nice long hot shower…

"Whoa, girl," said McBride.

"What?" Khia turned.

"You go around one more time," he ordered.

"Bu-but," stuttered Khia, "we just ran ten miles!"

"Yes," McBride nodded, "and you're going to do it again."

"No way, mon," groaned Harold.

"You *have* to be joking," Catherine said, thinking he really was.

"Nope." McBride looked at Norbert and winked. "This is how we whip 'em into shape."

"I refuse," Catherine said stubbornly, about to make her way into the house.

"Told you she was a liability," said Norbert.

Catherine went rigid. She turned and glared at Norbert. Without saying a word, she followed Khia and Harold to repeat the exercise.

Two hours later, it was dejà vu all over again, as Khia, Harold, and Catherine found themselves once again at the end of the long driveway, lined with cypress trees, staggering towards Salazar's house, and up the stairway, step by painful step, to the blue door.

Every muscle in Khia's body throbbed. Part of her hated Norbert and McBride's version of boot camp, but another part of her liked it, because she was seeing results; she was getting really fit. Her endurance level had improved significantly, and perhaps more importantly, she was feeling more confident because of it.

She felt safe at Salazar's house, but who wouldn't? His place was a modern-day fortress, and it would take an army to break through. Being there made it easy to forget the outside world—easy to forget what was out there. Once she'd believed that the monsters she'd created in her imagination were worse than the monsters in the real world, but Khia had learned the hard way that the monsters in the real world were much much worse.

As for Harold, he may have grumbled and complained and thought about going his separate way, but he also believed that in life there were no coincidences; there was a reason for everything.

Catherine, the last to set foot on the landing, was slower than the others. Secretly she wondered if Norbert was right. Was she a liability? Should she leave? Would Khia be safer without her? Persistent doubt clouded her thoughts. More distressingly, she kept thinking of The Book, missing it like an addiction. Deep down inside of her, she felt it was slowly taking her over.

Each in their own worlds, their thoughts were interrupted when the door opened and Salazar stepped out to warmly greet them. "Come, come my beloved and noble friends, dinner awaits you… but first," he paused as he looked at Khia, Catherine, and Harold, "glorious baths with essential oils to renew your spirits. Dinner can wait."

Just a few minutes short of an hour later, Catherine made her appearance. McBride glanced up at her and smiled. She looked radiant, acting as if all was well. She took her seat at the opulent table as servants appeared with refreshments.

"To refresh and restore the spirit," said Salazar, holding a glass in the air. "Nectar from the gods. Not too sweet, not too tart, quenches the thirst."

†

Khia sat on a luscious pillow. A long low sigh of pleasure escaped her lips. Salazar was the perfect host, she thought, as she dozed off for what seemed like a few moments but turned out to be a few hours. When Khia opened her eyes, everyone had gone except for Norbert, McBride, and Salazar. They were having a conversation in low tones when Roo walked into the room. Roo approached Salazar and whispered words that Khia couldn't hear. With half-opened eyes, Khia saw the brief note of surprise and then anger that rose in Salazar's face.

"Impossible," said Salazar.

"Upsy daisy, Sleeping Beauty," said McBride.

As Khia grudgingly stood up to go to her room, she caught the unmistakable turn of McBride's gaze to Norbert and the nonverbal communication that flashed between them. Having spent time with Norbert and McBride, she knew that they had something planned. She was starting to read them.

Pausing at the foot of the stairs, she saw Salazar, Norbert, McBride, Roo, and Stiff spreading papers and maps across the large table, hearing snippets of their conversation—words like Blackwood, mercenaries, and the Vatican—and then the door clicked shut.

†

"You are late," said Harold, as Khia made her way to the stables.

"I'm sorry." Not only was she late for her riding lesson, she'd totally slept through her sparring lesson with Norbert. This was highly unusual. Norbert would never let her miss a practice, which could only mean one thing: They were up to something.

Elinor (Salazar's second wife and Sartouche's stepmother) smiled and told her to tack up.

"Where are Norbert and McBride?" asked Khia.

"Norbert and McBride have no need of lessons," said Elinor. "They are both accomplished riders."

After what she'd heard last night, Khia was not surprised that Norbert and McBride were absent, but it upset her that they always kept her in the dark.

Harold's voice brought her back to the present. "Elinor, we men of the Caribbean are not born for the saddle," Harold said, trying to get out of his lesson. His horse nudged him, knocking him off balance.

As Khia sat on her horse, she vividly remembered the time she'd leapt atop the ethereal Grey Horse. It was during the battle in the eerie world of cold white mist, and the supernatural mystic power of the shamans—Rainbow Walker, Grey Horse and Timothea—when they had fought the Red Bear Shaman. It almost felt like a dream, but it had really happened.

"Khia," snapped Elinor. "Concentrate."

"Horsey... *nice* horsey." Harold rubbed its nose and it promptly tried to bite him. "Mon, I hate horses," he muttered under his breath.

"Horses know when you don't like them," said Elinor.

Elinor was firm, but she was also patient.

"Khia, heels down and hold on tighter with your knees."

"Harold, sit up straighter."

"Catherine, shorten your stirrups a notch."

"Harold, don't tug so hard on the reins; their mouths are sensitive."

Salazar's wife would not allow her horses to be used in their venture unless the group were able to ride. She didn't expect them to be competent riders, that would take far too long, but they at least needed to learn the rudimentary skills and treat her horses kindly. This meant keeping them brushed down, watered, and fed, no tugging at the bit, and no use of spurs.

"Good. Yes. Now bring the horse to a trot."

Catherine lost the reins, Harold lost his seat and ended up sideways on the saddle, and Khia bounced uncomfortably on Skye.

"Whoa," said Elinor.

All three horses stopped at her verbal command.

Khia winced. They had been so eager to learn to ride. With novice zeal the three of them had not realized the amount of effort and skill required.

†

By the following week, they followed Elinor out into the desert. Cantering to the top of a ridge of sand, Khia's purple scarf whipped in the breeze. All around them there was undulating sand as far as they eye could see. It was pretty amazing, but soon Khia knew, they would be out on their own without Elinor's help, or the protection of the house of Salazar.

CHAPTER 21

# Dreams and Nightmares

Dreams—are well—but Waking's better,
If One wake at morn —
If One wake at Midnight—better —
Dreaming—of the Dawn
Sweeter—the Surmising Robins —
Never gladden Tree —
Than a Solid Dawn—confronting —
Leading to no Day —

~ Emily Dickinson (450)

Despite the roaring fire at her side, the Sylph curled up on the hard ground, shivering. She was so cold, so hungry. She craved warm human flesh but anything would do. She hadn't eaten in days. She sniffed the air, unable to detect a living soul.

She was in her human form—her favored appearance—so pretty and delicate like her mother, Katrina. Lovely, pretty, Katrina...

Falling in and out of sleep, the Sylph saw Katrina's face; her loving smile… but then the image distorted and turned into Ezrulie... and then into Valerie. The three faces merged and separated until it froze on Valerie's image. The Sylph recoiled.

She opened her eyes.

*"Spawn."* She heard the soft whisper penetrating her altered thoughts.

Instantly, the Sylph was in a crouching position… waiting, watching. Her human arms transformed into powerful muscles, the hackles on the back of her neck splayed out, her slender hands turned into sharp extended claws ready to attack whatever or whoever it was that spoke in the darkness. She sniffed the air… but there was nothing beyond the chaotic dome of light cast from the fire.

*"Spawn."* She heard the word again.

"Who calls to me?" asked the Sylph, circling the fire, looking in every direction.

It came not from the vast darkness but from within. She looked into the fire and understood its genesis.

The fire surged. Tongues of flames stretched up to the heavens in a pretty display of sparks and puffs of smoke, which spread out like dark wings. *"Where there is fire, we are with you."*

"Who are you?" growled the Sylph. The Sylph heard the billowing voice of Smoke and the higher pitched voices of Sparks, lifted by the soft wind. *"Invite her in. Invite her in."*

The face of Flame turned to the Sylph. "You are cold. Feel our embrace. With us, you need never feel cold again." It lured the creature with its words.

"Why do you call me?" snarled the Sylph, though enticed by the warmth.

*"We come to free you; we come to free you,"* sang Smoke and Sparks in unison.

*"It is time... time to free you from your bonds,"* said the commanding voice of Flame.

"Free me!" said the Sylph, anger rising within her. "Do you think I'm stupid? You seek to *control* me."

*"You are clever for one so young,"* spoke Flame. *"And have grown since we watched your birth."* It sounded pleased. *"The church fire... was it not beautiful? Ah,"* it paused, *"but you would not remember, encased in your shell."*

After a long moment, Flame continued. *"You are a creature of fire. You are one with us."*

"*Creature of fire. Creature of fire,*" chanted Smoke and Sparks, as if they were the chorus in an ancient play.

"Perhaps," said the Sylph.

*"We come to free you,"* Sparks cried out, and in its excitement was lifted by the wind and snuffed out, only to reappear again in the heat of the

crackling flames. With a burst of energy, the fire expanded and Sparks jumped up again, but stayed closer to the flame. *"You don't need your mother."*

*"Sever the ties that bind you,"* said Flame. *"We can help you."*

Turmoil grew within the Sylph, for the bond with her mother was strong. Growing hotter, feeding off the Sylph's emotions, the flames roared up in impatience. Smoke puffed out and hovered above like a small gray cloud, casting the Sylph in partial shadow.

"Arhhgged!" screamed the Sylph. "Why do you torment me so?"

*"To free you, to free you,"* the baritone voice of Smoke and the high-pitched voices of Sparks sang harmoniously.

In human form, she took a step towards the fire. The fire reached out to the Sylph, tornadoes of flame spiraling around her, caressing her.

Her clothing burst into flames... and she swirled around in ecstasy.

Her skin began to glow a rich saffron and gold. The fire held her like a protective cocoon, and she felt warm and safe like a child wrapped in her mother's loving arms.

The Sylph screamed in enraptured pleasure.

The fire that had roared intensely was soon spent... blackened coals and ash.

†

Thousands of miles away in a penthouse apartment, Katrina felt severe cramps in her abdomen. Doubled over in pain, she stumbled out of the room. Nausea swept over her; she did not want anyone, especially Ezrulie, to see her like this.

Locking the bathroom door, she bent over the sink and splashed cold water on her face. She stood up and saw her face looking back at her in the mirror. She looked so pale.

*"There's no more time. They're here," Katrina heard an urgent voice, but it was like it was coming from the other side of the mirror. Then two gunshots, so loud they could have been fired from her own hand.*

*Excruciating pain surged through Katrina's body. She slumped against the bathroom door and watched the red blood soak through her dress. In disbelief, she touched the blood and looked at her hand, red and sticky. Her arms fell limply to her sides. It was hard for her to focus. A deep tiredness was overtaking her.*

*She heard muffled voices and became aware of a figure approaching, towering over her.*

*"The Harbinger has escaped."*

*"Find him."*

*Through blurred vision, she tried to see his face, but it was in shadow.*

*"Lady Eupheme, we meet again."*

*Katrina tried to correct him, tell him he was mistaken—she was Katrina—but words that weren't her own escaped her lips, "You have failed."*

*"No, Eupheme," he laughed, "you have failed. Though, I compliment you on your efforts. Impressive but futile. Look around you. Your people... dead."*

*In near delirium, Katrina was no longer leaning against the bathroom door but against a shattered tree. She looked around. It was a wasteland. The scale of destruction was epic. The multitude of fallen warriors, her army, lay scattered.*

*He spread his arms wide. "Your Kingdom has fallen."*

*Despite the pain she felt, she gnashed her teeth, trying to stay conscious.*

*He laughed at her. "Still trying to defy him."*

*Katrina looked at her stomach, oozing with blood, "What you want is… gone."*

*"Ahhh, but that is where you are wrong. You may have tried to destroy the last vestiges of your line," he said, looking at the bullet holes Eupheme had pumped into her own abdomen. "So powerful, yet so weak. You suffer such trauma and still you linger. Why do you fight?" He bent down to her and whispered into her ear. "Eupheme, you could have been by his side. His bride."*

*"I'd rather be damned," said Katrina, and she spat at him. Blood trickled from the side of her mouth.*

*Wiping the blood splattered phlegm from his cheek, he smiled coldly. "You could have had worlds. Instead you choose this—death. Such a waste. And for nothing… He will have his progeny."*

*"Over my dead body."*

*"So be it," and she felt his hand reach inside of her…*

Knock. Knock. Knock.

Katrina found herself on the bathroom floor. "What do you want?" she snapped.

"You're late!" Ezrulie yelled from the other side of the door.

Katrina pulled herself together, smoothing out her dress. It was time for another boring lesson with Ezrulie. She was a really lousy teacher. She took a breath and opened the door.

"Pay attention," demanded Ezrulie. "What's wrong with you? You have the attention of a gnat. I asked you to tell me what it is!"

"It's a door. What do you think it is?" Katrina answered acidly.

"It's more than that," Ezrulie pushed her staff aggressively into Katrina's ribs.

Hatred in her smoldering eyes, Katrina held her ground.

Ezrulie pushed harder.

With clenched teeth, Katrina said, "Do you really want me to show you how I feel about these stupid endless lessons?" she asked, in a tone that mimicked her aunt.

Katrina raised her hands in a dramatic display. Drawing in the energy from the room, her hands started to shake. The lights started to flicker on and off. The room crackled with electricity, dimmed, and then started to grow brighter. The air screamed in protest… and the door she had conjured exploded, knocking Ezrulie to the ground.

Katrina stood over the older woman and Ezrulie knew that she no longer had control over her young apprentice.

"Let this be a lesson to you," smirked Katrina, and started reciting one of Ezrulie's speeches, verbatim. "Controlling the weak minded, the mad, and the dispossessed is easy, but outcomes can be unpredictable. The domination of the intelligent, the wise, and the clever is another matter. More—much more—difficult to control, but with patience they can be led. And how? Through truths, half-truths, and well-positioned lies. Plant the seed and they will willingly sacrifice themselves for our purpose. But they can also make us vulnerable." Katrina looked into Ezrulie's eyes. "And there's the flaw in your logic, Auntie Dearest."

Katrina laughed. Ezrulie looked dazed.

"Goodbye Auntie. I'm going away. Far, far away from you."

CHAPTER 22

# When The Cat's Away

Khia was getting worried. There was no sign of Norbert or McBride. Looking out from her second floor balcony, she saw guards positioned along the fortress wall, protecting the compound like gargoyles. Beyond the wall, she scanned the desert. It was like looking at a painting, nothing had changed.

Padding across the floor in her bare feet, the tiles felt cool. She slipped into bed and pulled the covers up and over her. The white sheets fluttered in a graceful arc, settling on her outline, and she fell asleep to the sounds and sweet aromas of the desert, which crept into her room.

†

Khia opened her eyes. It was like she had been drawn into a *dream… strange and familiar—strange in that she didn't know where she was, but familiar in that she'd been here before.*

*Standing high upon the ruins of a great bridge, she looked upon a blackened blasted wasteland. The scale of destruction was horrific—the final battle, epic and cataclysmic.*

*A small breeze caused the dry earth to swirl and the images to speed backwards in time. When it stopped, the bridge shone golden in the fading sunset and led to a beautiful city in the sky.*

*And like time repeating itself, she watched it happen. The horde, like a black tide, breached the bridge and attacked the city.*

*Fine cracks emerged and stretched from one end of the bridge to the other. The fault lines deepened and the fissures fanned out like the branches of a tree. Ash from the burning city flew up into the sky and fell back to the earth like snow, and the bridge, not being able to bear any more weight, collapsed… and the city fell from its dizzying height.*

*Khia once again found herself standing high upon the ruins of the great bridge, looking at the scorched landscape. Nothing was alive; there was no heartbeat. But this time she saw something different—something that she hadn't noticed before (or maybe it was something that hadn't been there before).*

*Next thing she knew she was on the scorched land, standing amongst the remains of the fallen. They were scattered upon the arid land like fallen leaves. It was eerily quiet. Walking amongst the fallen, she made her way to a tree, old and gnarled by time. Slumped against it was a woman—young, beautiful, and dead. There was blood everywhere...*

"Khia."

Khia opened her eyes. Someone had called her name. She was sure of it. But there was no one there. She glanced at the clock; it was 1:21 a.m.

Swinging her legs out from under the sheets, and sitting at the edge of her bed, she noticed that the balcony door was wide open. As if she were still within her dream, she quietly made her way out onto the balcony. She looked over the edge of Salazar's compound and thought she saw something scurrying along the wall, but decided it was nothing more than a shadow. At that moment, the compound came alive with lights and sirens. Search lights scoured the area, and urgent voices in Arabic drifted up towards her. On the thick wall, security personnel had their weapons ready. On the ground, Roo appeared and shouted orders to her men. Someone had penetrated their sanctuary.

Mid-stride, with one foot in her room and the other foot on the balcony, Khia froze. She wasn't alone. She couldn't hear or see anything, but she could feel it. Someone was in her room.

Paying particular attention to the shadows in the corners, her senses were sharp. And then, seeing who it was, Khia sighed with some relief. "What are you doing here?"

"Your perceptions are good." He stepped out of the shadows. "Few know when I am present."

Khia's eyes narrowed critically. "What do you want?"

"I have been trying to get you alone."

"Do you know how bad that sounds?"

"Fire and darkness fast approach and you will be in the center of it," he said cryptically.

"You sound like a fortune teller, and not a very good one," Khia shot back.

"Predicting the future has its complications. The variables in play have a tendency to change too quickly. If we hope for a future, we must stand up against this together."

"What are you talking about?"

"By not going through the portal with Devon, you changed everything," he replied. "I offer you an opportunity, but it is not without its risks."

"What kind of risks?"

"Death," he spoke coldly. "But I do have some ability. I can manipulate events in a small way, so that when the end does come for you, it is merciful; it'll be quick and you'll hardly feel a thing."

"You're not selling me on the idea," answered Khia. She held her ground.

"I can teach you—"

"Not interested," said Khia. "Get out of my room or I'm going to scream for Norbert, and he'll be here so fast you won't know what hit you."

He laughed, because he knew it was an idle threat. "Do you ever want to see your brother again?"

Khia stopped.

"I can teach you… about the Corridor."

A part of her wanted to leap at his words, but she spoke slowly, trying not to sound too excited. "You can teach me?"

"Yes."

She hesitated.

"You'll have to trust me," he said.

Her bedroom door swung open, staining half his face red with the light that entered.

Aloysius held out his hand, and Khia, as if she were a reluctant bride, reached out her hand to his.

†

In a far-away recess of the Corridor of Doors, something stirred. A sliver of silver light framed the door of a world that had been abandoned long ago, its key lost or stolen.

It flared brightly, one last time, like a dying star starting to fade. Enveloped in blackness, a dark cold vacuum of nothingness started to creep along the cracks on the door, like black veins.

And in the Corridor, the lights started to flicker on and off, leaving a growing stretch of silence in the expanding darkness.

CHAPTER 23

# Endless Loop

Norbert and McBride were eating breakfast. It was as if they had never been gone.

For Catherine, the time they had been away had weighed heavily on her. The Book was strengthening its hold on her, growing more pervasive with each passing day. Most disconcerting, brief moments of time were lost to her. She was experiencing blackouts—not knowing where she had gone—followed by feelings of fear and regret.

Not having McBride around had been an agony beyond measure. She had kept busy, doing anything to distract herself, so that at the end of the day she was exhausted: early morning sparring lessons with Khia, running, strength training, and spending extra time with the horses, even mucking out the stables (though there were grooms to do the work). Above all else, she had to prove to Norbert that she was not a liability... but deep down inside, she feared that he could be right.

The night before, she had seen it again: the Rand. While staring in the mirror, she saw it standing behind her. "Catherine," it whispered into her ear, bringing cold terror, "I've missed you. I've waited a long time for you, Cathy. You're going to crawl to me. Would you like that? Ah, you're gonna love it," it said, licking its thin lips. She felt its cold sinewy fingers caress her neck.

"Catherine," McBride's voice brought her back. "Are you all right?"

"Yes, yes of course," she smiled weakly as she became aware that she was sitting next to McBride at the breakfast table. She was unaware of how much time she had lost. She had promised to be truthful with McBride, but how could she tell him? She didn't want to look evil in his eyes.

"Where's Khia?" asked Norbert.

†

What had possessed her to follow Aloysius? Placing her hands on her temples, she squeezed her eyes shut trying to block out the pain in her head. Gradually the sensations subsided.

"What are you doing to me?" Khia asked through gritted teeth.

"Suppressing your memories," he spoke casually. "With time your conscious mind will remember."

"Remember what?"

"You are a bright beacon drawing both good and evil to you. We are drawn to them through their magic as they are drawn to ours."

"Magic?" asked Khia, feeling the words pass through her lips. What was he talking about?

"You are a danger to yourself and to others, until you learn to control your powers."

"I don't have any powers," said Khia.

"Oh my dear, believe me, you have powers."

"Am I a wizard?" she asked.

He shook his head. "Nor magi, mage, or shaman." He looked at her thoughtfully. "You are something different. Coveted." He paused for a moment. "A most unique kind of bait."

She didn't like being referred to as bait, and was about to say so when her memories started to return. They had had this conversation before... and then she knew what he was going to say next.

"You're using me," accused Khia.

"That I could be," Aloysius answered.

More pain shot through her. Khia fell to her knees. Pain was good. It was something she could hold onto. A few moments later, the pain subsided. Breathing hard, she became more aware of her surroundings. She was in the middle of a rectangular slab about twenty feet long and ten feet wide. Fading, the sapphire sky turned to gray, and beyond it, all there was was an endless void.

"Where are we?" asked Khia. "I know I've been here before."

"Good," Aloysius nodded. "You're starting to remember."

"Aloysius, how many times have I been here?"

"Many."

"Give me a number," snapped Khia, her anger rising to the surface.

"So much anger," Aloysius lifted up his hand to stop her from saying more. "I know what you'll say, for you always say the same thing." He was growing impatient. "You do not trust me and that is wise, but you need to accept your role, and until you do so, you will be trapped in this endless loop."

"How can I accept lies?"

"Lies?"

"You twist the truth," accused Khia.

"That I may." He laughed softly.

"How many times have I been here?" repeated Khia, her voice trailing away.

"Six or seven, or a thousand times or more; it is of no importance," answered Aloysius. "It is a place for you to learn and test your abilities." Aloysius looked at the pendant that began to glow around her neck. "Did you ever ask yourself why you would receive such a precious gift? You? A little girl who takes the long way to get to her grandmother's?"

Protectively, she wrapped her hand around the glowing pendant, and in that brief moment, she thought she saw a spark of longing in his eyes.

"Why do you want it?" Khia asked.

Aloysius' eyes narrowed. "If you saw the object the way I see it, you would be quite impressed. A unique bauble. Interesting how it moves of its own volition, as if it were in two places at once. The finest that I have ever seen," he said wistfully. "The knowledge of such magic no longer exists. Not even for Timothea."

Thoughts were jumbled in her mind. How was it that he knew so much? How did he know that Timothea had given her the pendant?

The wizard's cold eyes met hers. "You can't imagine what I could do with that pendant."

Khia faced him squarely. "Enough. I've had enough of your games," she said, raising her voice in frustration.

Unexpectedly, he laughed.

She felt herself deflate.

"We're wasting time. I have no use for pendants," said Aloysius. "Your path, one way or another, is leading you to a door and you shall either die before it or you will go… beyond. Now follow me. Or not. The choice is always yours."

*Yeah, some choice,* she thought and followed Aloysius.

Out of breath, she came to a stop a few feet behind him. Thick fog encased them. It was hard to tell if they were moving or if the world around them was.

"Is this for real?" asked Khia.

"Real? Unreal? Neither is true. Neither is false," said Aloysius. "You, me, everything, and nothing. You must look deeper."

Puzzled, Khia looked at him. What was he trying to teach her? It was like a test and a trick all at the same time—designed for her to fail.

"Observe and learn."

What did he think she was trying to do?

"Illusion?" he asked. He raised his forearm and she saw the wizard's mark there. "Perhaps. Maybe illusion is, in fact, everything that you believe is real. Do you believe you are sleeping in Salazar's compound? In your bedroom under warm blankets, which are protecting you from the things outside your window? Or are you here with me?"

Khia didn't answer, for a wave of nausea had washed over her.

"Things are moving quickly," he continued. "You placed yourself on this path the day you chose not to follow Devon through the portal. Had you gone through… interesting how different your life would be, but it is a moot point. Unlike your beloved mother, you cannot choose madness to protect yourself, although you may try."

"Don't speak about my mother," said Khia. "She didn't choose to go crazy, no one does."

He arched his eyebrows.

"Whose side are you on?" accused Khia.

"No side."

"Are you telling me you're neutral?"

"That I am not. The more pertinent question," he emphasized, "is how you fit in this complex equation?"

Khia said nothing.

"Doors that have been closed for a very long time, you will one day be able to open. The fluid that runs in your veins makes it so."

"I have blood running through my veins just like everybody else." He did the eyebrow thing again, which really pissed her off. It was a look that said she was like... stupid or something.

"Your mere existence is a threat," he said. "There are many who desire your ending."

Pieces of the puzzle started to click together. Strange and unusual things had happened to her over the last year. There had been a string of weird events, which had included the mist wraiths aboard the Abraxis, those deformed creatures in the catacombs, and the seven vultures that she was sure were somehow connected to her mother. Is that how they had found her? Through her magic? And was that why they wanted her dead?

"And," he pointed out, "whether you live or die is of no consequence to me."

Khia looked at him in shock. Maybe he was joking, but there was no compassion or pity, just indifference.

"There is no time to grieve the fallen."

"Norbert and McBride will protect me," said Khia.

"They will try." Suddenly Aloysius smiled. "You have most unusual guardians, one of the blessed and one of the fallen."

"Why don't you just say it?" she snapped at him. "An angel and a demon."

"So you know!" He sounded a little surprised. "Beware of them."

"And what of wizards?"

"Touché." Aloysius laughed, but quickly brought her back to task. "Look at your hand. What do you see?"

"My hand?" She lifted it and turned it to look at her palm.

"Look deeper." He waited a few moments, giving her a chance to focus. "Now what do you see."

Khia looked at her hand and saw the lines of her palm. They had always been there, but she was seeing it differently. Somehow similar to her pendant, coming in and out of existence, she was able to see through layers upon layers of skin, cells, blood, and life. Khia looked deeper and saw coils of strings, DNA, and going deeper yet by orders of magnitude, all of it vibrating, give off light, giving off energy, absorbing it. It was a complex balance of forces and fields—its own kind of magic.

"Yes," he said. "I think you see. Impermanence. Movement. Everything is moving, always moving, in and out of existence... and you can see it. Good. Now find your way."

The ground under Khia suddenly gave way. Khia reached out and grabbed the ledge, her feet dangling in the air. Aloysius stood looking down on her with cold emotion. He had a talent for keeping her off balanced.

"Aloysius, help me!" cried Khia. "Please, don't let me fall." She felt like crying, but held back her tears.

"There is power in tears." He looked dispassionately down upon her. "But they have no power over me."

She couldn't hold on anymore and fell through the air.

"You are in a gravity well," he informed her. "Find your way out."

"Aloysius!"

Kicking and screaming, Khia woke up… and like with a dream that quickly fades, she could not remember anything at all.

## CHAPTER 24

# Shimmering Land

The desert is a true treasure
For him who seeks refuge
From men and the evil of men.
In it is contentment,
In it is death and all you seek.

~ Passage from a Sufi Song

Khia slowly made her way to the courtyard. In the center, the large rectangular pool looked like a gilded framed mirror, reflecting the blue sky above. The sun broke over the horizon and the stately statues that mutely lined the garden seemed to come to life. In the shadows, seven Arabian horses, saddled and ready, snorted impatiently.

It was bitter sweet, leaving Salazar's fortress. Salazar and his wife had made her feel like she was home. She'd felt the same at Nora's. She and her brother had been to one foster home after another for years, and then on the run with Norbert and McBride. She hoped for a home one day.

"I will ride with you," Elinor said, approaching. Her blue eyes were as brilliant as the mirrored pool.

In a single fluid motion, Khia mounted her horse.

"My beautiful wife has trained you well," Salazar said proudly, as he walked into the courtyard followed by Catherine and Harold. Raising his arms to the sky, he proclaimed, "It is an auspicious day to begin your desert crossing."

One of the attendants opened the heavy steel gate as Norbert and McBride made their appearance. Aloysius was trailing behind them.

Salazar smiled broadly at the group. "My door is always open to you and you will be embraced as family." He waved as Elinor led them boldly into the desert.

†

It was exciting to be part of another one of Norbert and McBride's adventures. Khia felt confident. Under their tutelage, she had learned to handle a sword, throw a knife, shoot a gun, run for miles without tiring, and had fundamentals in various forms of martial arts. She felt ready—ready for anything.

It was going to be a good day; Salazar was right. Khia looked over at Catherine and Harold, and she had to admit that they looked pretty good on horseback. The intense training with Elinor had definitely paid off. They weren't groaning or complaining; their muscles had adapted and they glided over the sand like they had been born in the saddle (okay, even she had to admit that was a bit of stretch, but they did look like they knew what they were doing).

A few hours later, Elinor stopped. "This is where I leave you." With that minimal preamble, she turned and rode away.

Elinor looked like an Arabian princess, thought Khia, with her flowing headscarf fluttering in the breeze. "Will she be all right on her own?" asked Khia, as she watched Elinor and her horse get smaller and smaller.

"Who says she's alone?" answered Norbert.

Far in the distance, the sun caught something that glittered like silver. Khia smiled. She saw a man on a motorcycle cresting a ridge, six body-guards merging into a triangular formation behind him.

"Salazar!" exclaimed Khia.

"And Roo and the boys on Harleys," said McBride.

"How come I didn't hear them?" asked Khia.

"Wind in our face, not our backs," replied McBride.

It was a reminder, yet again, that she needed to be more aware of her surroundings.

Khia waved, and in the elusiveness of the Saharan wind, she heard Elinor's blessing, "May the desert protect you."

The six of them continued on their journey. After a few more hours in the saddle, the reality of the situation started to sink in. Khia no longer felt so positive or so confident. The reality of crossing thousands of miles of desert to get to a small Atlantic port in Morocco was daunting to say the least.

"Don't worry," said McBride, interrupting her thoughts. "You're going to get wrinkles."

"Do you think we'll make it to Morocco?" she asked.

"How can you have any doubts? They may control the sea and sky, and use the latest in technology—satellite, radar, infrared heat sensors—but no one can control the sands."

"It's that bad is it?" asked Khia.

"On horseback, with Salazar's connections, using paths that the nomads have used for thousands of years…"

"So you're saying we have the advantage," said Khia.

"You bet ya," laughed McBride.

But no one else was laughing.

"When do we stop?" asked Harold, for the umpteenth time.

"Oh for God's sakes," said Norbert impatiently, "will you stop your complaining. Distract yourself and… sing Ninety-Nine Bottles of Beer on the Wall."

"But that will only make me thirsty."

Norbert shook his head and muttered to himself. This was only day one. It would get a lot worse. *Day after day of this! Give me patience.* Norbert didn't think they were anywhere near being ready. A simple assignment to get Khia to her grandmother's had gotten complicated. At least he had McBride. He could always count on McBride. But when he looked over at McBride, he had to admit that he wasn't so sure anymore. With a little too much force, Norbert dug in his heels, and his horse quickened its pace.

†

Sunrise ... Sunset ... Sunrise ... Sunset ... The days merged into each other. Khia lost track of the days and the nights. Pictures she had seen of the desert had looked smooth and flat, with soft inviting mounds, but in reality, it wasn't so. The sand invaded every part of their bodies, and if you let it, could also invade your mind. It was a harsh and unforgiving environment, but the desert had its own rhythm, a pulse all to itself—a world locked in its own time.

No one spoke. The only sound came from the horses snorting, the stirring of leather, and hoofs softly clomping on the sand. Relentlessly, the sun beamed down; sometimes the light reflecting off the sand was blinding. Often Khia glanced back to see their path being erased by the wind, leaving no trace that they had ever been.

McBride's voice broke the silence. "We're here."

*Oh, thank God,* thought Khia. They'd made it. She felt so tired.

As usual, their cache had a surplus of supplies. Salazar, with his many desert connections, had kept his promise to supply them with provisions. He was a man of his word. Norbert, McBride, and Salazar had spent many nights bent over a map planning this. They had planned well.

Upon arrival at the cache, they followed the usual routine. Horses first. Norbert was always the last one in. He'd spend a few minutes scanning the horizon, looking intently from the direction they had come as if mentally retracing their steps. Then he'd go down on one knee and feel the heat drain from the sand. His ritual was always the same and it would be a while before he finally walked his horse into their rocky and protective alcove.

After a small supper, Khia sank into her sleeping bag, exhausted. She fell asleep before her head hit the pillow, but before she knew what was happening, she felt McBride nudging her awake. It felt like no time had passed.

"Am I going to have to kiss you awake?" he asked her playfully. "Rise and shine."

Khia made a sleepy face. "It's not morning."

"Watch duty."

"Oh, yeah. What time is it?" she asked, as she struggled out of her sleeping bag.

"One oh three," he answered. "You should be thanking me for those extra three minutes."

Too tired to smile, Khia followed McBride to the top of the crest, where they traded places with Harold and Norbert.

"Khia," Harold welcomed her with a smile, "old enough now to do yo share of lookout duty."

She was too tired to comment. She'd asked for this.

The desert was cold at night—so cold that she could see her breath. The moon shimmered eerily across the barren landscape, giving it an alien look. From atop a ridge that afforded them a 360 degree view, McBride settled in, looking rather relaxed and comfortable. He closed his eyes. Khia scanned for anything in the slowly shifting sand, but nothing was evident and there was little sound except for the haunting far-away howls of wild dogs.

About twenty minutes had passed when McBride stiffened.

"What's wrong," whispered Khia, not aware that anything had changed.

McBride, using the telescope of his gun, scanned the south east. "Someone's found us."

"Impossible," whispered Khia, looking through her binoculars and seeing nothing unusual.

"He's good. And he knows that I know he's out there."

"How do you know that?"

"I just do."

"You want to go out and get him, don't you?" asked Khia, excitement rising in her voice.

McBride grinned. "You're pretty smart for a girl." He put his hand on her shoulder. "But you're staying here. He may have friends." He handed her his spare rifle. "You remember how to use this. I want you to cover me. Watch out for the ridge." He pointed to it. "We're most vulnerable from there. That's where I would go if I was pursuing us. We're going to see how good he really is." Winking at her, McBride slipped away like a nocturnal animal with night vision, disappearing into the shadows.

In the dark, looking through the binoculars, it was difficult to see McBride. Attentively, Khia watched McBride make his way over the crests of sloping hills, and then he disappeared from sight. She was supposed to watch his back, but where was he? She'd lost him. She heard a gunshot in the distance. Khia bit her lower lip. So intent had she been, scanning for McBride, that she jumped when Norbert suddenly appeared at her side. He grabbed her binoculars (practically choking her as he pulled the strap, which was still around her neck) to scan the area.

"Pay more attention next time," he reprimanded her. "Always, ALWAYS, be aware of what's around you."

"Well you shouldn't be sneaking up behind me," argued Khia defensively.

"And what if I was an ax murderer?"

She'd made a beginner's mistake—again. But what was the deal with Norbert being able to sneak up on her so easily without detection? Maybe she *wasn't* ready for this; doubts clouded her mind.

"McBride out there?" he asked her.

Khia tried to nod but nodding was a little difficult sitting cheek to cheek with Norbert.

After a few moments of scanning the area, Norbert let go of Khia's binoculars; the cord around her neck released and she could breathe again. Then he got up and walked back to camp.

"But, but... where are you going?" she called after him.

"Keep an eye on the ridge; we're most vulnerable from there," he said, repeating what McBride had said almost verbatim.

"What about McBride?"

"What about him?"

"Aren't you going to go after him?"

"Nah," said Norbert, who turned and left her all alone to wait and to watch.

Nearing the end of their shift, Khia, restless and fidgety, finally saw McBride making his way towards her.

"He's good, but I'm better." McBride held a fragment of black cloth.

†

"Help the horses, quick."

Khia woke up with a start. Without thinking, she reacted. Slithering out of her sleeping bag, she ran after Aloysius. Gabbing one of the horses by its halter, she coaxed the animal under the rocky overhang.

Three large helicopters appeared, flying in formation. The three crafts hovered over the ridge, flashing their high beam lights in the darkness and scanning the area. Tucked in the shadows, no one moved.

The decision was made to wait the day out and set out again at nightfall. Khia couldn't wait to get back to sleep.

All day, Norbert and McBride had waited and watched, but there had been no sign of anything.

At nightfall, Khia mounted her horse. It was much harder riding at night. Not only could you not see where you were going, it was cold. Khia noticed that Catherine was shivering, her teeth chattering.

"Are you all right Catherine?"

"Just cold." Catherine gave Khia a weak and tired smile.

"Here, take my blanket," offered Khia generously.

"Thank you." The extra layer didn't seem to do her any good. Khia watched her for a while, but Catherine was shaking just as much as she had been before.

Aloysius rode closer to them. At first Khia was a little annoyed, but then he started talking softly, his voice soothing, like a lullaby. "Have you heard the story of the Wyvern Wizard and how his grief was immortalized in the night sky?" He pointed to a group of bright stars that Khia had never noticed before.

Khia shook her head. Linking the stars, she indeed saw a wizard with his hat askew and a magical book in his hands. She could almost imagine the staff at his side, surrounded by stacks of books and a black cat as he absentmindedly did whatever it was that wizards do.

"Few have heard of the Wyvern Wizard," said Aloysius.

"Will you tell us the story?" asked Khia.

"If you wish."

CHAPTER 25

# A Young Man's Wishes

When shall we three meet again?
In thunder, lightning or in rain?

~ Act 1, Scene 1, *Macbeth*

"The beginning of any story is merely an arbitrary starting point," said Aloysius. "Where to begin? That is the crux." Aloysius paused, then snapped his fingers. "The conflagration—that would be as good a beginning as any."

Not feeling quite as tired anymore, Khia felt a warmth move through her, and Catherine forgot how the cold was penetrating deeper into the depths of her marrow.

"Long long ago," the soft clomping sound of horses' hoofs on sand faded to the background as his voice carried in the cold desert air, "... in a different place and a different time, there were two great wizards."

Aloysius stopped. "Perhaps great is somewhat of an exaggeration, suffice it to say... there were two wizards and their names were Mathyssen and Swivet. What they had in common? Only that they taught at the same school of wizardry and both wore the three purple bands around one sleeve of their white robes, denoting their high teaching order. No two could ever be so different. Mathyssen may have had the qualifications but arguably should never have been a teacher. Swivet, a great concocter of potions (on which he was rumored to indulge himself, on occasion) was a better teacher but not a better wizard."

"On this particular day that I speak of, Mathyssen and Swivet were walking through the back alleys of the great city of Kalise, arguing about something or other, or perhaps about nothing at all, when a great conflagration cast them from their feet.

"'*What is it this time?*' asked Mathyssen, sounding irritable (she mostly always sounded irritable, so perhaps we could say it was her normal voice).

"The growing crowd of students parted for Mathyssen and Swivet like the Red—" Aloysius stopped suddenly to clear his throat.

Catherine, starting to get into the story, repeated Aloysius' words, "Like the Red...?"

"I was going to say 'like the Red Sea parting for Moses' but that is just too much of a cliché even for me. So where was I?"

"The crowd of students parted..." said Harold.

"And the cause of the disorder," Aloysius continued, "was none other than a skinny little seven-year-old boy, with smudges of coal on his face and wisps of smoke rising about him.

"'*Are you stupid?*' Mathyssen shouted harshly. She raised her hand and struck the boy a backhanded blow that sent him back a few steps. About to be struck again, the boy didn't cower, cringe, or flinch. He had learned (even at that early age) that it was better to take the punishment sooner rather than later.

"'*Easy Mathyssen,*' said Swivet stopping her.

"Mathyssen glared at Swivet, but her glare had no effect on him whatsoever. The students quickly dispersed, leaving them alone with the source of the conflagration.

"Her flaming eyes met Swivet's steady but somewhat glassy gaze. '*Why?*' *she complained.* '*Why do they send us these pathetic children with so little skill? They would be more suited as laborers, beggars, or thieves. And,*' she looked at the young boy's handiwork and spread out her arms dramatically, '*we get this.*'

"She shook her head. '*How in the heavens did the stars choose you to be one of our students?*' Mathyssen didn't need or want an answer.

"But it was a good question. If not for the war that had scarred his family and reshaped his world, he never would have been a student at the school of wizardry in the great city of Kalise, he never would have caused the conflagration that attracted Mathyssen and Swivet's attention, and he never would have become the Wyvern Wizard.

"When we are young, we cannot know where the twisted path of life will lead. At critical junctures in our lives, we can choose to walk by closed doors or choose to see what is on the other side." Aloysius looked at Khia. "Sometimes we are guided in that choice, and sometimes influenced or even manipulated. We are streamed into places others deem suitable, perhaps with good intentions and perhaps not. We are labeled, graded, and judged like various items on a grocery store shelf."

Aloysius looked at Catherine and Harold. "This young boy was born in an uncertain time, as can be true for all of us, and he had to play the cards he was given… We never know when the next card dealt, like a page being turned, will change everything from impossible to possible.

"'*He's yours Swivet,*' announced Mathyssen, as if she'd picked him up off the pantry shelf and discarded him for being past his sell-by date.

"'*But, I warn you,*' Mathyssen pointed her staff at Swivet, '*it would be a mistake to spare him. He will need discipline, that one.*' And with that, she made her grand exit. Mathyssen always liked a grand exit, perhaps even more than a grand entrance.

"'*Well boy, are you the one responsible for this?*' Swivet tried to hide the smile that threatened to creep onto his lips.

"'*Yes sir,*' responded the boy, his bottom lip quivering.

"'*No use crying about it lad. What's done is done.*'

"'*Yes sir.*'

"'*What in the name of the great magician were you doing anyway?*' asked Swivet.

"'*I… I was taking out the trash, sir,*' the boy replied, in a tiny voice.

"'*Taking out the trash?*' Swivet roared, trying to sound fierce, but despite his best efforts, he burst out laughing. '*You know it's less trouble lad, if you take it out the old fashioned way.*'

"'*Yes sir.*'

"'*Well, spit spot, clean it up. No short cuts this time. You'll find water and buckets over there in the shed,*' he pointed.

"'*Yes sir,*' complied the boy, who ran off to do his work, relieved that he'd not been more severely punished.

"And that was how the Wyvern Wizard was introduced to his not-so-great Master Swivet," said Aloysius.

"Of course, he wasn't yet known as the Wyvern Wizard. Not until he could make it rain," smiled Aloysius. "Oh, but I do get ahead of myself. As a young boy, believe you me when I tell you, he was not remarkable in any way... except perhaps in his tenacity; in fact, he possessed negligible magical abilities. No one (except perhaps for Swivet) thought that he was destined to be a wizard of any kind. And as far as a great wizard? Not even Swivet thought that possible. He was just a normal and very average boy. Sadly, the young boy had no reason to be very confident, for he was not very good at most of the things he tried… except in his dreams..." Aloysius trailed off for a moment before continuing again.

"Now most worlds have little time for dreamers. It's the value of study, achievement, and wealth that matters. But if not for dreamers, where would worlds be?" Aloysius took a deep breath and fixed his gaze on the distant stars; they hung above the desert floor and would soon sink below the horizon, but they still had many miles to cover before they reached the next cache.

"As a young boy," Aloysius continued, "the boy was most undisciplined… but he had imagination. He visualized feats of greatness as he trudged to and from his dormitory to his classes. On sunny days, spring showers, and fierce winter storms, he dreamed of scaling great mountains... of crossing vast seas and visiting other worlds. Lost, he was, in idle pursuits... not in the huge dusty magical books or the tasks that his teachers set before him. In his daydreams, and the clandestine books he read when he should have been studying, he was the hero—brave and selfless—who slew dragons and rescued beautiful damsels in distress.

"In his eleventh year of study, which would make him about eighteen—everything changed."

"Is that when he became a wizard?" asked Khia.

"He fell in love." After a long pause, Aloysius continued. "The universe, in a kind of twisted comedy, caused their paths to cross. She came from a magical and powerful family, and not only was she very beautiful but she was very clever too. She kissed him once, but he never told her how he felt."

"Why?" asked Khia.

"He felt he had nothing of worth to offer," said Catherine, answering for their storyteller. She didn't know the story any more than Khia, but was old enough to know how these things worked. "How sad… because everything could have been so different."

Aloysius nodded, no truer words had been spoken. "Early in the boy's childhood, he had learned a very harsh lesson. In the real world, he believed that young men of modest lineage were worth no more than a penny, and young men who lacked ability and drive half as much so. But he vowed that he would prove himself worthy and return one day a hero… and win this lady's heart. With only the clothes on his back and his meager possessions (wrapped in a bundle tied to the end of his staff), he left like a vagabond with only his hopes and his dreams.

"For years he struggled. There were no feats of greatness, traveling to different worlds, or saving damsels in distress. Alone, he found himself on the outskirts of a town. Standing on a muddy sidewalk after a downpour, he paused to look at the day's fading sunset. It had been one of his favorite things to do, but now it only saddened him more… for it was a reminder that another day had passed and his dreams had faded long ago.

"Few are destined for greatness, most live in the realm of mediocrity, and others fail miserably. He had failed miserably. But the strange thing about the universe is that we never know when things will change.

"*'You!'* a drunk in the street hollered. *'Garbage boy! Help an old man up.'*

"The young man looked around.

"*'Yes, you!'* shouted the drunk.

"The young man walked over and helped the man to his unsteady feet. The stench of liquor on the man's breath almost knocked him over. *'You're in pretty bad shape old man.'*

"*'I'm in better shape than you, garbage boy,'* was the drunk's nasty reply.

"Hearing something in his voice, the young man looked more closely at the man, seeing beyond the drunk. He saw the red beard, a little more gray than he remembered, and the bloodshot eyes. *'Master Swivet?'*

"*'Yes, it's me you fool,'* said Swivet, none too kindly."

Aloysius glanced at Khia. "They say that, when the student is ready, the teacher will appear. And he got Swivet… not once but twice in a lifetime! What *was* the universe trying to tell him?

"Swivet had to be steadied and held upright lest he fall, not only because of his intoxication but because of his advanced age. *'Almost drank myself to death waiting for you. Pick up my bags.'*

"*'But...'* protested the young man.

"*'I see you've made extraordinary gains on your own. Come or stay. The choice is yours.'*

"The young man needed no one to remind him of his failures. He had himself for that. For years he had wandered aimlessly. Perhaps an old drunk teacher was better than no teacher at all. Stooping down, he complied and picked up Swivet's things.

"Those early days with Swivet were trying, to say the least. Most of his lessons seemed to have no rhyme, reason, or purpose. He was forever telling him that wizards 'pay close attention to every little detail.' I'm sure if there were automobiles in his time, his master would have made him polish a car clockwise with his right hand and anticlockwise with his left, fifty thousand times and more…

"As it turned out, without knowing it, the young man learned much more than he would have learned in sorcerer school, for although such places are generally quite good, not one wizard destined for greatness (well… perhaps there were three or four) studied within the walls of a school.

"He learned that what appeared to be menial work could be most enlightening. Everything was of equal importance… nothing, absolutely nothing, was more or less important… and that included cooking, cleaning, caring for things, cutting firewood, building fires, painting, and fixing leaky roofs. Embedded in the physical manual labor were lessons about patience, and even greater tenacity... and he learned not just to hear but to listen.

"The Wyvern Wizard earned his name under the tutelage of his teacher, the hard way. But it didn't happen until after he had run out of patience and cried out in frustration about how the old man had used him as a fetch-this boy and accused him of not keeping his promise: to teach him how to be a real wizard.

"'*Really,*' said Swivet, scratching his red beard, now streaked with even more gray. He took another deep swig from a whiskey bottle that was wrapped inside a plain brown paper bag (as if that would hide the truth). Empty. He threw the bottle at the young man, who narrowly dodged it. The glass shattered behind him. Swivet rose to his full imposing height (and he was *really* tall, perhaps 6'7"... uh maybe 6'6" as he most likely had started to shrink a little by then). He stared into the face of the young man and his voice boomed. '*You think you've learned nothing. Let us see if it is true and you have indeed learned nothing at all.*'

"The young man stood his ground.

"'*Make it rain,*' Swivet demanded.

"'*I can't,*' the apprentice wizard said, '*I don't know how.*'

"'*Then you are no longer my student, and you can go,*' Swivet announced, as if he didn't care.

"'*What?*' Never in his life had the young man been so shocked and baffled by the words spoken to him. '*You've got to be joking.*' The abuse that Swivet had rained down upon him, the years of labor and long hours, had amounted to nothing. Nothing. What hurt the most was that he had placed his dreams in the hands of an old drunk. He had so wanted to become a wizard. It struck him like a powerful blow in the very middle of his being, which spread out throughout his body. An anger deeply hidden (so deeply hidden that he hadn't even known it was there) rose up within him.

"Dismissing him with a wave of his hand, Swivet turned his back on him, appearing more interested in finding another bottle in a brown paper bag.

"The young apprentice had reached his breaking point. In blinding fury, the young wizard raised his staff to strike the old man. Swivet moved with such speed that the young man's staff struck nothing but the ground. The impact was jarring.

"Driven back, he fell. Before he could get to his feet, Swivet was on him like a rabid dog, bombarding him with his staff, blow after blow, which he could hardly defend himself against.

"Useless. Even drunk, Swivet was much too wily for him. He couldn't even best an old drunk. His staff tumbled from his hands. On his knees, he was on the point of tears. His rage spent, his anger spent… he was utterly and totally defeated.

"'*Make it rain,*' demanded Swivet.

"'*I can't,*' replied the young man. '*You never taught me.*' He looked up at Swivet with tears blurring his vision. '*I can't.*'

"Saying nothing more, Swivet turned and walked away.

"'*Make it rain.*' Swivet's words echoed in his mind. Raising his face to the heavens, the young man closed his eyes to try and shut out the pain, and something small and hard hit his cheek… and struck him again… and a half second later again… and then again and again.

"Thinking Swivet had returned to inflict more pain and punishment, he looked up and was amazed to discover that the sky, which had been clear and bright, had turned into a maelstrom of clouds that seemed to have ripped the sky apart... and there was hail falling in great sheets from the sky.

"Swivet turned and looked at the young man. '*I asked for rain. But hail will do.*'

"'*Yes sir.*'

"'*Took you long enough,*' Swivet muttered, then laughed his laugh.

"'*Yes sir.*'

"You see, Swivet never needed to teach him; it was in the young wizard all along." Aloysius looked at Khia. "It just had to be awakened in him."

He looked back at the sky. "And from that day forward, their lessons began in earnest. The young wizard, for that was what he had become that day, could make the heavens shriek with electric storms and could make the ground shake. Acts of great power were his, but also of gentleness… like making a single seed sprout. Eventually... the inevitable day came when the young apprentice was the more knowledgeable and skilled than he who had chosen him.

"'*Lad, it is time,*' said Swivet.

"'*No.*' He held Swivet's old hand.

"'*Do you know why I chose you?*' he asked. '*It's because I knew that any child who could cause such havoc at such an early age could change the world.*'

"'*Swivet,*' he said, '*you need to rest.*'

"'*I want you to… do something for me.*'

"'*Anything,*' promised the Wyvern Wizard.

"'*Go back.*' He labored for breath. '*Show Mathyssen... she needs to know… before she does something stupid.*' Swivet closed his eyes, and like the gentle shudder of an autumn leaf finding freedom at last free and falling, the wizard died.

"Such are the vagaries of life. So he went back, intent on fulfilling Swivet's last wishes. In some twisted tragedy, the universe caused his path to cross with hers once more—the one who had stolen his heart. She had not only grown more beautiful but she had become a powerful witch. He had hoped to impress her with his feats of greatness, but she had no time... for she had her own destiny to fulfill.

"Hiding his disappointment, he turned and quietly walked away. Some say the universe (being very cruel to him for even allowing their paths to intertwine) took pity on him. Perhaps the universe did understand his loss. From inside of him surged an amazing amount of energy, and in one magnificent blast of magic, he willed his grief into the heavens and nine new stars were born.

"Alone, he wandered… for wizards are for the most part solitary beings. He climbed great mountains to listen to the wind; he crossed great seas and traveled to different worlds."

"Did he slay a dragon?" asked Khia.

Aloysius smiled. "No, but he may have met a dragon and saved a damsel or two in distress."

His story ended there. They had reached their cache.

†

The world about Sagar stabilized. This sort of travel still made her a little woozy, but she was where she was supposed to be: the Ice Palace of the Mist Wraiths. Sagar had no hesitation, but that wasn't to say she wasn't scared. This was indeed a desperate and desolate path that she had chosen. This was one place in which she could get eternally lost. She took a deep breath, stepped forward, and did not look back. As the eyes of the mist wraiths turned upon her, anyone else would have frozen in fear.

"Hello Grinspoon," she said, as mist wraiths swirled around her.

"And what brings you to my doorstep?" asked Grinspoon, in a strange and ancient language, as he slowly turned towards her.

"You know why I have come," she replied, following him into his ice chamber.

Grinspoon went to his vault. As it opened, cold white mist spilled out. He filled the silver chalice and brought it to her.

The mist wraiths danced around her as Sagar brought the cup to her lips and drank. Her face turned pale and the cup fell from her hand.

CHAPTER 26

# Lest We Forget

'Tis a lesson you should heed:
Try, try, try again.
If at first you don't succeed…

~ Credited to William Edward Hickson (1803-1870)

Their journey into the desert had not been easy. At the beginning, when they had been following the contours of the Mediterranean, it had been tough, but they had made excellent progress. Stepping inwards, into the unforgiving sand and sandstone-sculptured interior, that's when things had gotten tougher… and traveling at night tougher yet.

As the sun was setting, Khia stirred, half awake and half asleep. She tried to remember her dreams, but all she could recall were discordant fragments that made little sense. She wasn't used to sleeping during the day and felt tired all of the time; dark circles rested under her eyes. She glanced suspiciously at Aloysius.

Sensing her eyes on his back, he turned to look at her.

Khia quickly looked away. There was something about him that she couldn't quite work out. It was no secret that Norbert didn't like him, or trust him for that matter, and it seemed like the icy animosity between them was mutual. But Aloysius had proved himself useful in the desert. Somehow, he knew things well before anyone else (even before Norbert and McBride, which was saying something). It was like he didn't just have a sixth sense—he had a seventh one too.

She'd lost count of how many times he had forewarned them of approaching danger. Once, however, it was only a harmless caravan of Bedouins who had been following their ancient paths, with their camels loaded with salt, carpets, and merchandise. That day the only risk had been McBride: holding him back from his urge to haggle for a few bargains. But the other times had been very real. They had managed to avoid a small convoy of military vehicles that had plied the dunes, helicopters that circled above like vultures rising on thermals, military jets that screamed low across the horizon, and the random scouts on motorcycles too. Most concerning (and the reason they had remained hidden) was the stealth drone and its surveillance technology, sensors, cameras, and listening devices.

The desert was their menace… and their ally. Aloysius, in simpatico with the desert, understood its natural ebb and flow (somewhat like Salix and the sea). He used the natural variations of its wind to erase their steps, and with its blanket cover of darkness, conceal them… but he had no power over time, and time was running out. They were fast approaching the time of the crescent moon and they hadn't moved in days. Running out of food and water wasn't their only problem. Catherine was becoming more despondent. The difficulties of their journey, the heat of the day, and the cold of the night had taken their toll, but for Catherine, it was exponentially worse… and no one spoke of it.

It was as if Catherine was trapped in a perpetual nightmare. Khia wanted to help her, but she didn't know how. Harold, a few feet away, was ever watchful and attentive; McBride, at Catherine's side, gently placed a blanket over her, but in her delirium, she threw it off. He lightly brushed her cheeks with his fingers. It may (or may not) have been in Khia's imagination, but the pain that creased Catherine's face seemed to ease and it looked like she fell into a less troubled sleep.

Norbert stood alone, his rifle resting rigidly over his shoulder, and stared moodily into the distance. The horses pawed the ground, restlessly.

Khia wanted to go over and speak to Norbert, but decided it was best to leave him alone with his demons.

The alternative was Aloysius, who was sitting quietly by a small fire. Curiously, she asked, "What are you doing?"

"Just passing time," Aloysius said, but as he looked up at her, his eyes flashed. "It's as easy as making an angel dance on a head of a pin." He said it loud enough for Norbert to hear.

A wave of apprehension swept over Khia, and she had a strong urge to get away from him… but she couldn't. It was as if he had placed a powerful spell around her—a strong magnetic pull drawing her closer to him.

She blinked. She shook her head, wondering if her eyes were playing tricks on her. Had she just seen a black aura absorbing all the light around him? Whatever she saw, was gone.

The small fire glowed and tiny sparks flew into the air. The wind seemed to hesitate and the tiny sparks, suspended in the air, fell ever so slowly back to the earth.

"Would you like me to show you?" asked Aloysius, his smile deepening and showing the creases around his eyes.

Khia nodded slowly.

"Come then," Aloysius invited her closer, motioning with his long sinewy fingers. "Sit beside me."

She sat across from him on the sand.

Aloysius looked into her eyes. It made her feel uncomfortable, as if he was inside her head. "Imagine space before you." His voice seemed far away. "The universe is without beginning... without end. Absolutely anything imaginable is possible..." Being guided by his words, she followed them like bread crumbs scattered along a forest path.

He spoke the words slowly. "You know that most things are hidden… hidden right in front of our eyes."

Instinctively, Khia raised her hand and touched the pendant that hung around her neck. She remembered Nora using those exact words. What else had Nora told her? For some reason she couldn't hold onto the thought. Khia's heart blipped and a feeling like an electric jolt coursed through her. As she breathed, she felt the air flow down her throat, expanding in her lungs, and then she felt her lungs compress again as the air flowed up and out again.

Khia opened her eyes. She wasn't in the desert anymore.

Aloysius was nowhere to be seen, nor was Norbert. Instead of sitting on the sand, she was on a hard surface. Above and below the sky, everything was gray and opaque.

Where was she?

She must be in a dreamscape. Instinctively, she looked for the beacon of light… but this was not the Dark World (to which Nora had brought her). This was different. Suddenly, pain shot through her head like a tidal bore. She felt an odd sensation, as memories flooded back to her... and then she remembered that she'd been here before, many times in fact. No wonder she was tired all the time. Ever since that night in Salazar's House, Aloysius had been bringing her here. Teaching her things that she needed to learn.

And then she saw Aloysius. And what was really weird is that she knew what he was going to say before he spoke the words—and she knew her answer too. How often had she been in this endless and repeating loop? She knew the loop wouldn't be broken until she learned whatever it was she was supposed to learn. But she wasn't sure what he was trying to teach her. She had tried to follow him, match him, best him. She had tried everything: screamed, cried, and coaxed… but such things had little effect on Aloysius.

"You're a lousy teacher," accused Khia.

"Am I? Perhaps it is the student."

"How come you always bring me to this dreary place?"

Aloysius raised his eyebrows, and with half smile on his face, he took a step back and plummeted over the edge.

"Aloysius!" she screamed.

There were no options to weigh. She flung herself over the edge after him. Falling through empty space had been scary at first (it was like falling in a dream), but she was getting used to it, able to release the fear and control her movements a little more. She needed to close the gap between them. As she did so, the world transformed from a gray void to a world full of doors. She needed to be in position.

Gliding towards a doorway, Aloysius shuffled through a set of keys in his hand. He paused a moment and turned. It was as if he were asking, *Will you make it this time?*

A second later, she landed on a platform. Rolling to absorb the impact, she skittered close to the edge. She looked over and saw thousands of doors below, above, and around her—every one of them mirror images of themselves floating around in empty space.

Khia leapt to her feet, sprinting after Aloysius trying to reach the door before it closed.

"Damn!" Too late.

How was she supposed to get through a locked door without a key?

"I can do this," she said, trying to convince herself without really believing that she could. "Think, think, think."

The pendant that hung around her neck started to glow. It always glowed at this time, but what was it trying to say? She remembered how she had felt in the Dark World when Nora had left her to find her way back. Nora had said it was its opposite… and yet it had felt impossible to figure out. The world had seemed dark, but it hadn't been.

The answer had always been there, hidden right in front of her eyes… and then she saw that this place too wasn't as it seemed. Everything was moving in and out of existence. There were forces and fields of energy, some large, some small... pulsing and turning around themselves... each in an intricate and balanced dance that made everything possible.

Khia touched the door with her hand, and watched in fascination as she moved it in the space between. She was able to break through a thin invisible veil, almost (but not quite) like dipping her hand in liquid. Its shape distorted and she was able to put her hand through countless layers.

She focused on the door and discovered that it too changed from a solid to a veil. She stepped forward and went into the fabric of the door. The ripples moved away from her touch. She could see the patterns, their brilliant intricacies, their swirls and twirls of exponential expanding and contracting forces and fields... all of it simple... and complex.

"There," she said to herself, as she altered the field around her hand. The effect surprised her. The field in that small section collapsed. She had interrupted the field; it separated outwards and the door dissolved. "Cool!" She was manipulating the energy and matter of this place.

Floating about her were fifty or so doors… and farther out, for as far as the eye could see, more and more doors.

"Wow." She'd never made it this far before.

She watched, in some awe and fascination, as the fifty or so doors formed a tier. The doors stacked one on top of the other, ascending, like a stairway. At the very top was a door that stood upright and slightly ajar, and through which a sliver of silver light spilled.

As she stepped on the first door-step, she felt it shift... but it held her weight.

Her first few steps were tentative. She looked back and noticed that the first two doors were starting to dissolve. She ran up faster and faster. Out of breath from the exertion, she reached the last step and pushed her way through the door. As she stepped over its threshold, the stairway of doors collapsed.

Taking a moment to catch her breath, she saw Aloysius on a large terrace leaning on a railing that overlooked a view of a beautiful lake, and high mountains in the distance crowned with snow.

"Well done," he congratulated her.

She'd done it! She was so excited that all she wanted to do was jump up and down and savor the moment... causing her to forget rule number one (a lesson drilled into her by Norbert): Don't let your guard down, ever.

Catching her unawares, Aloysius grabbed both of her wrists.

"What are you doing?" Khia tried to wrench her arms from his grasp, but his grip was too strong. He was scaring her. He twisted her arms until he could see the inside of her forearms. She saw the faint white scar on his forearm: the wizard's mark. Perhaps he'd wanted to see the wizard's mark on her arms… but they were bare. It seemed to her that his face changed then, from an expression of pride in her accomplishment to one of disappointment... that she wasn't what he thought she should be.

Khia wrenched her arms from his grasp, yelling at the sudden pain.

A voice called her name… and she was sitting cross-legged in the sand by the embers of what had been a small fire, with Norbert's fingers wrapped in her hair and pulling her to her feet.

"Khia!" shouted Norbert, releasing her. "Stop fooling around. We have to get out of here. Now!"

Disoriented, Khia thought she must have fallen asleep.

It was dark and the stars were bright in the night sky. Hours must have passed... yet it had only seemed like a minute or two since she had joined Aloysius by the small fire.

Khia went over to the horses and cast her gaze towards the eastern horizon. She saw a growing light. Was the sun rising? The light separated then into a growing line of military vehicles, their high-beam lights blazing and converging on them.

They had been found!

## CHAPTER 27

# High Noon

Helicopters, like angry wasps, crisscrossed the sky to a staccato soundtrack of submachine guns and grenade explosions.

Doggedly pursued, they had been forced along the edge of a canyon. A wide array of tricks and deceptions had failed. They had been riding for hours, the horses tiring after a failed last-ditch attempt at drawing out their attackers. There was nowhere else to go. Norbert and McBride fell back.

"I'm all out of ideas," said Norbert, feeling the circle around them tightening.

"You? Out of ideas!" cried out McBride. "Norbert, this is not a good time to be out of ideas!"

"What are we going to do?" asked Khia, as the rest of them pulled up around them.

"Beats me," both men responded at the same time.

"Jinx," said McBride, but Devon wasn't there to laugh.

"We're dead," lamented Harold.

"Come on Harold, cheer up." For the first time in days, Catherine was alert and had a heightened awareness of everything that was happening. "We're still breathing."

"But for how much longer," Harold muttered under his breath.

"We gotta wait for the fat lady to sing," said McBride, his playful smile exuding confidence. "The last act in an opera—"

"McBride, not the right time," said Norbert.

"I prefer chess," added Aloysius.

Bullets splashed the sand and echoes ricocheted off the canyon walls like a crescendo.

"The lady is singing!" shouted McBride. Harold's horse spooked. Norbert and McBride simultaneously drew their weapons.

Two muffled shots were heard and two bodies fell through the air.

Norbert and McBride looked at each other. Neither had pulled the trigger. Both looked at Aloysius.

"Wasn't me," replied Aloysius.

McBride shrugged his shoulders.

"Who took those shots?" asked Norbert, with a puzzled look on his face. Norbert calmed his horse, letting her walk in circles while he looked around. But he saw nothing.

"Never look a gift horse in the mouth," smirked McBride.

"Yeah, you're right," answered Norbert, looking around and spotting a horse that was still freaking out from the sound of gunfire and a desperate New York City taxi driver hanging on for dear life. "Oh for God's sake, will someone go and help Harold."

†

Catherine looked over the edge. Several hundred feet below, she saw what had once been a meandering river that had etched its way through rock and ancient sandstone.

"What we going to do now?" asked Harold. "We can't go forward and we can't go back."

"Zugzwang," stated Aloysius flatly.

Harold looked puzzled.

"A term in chess where there are no good moves left to play," explained Aloysius.

"I like that word," said McBride, trying it on for size, "zugzwang. I should use it some time."

Catherine sidled up beside McBride, leaned over, and kissed him seductively before pulling abruptly away. "Let's see how close we can get to the edge, honey." With a wild woman's cry, she kicked the flanks of her sweated horse and coerced the animal over the edge.

"Catherine, nooooo!" yelled Harold, shock written on his face.

Because of her vantage point, Catherine had seen what no one else had: a narrow path snaked an almost suicidal route down to another level below.

McBride looked at Norbert as if to tell him, *I told you so. She's not a liability*.

"McBride, don't be a smart-ass. Nobody loves a smart-ass," Norbert gruffly responded.

"I didn't say anything," McBride protested.

"Yeah, but I know what you were thinking."

McBride ignored him and took to the path, looking like he'd simply plunged over the edge. In quick succession, Norbert, Khia, and Aloysius followed suit.

Harold hesitated. Astride his horse, which nervously pawed the ground, Harold cautiously looked over the ledge. "Oh mon, how is it I get myself in these bad situations?"

"Come on Harold," shouted Khia encouragingly. "It's not as bad as it looks."

"I'd rather be driving a cab in New York City during rush hour, on a Black Friday, in a snowstorm, when there's a sale at Macy's," he muttered.

A glance behind him was his determining factor. Dust clouds were approaching, which meant military vehicles.

"Disaster ahead and death chasing." Harold shook his head and reluctantly kicked his horse. As he did so, he yelled, "Geronimo!"

Eluding their pursuers had been only a temporary measure. The horses were frothing and needed water and rest. Everyone looked tired, except for Norbert and McBride who looked like they were actually enjoying this. In reality, they were no better off than if they had gone around in a big circle, ending up in exactly the very same place. The difference was that they had bought themselves some time.

"Checkmate," said Aloysius.

Seven helicopters circled above like black vultures. Professional mercenaries (Blackwood employed soldiers), carrying an arsenal of weapons, blocked their way.

In one of the vehicles, the Monsignor, protected behind bullet-proof glass, sat in air-conditioned comfort. He prayed that this would soon be over, with no harm done to others. And not for the first time, he doubted his superior's orders.

"You see the size of their weapons," commented McBride.

"Honey, I thought you told me size didn't matter!" replied Catherine.

"It's what you do with it," replied McBride, meeting her quirky response, but Catherine's smile froze on her face and her body convulsed. McBride grabbed her before she fell off her horse.

McBride looked at Norbert. "Don't say it."

"Say what?" asked Catherine, as if nothing had happened.

"No place left to hide. No place left to run," said Harold.

"Zugzwang," said McBride. "That is such a great word—"

"Shut up! I've got to think," snapped Norbert. "The good news is it's the Monsignor and not Burdock and Cocklebur out there."

"Yes, I agree," answered McBride. "If it was Burdock and Cocklebur, then we really would have a problem."

"They're bound to show up some time though," said Norbert.

"Makes me wonder what they're up to," pondered McBride.

†

"You should have an image now," spoke Father Tobias.

Almost imperceptibly, Sister Ashema nodded. She heard the soft words of Father Tobias as if he stood next to her in the room. She made a small adjustment to her ear-piece. It was highly sensitive surveillance equipment provided courtesy of Vatican Intelligence, which could have easily been mistaken for a hearing aid. Accessing satellite images was like her eyes looking down from the heavens. She could see the image of the Earth in its rotation, and the growing darkness. She inputted the coordinates and the image zoomed in on the Mediterranean.

Tipping her glasses to the tip of her nose, she glanced over at the Nigerian Cardinal who stood beside her. They were in a small room in Vatican City. He was pensively looking out the window. She saw the golden elongated rays of an Italian sunset casting long shadows.

She returned her gaze to the satellite image. As the image zoomed in closer, Sister Ashema easily identified the Nile River basin. Because of the hour time difference, it was already dark and she could see the lights around the Nile River, looking like the stem of a flower, its delta where it reached the Mediterranean Sea expanding out like yellow petals.

Scrolling westward, Sister Ashema followed the contours of the Mediterranean. At Tunisia, she split the screen in two so she could simultaneously scan the North African coastline (heading towards Gibraltar) and have a visual on the Pope's death chamber. All those in the Pope's apartment were drawn to the Secretary General, who knelt beside the gaunt, unconscious figure. The Pope would soon take his final breath in this world.

"We don't have much time," Father Tobias informed Sister Ashema.

Ninety million miles away, a huge magnetic storm (which had erupted eighteen hours earlier on the surface of the sun) was traveling at a terrific speed directly towards the third orbiting planet.

The leading edge of this huge electromagnetic solar storm was starting to interfere with highly sensitive electronic equipment. Hours before, most national and international satellite providers had turned their electronic masterpieces off, praying they would not be harmed. Otherwise the cost would be potentially ruinous. Scientists from around the world followed protocol, preparing for one of the deadly plagues that inner space could throw at them.

Sister Ashema worked quickly. She had no idea how long she had before communication would be cut off. On one side of her screen, she located Norbert and McBride and knew they were in trouble. Adding another panel, she focused her attention on finding the Abraxis. And there it was, near the Strait of Gibraltar.

Readjusting the screen brought the two separate images into sharper focus, and she scrolled a little more to the south and out by several orders of magnitude. With the enlarged image, she saw the enormity of the storm in the desert and on the sea.

"My God," she prayed, "protect them."

†

No one moved; it was like a Mexican standoff. Norbert looked at the vehicles arrayed before them. A wry smile appeared on his face, for he saw something, that as of yet, no one else had seen.

Harold was about to move, but Norbert grabbed his reins and yanked him back. It was a good thing too as bullets flew through the space where Harold's head would have been.

"I almost met my maker," said Harold, nervously rattling on.

Catherine suddenly laughed, no longer in possession of her faculties.

Norbert ignored her; she wasn't his priority. "Ropes. Get the ropes." McBride already knew what Norbert was thinking.

"No matter what you do, do not let go," said Norbert, as he uncoiled the nylon rope and passed it to Khia and Harold. McBride did the same with Aloysius and Catherine. "Do you understand?"

Khia nodded.

"You two," he pointed at Khia and Harold, "stick with me. We're going to give 'em a show they never expected. Are you ready?"

No one nodded.

†

Sister Ashema's equipment started to flicker on and off. At most she had another minute or two but had enough time to see that a sandstorm of incredible magnitude had sprung up in the Sahara desert.

Sister Ashema heard the Secretary General. "Padre Eterno."

There was no response…

†

Near the Strait of Gibraltar, Salix's fingers, stained yellowish brown, trembled. He was out of time and he knew it. He was being constantly harassed by land, sea, and air.

Salix smiled to himself. More than once, he and his crew had gone around the world. He had had many adventures, a few with Norbert and McBride. Today, it was a different world. The risks had always been high. He needed no fortune teller to foretell the future.

Salix took another deep drag of his unfiltered cigarette; it burned his fingers. He worried that he might not be able to keep his promise to Norbert and McBride and meet them in Morocco.

And so he had sent out a call, not knowing if anyone would answer…

The storm was almost on top of him. He could feel the choppy movement of the waves. The Abraxis, his beautiful old ship... her days (he feared) were numbered.

†

For the second time, the General Secretary called out the Pope's name.

†

Hope rose in his chest. "Power full," shouted Salix, laughing out loud. Six captains had responded to his call.

The storm struck. Angry storm clouds, the churning sea, and the thick fog rolled in. The sea boiled as their powerful diesel engines screamed, their pistons rising and falling. Their giant propellers cut through the rough waters. In a tightly choreographed dance, six ships plus one, the Abraxis, formed a moving circle. In the fog, the ships dispersed in seven different directions.

Salix lit another cigarette.

Melalaia stood at his side. "Poppy, you know those things will kill you."

Salix looked at his daughter. "We all to die one day," he said, fatalistically.

†

High above, a satellite closed its eyes as the massive coronal ejection of charged ions rained upon the earth.

Seven ships, as if bowing to each other at the end of a dance, parted, moving in different directions. The Abraxis moved beyond Gibraltar towards the ocean. This great ruse was designed so that Salix could escape and foil their pursuers.

Allah and God willing, they would make it to Morocco.

†

The General Secretary called out a third and final time.

Calmly, the Secretary General slipped the Ring of the Fisherman from the mortal man's emaciated finger. He held the ring in his hand, and without another word, slipped it into his pocket and walked from the room.

CHAPTER 28

# Desert Storm

To see a World in a Grain of Sand
And a Heaven in a Wild Flower,
Hold Infinity in the palm of your hand
And Eternity in an hour.

~ William Blake (1757-1827)

At a full gallop, two groups led by Norbert and McBride, holding onto their ropes, made their move. By hoofs and fury they confronted their adversaries with a surprise attack. And like the charge of the light brigade, rode right through the Monsignor and the mercenaries and into the storm. The sand kicked up by the horses merged with the sand of the intense storm. The Monsignor, although protected by a thick bullet-proof windscreen, cowered in his vehicle. Bullets, fired off in quick succession, cracked the windshield. Seeing his reflection in the cracked glass, he made the sign of cross.

The storm struck. Whipped by the sandstorm, men who had only moments before been full of smug confidence, dove for cover.

Helicopters crisscrossed the sky. Their sophisticated RADAR screens went static and they watched in horror as a tsunami of sand moved in like a wave. Rotary blades started to sing as they cut through the blowing sand. Before their intakes clogged up, the helicopters turned around and fled the ferocious Saharan storm.

The Monsignor looked on in disbelief as the six on horseback rode by them and into the storm. Again, doubt clouded his convictions. The fury, and the speed of the storm, was like the hand of God descending upon him like a fist. In horror, the Monsignor sat in his vehicle. It might as well have been his coffin, and the sand the dirt on his grave.

†

Blinded by the sandstorm's ferocity, Khia's horse reared. Flying through the air, Khia landed hard, the wind knocked out of her, but she never let go of the rope. This was her life line, and no matter what, she wasn't going to let go. She rolled to her feet. The terrific storm had saved them and damned them at the same time. Her clothing flapped angrily in the whipping wind, loose strands of hair flailing madly about. Searing blasts of sand struck Khia's reddened skin, stinging as if coarse sandpaper was scraping off the top layer. Her eyes were gritty. She raised the crook of her arm to try to protect her face.

"Norbert!" she called out.

†

"Khia!" yelled Norbert into the raging wind.

There was no response.

"McBride!"

"I'm here!" answered McBride.

"Aloysius?"

"Here!"

"Me too!" called Harold.

"Khia!" Norbert yelled again, even louder.

No response.

"Catherine!" yelled McBride.

†

Khia pulled the nylon rope; it had become slack. She followed it as it moved like a snake in the sand. She reached the end of her rope and looked at it in disbelief. It had been cut.

"Norbert!" yelled Khia. "McBride!" She waited but could hear nothing but the storm.

"Norbert! McBride! Catherine! Harold!" she called out, as if calling out to the four winds. They couldn't be that far away. But in the blinding sand storm, it was impossible to see or hear anything.

"Catherine! Harold?"

Nothing.

"Anybody?!" she cried.

†

Without warning, Norbert lunged at Aloysius, dragging him off his horse. "You had something to do with this!" yelled Norbert accusingly. "Tell me now or you're never going to live to see the end of this day."

Aloysius faced the angry angel. "Not now!" Aloysius shouted at full voice; the storm had intensified, allowing his voice to carry only the few inches between them.

"Not good enough," Norbert said, even as the folds of Aloysius' black keffiyeh flapped and whipped wildly between them.

"Norbert," McBride grabbed Norbert's arm, holding him back, "let Aloysius do what he needs to do."

"I hate wizards; they can't be trusted."

"Then trust me," said McBride.

Norbert released his hold on Aloysius. Aloysius ripped his keffiyeh off, exposing his face to the full force of the storm. Raising his hands, he revealed his power. Inches from his hands, a clear sphere materialized. It expanded, pushing back the storm. The storm fought back against the translucent sphere he had conjured.

Expanding outwards, the sphere formed a protective dome around them. The storm fought back and Aloysius faltered, but only briefly. Miraculously, after an epic battle of wills, the sphere held firm, and they were protected from the storm. There was a magnificent display, as the sand that beat against the dome turned to beads of brilliant colored glass fell from the heavens like hail.

Norbert's jaw fell. "You're the Wyvern Wizard."

Sand swirled like a vortex nearby and revealed a partially buried female body.

McBride leapt out of his saddle and ran towards the unconscious figure, not sure if it was Khia or Catherine.

Then he saw, falling to his knees beside her. "Catherine!" He cradled her. Gently, as if afraid he might break her; he picked her up, climbed to his feet, and carried her to Harold. Without a word, he passed Catherine to him. Quiet anguish showed on McBride's face, for he understood more than anyone else what kind of battle was going on inside her mind. He knew what he had to do. And he knew that there was nothing he could do for her.

"Harold," his voice shook ever so slightly, "look after her for me."

Harold held Catherine's lithe form. He looked for answers from McBride, Norbert, Aloysius...

No answers were forthcoming.

With no farewell, McBride leapt astride his horse and rode into the storm.

"Where's McBride going? Is he gonna find Khia?" asked Harold, overwhelmed by all that had happened.

"No," replied Norbert, looking out into the storm and watching his oldest friend disappear into the swirling sands. Shaking his head, he turned back to the others. "Hold it together Harold. This is no time to lose it. You have to look after Catherine."

Aloysius withdrew an object from his saddlebag. It was a lantern. He held it out to Norbert, who took it without question. It came to light in his hand.

"This will lead you to the next cache," Aloysius said. "It's about two miles. Wait there. The dome will protect you for an hour or two... no more.

Norbert's shoulders stooped. Within the orb of protection, he walked away... holding the lantern like the Hermit in the deck of tarot cards, with Harold following silently behind, Catherine in his arms, and four horses in tow.

Norbert looked back just as Aloysius was swallowed by the storm.

CHAPTER 29

# Khia's Heel

Water is imbued with a wandering spirit
A stream, a river, an ocean
A single drop of water
A world unto itself

Visibility was no more than a few yards and the sand seemed alive with wraiths. The thought of being buried alive frightened her. She didn't want to die. Khia tried again to yell for help, but her voice was hoarse and barely audible. All she heard was the wind screaming at her as she struggled to stay upright. She needed to keep moving. She needed a place to hide—somewhere she could shelter from the storm.

She braced herself. She became aware of someone or something near. First a shadow and then a figure emerged.

"Aloysius!" Her sigh of relief turned to shock as he pushed her roughly to the ground.

While she was falling, she had a glimpse of his face. He looked cold and impervious, and in his hand he held a sharp silver knife. She hit the ground hard. She tried to roll away from him, but he'd anticipated her move. She felt his foot pressed against her back, and her face in the sand. She couldn't move. Then he grabbed her ankle. Holding her foot steady, he cut her heel repeatedly in swift succession… again and again.

He released her and then, like an apparition, he was gone.

Did what just happen really happen? Stunned, Khia sat up and looked at her heel.

Five razor-thin cuts.

Numbly, she ran her thumb along her heel and felt the thin cuts opening. Blood welled up and seeped onto the sand. And then she felt the pain…

"No use crying about it, girl." She heard Aloysius' voice as clear as day. "What's done is done. Now, what are you going to do about it?"

Using her scarf, she squelched the flow of blood. Slowly lifting the fabric, she peeked at the five thin cuts. Blood drops appeared on the scarf like the notes on short lines of music. Gently she dabbed the blood away and wrapped her scarf around her heel. Then, like a beggar in the desert, she got up and limped away. It wasn't long before her heel was caked with blood and sand. It was painful, but she had to keep moving.

She needed to find shelter.

†

Khia felt a drop of water rolling down her face like a tear. It didn't matter; nothing mattered... a dark forgetful bliss was what had found her.

"Khia," she heard a voice as if from far away. "Come back."

"Leave me alone," she murmured.

*"Khiaaa. Khiaaa. Khiaaa."*

A memory surfaced… of a little boy, no more than three, bounding towards her. She lifted the blankets up and over him as he dove into bed next to her.

"Devon!" She was so happy to see him. She'd missed him so much, but when she went to hug him he wasn't there.

She felt another drop of water roll down her face and raised her heavy hand to brush it away. Another image surfaced. It was of Catherine, tossing and turning in restless sleep. She wanted to comfort her, but the image changed into her mother.

She felt a warm hand on her shoulder. *"Let her be. She's having one of her bad days."*

"Daddy," Khia whispered. She turned around. He wasn't there.

"No," she cried, "come back. Please. Please, come back!"

The disappointment was heart wrenching, and Khia felt another drop of water roll down her face. *"Get up!"* a voice demanded.

No. No, she didn't want to. She wanted Devon back. She wanted her dad, she wanted her mom.

"*Get up. Now.*"

She felt another drop of water roll down her cheek. Khia groaned and slowly opened her eyes, like a sunrise ending the night.

*Plop*.

Instantly she was on her feet, ready to fight the monsters, but there was no one there. It was only a drop of water that had landed on the sand.

She wavered… Oh God... she was going to be sick. She dropped to her knees, bent over, and heaved out what little she had in her stomach. She wiped her face with her dirty sleeve.

"Devon!" she called, but her voice didn't carry; her lips were parched. "Devon!" she called again. She had to find her little brother.

Her mind felt muddled. She tried to sort her thoughts, but they were shuffled thoroughly like a deck of cards. Her brother was gone; she'd pushed him through a portal... and then she started to remember.

Memories flooded back: their escape from the Vatican, their journey on the Abraxis, and setting out from Salazar's compound… their trip across the desert, being pursued, the storm, the rope that had been cut… and she remembered what Aloysius had done. She looked at her heel. It was caked with dried blood.

"Aloysius." She spoke his name aloud like a curse. Swallowing hard, she tried to push away the feeling of abandonment and betrayal when she saw a drop of water, glittering like a precious white diamond, fall though the air.

Khia looked up into the sky; it wasn't raining. She had to blink a few times, wondering if her eyes were deceiving her. She stepped back a few feet and tilted her head to the side. Hanging in midair was a door.

*Wow, a portal!* When she stepped to the side, it became just a sliver of light, and when she took another step, it all but disappeared. All she could see were drops of water appearing out of nowhere, falling onto the sand. Khia approached it. On tiptoe, she reached up but couldn't quite touch the silver handle. Just as she was thinking she might be able to jump up and turn the knob, the door opened wide and she quickly skirted to the side as a cascade of water burst out.

"Hello! I was hoping you would be here. You're Khia?"

Speechless, Khia looked at the man. At first, she thought he was a knight, but when she looked closer she realized that it wasn't a suit of armor he wore; he *was* the armor—a mechanical man. His eyes were the color of white silver. Khia could hear the servos hidden under his metallic skin.

And behind him, on the other side of the door, was a dark and stormy world; lightning slashing across a gray sky.

"You don't know how many times I have tried this door and you were not here. But here you are. Come on then, they're waiting for you. No time to dawdle."

He whirred, cocking his head to one side, and studied her.

"Who are you?" asked Khia.

"I am Barwick of course," he said, lowering his hand to hers. "Some call me the Tin Man."

"Ah," she said, because she didn't really know what to say. She took his hand. Unexpectedly, it was rather soft and warm.

"Must be quick." He hoisted her up. "I don't particularly like sandstorms." As Khia stepped over the threshold, he closed the door firmly behind them. "Nor rain for that matter. Best to be prepared." He opened his umbrella.

They were knee-deep in the middle of a large fountain, with water cascading from stone walls of various heights.

Khia washed away the sand and the heat, but Barwick was eager to get out.

"Is this water safe to drink?" asked Khia.

"You've been without water. I do apologize. Yes, it is safe to drink."

She cupped her hand, catching its cascade, and drank. The cool water was refreshing.

"Not too much or you'll be sick... or so I've been told." His voice had little inflection, but the words he chose were of concern.

Khia nodded.

"Come this way," said Barwick.

Carefully making her way out of the fountain, she realized that they were not on the ground but the rooftop of a very tall building.

Drawn to the edge, the wet wind tussling her hair, Khia caught her breath. She was in a great city, dark, wet, and gray, and standing on the roof of one of its most imposing towers. There was a matrix of roads and thousands of buildings squeezed together. It was as if each was trying to break through the clouds. Electrical arcs were being thrown from one tower to another, and blue lightning slashed the sky.

"Where are we?"

"Welcome to the city of the Nephalim."

†

For three days, gripped in wind and sandblasting fury, Norbert waited impatiently with Harold and Catherine, who was trapped in a world of nightmares that she could not come out of and they could not reach. He thought it was ironic that the two he was left to guard were the two who should never have been on this journey. Now he was stuck protecting them… and Khia. Where the hell was Khia?

He knew Aloysius had everything to do with this. And if Aloysius did what Norbert thought he had done, he feared for his young charge. Khia would be tested to her limits. His only hope was that he had trained her well enough.

"Oh, now what," grumbled Norbert, as he spotted a figure on horseback riding towards them. Picking up his rifle, he lifted it to his shoulder. His eyes narrowed. "Well, well, well what do we have here?"

## CHAPTER 30

# Grave New World

Seeing the streets of the Nephalim was like watching an old black and white film. Everything was dark and grainy. Its buildings could have been towering monolithic monsters on a matrix of streets, the pavement glassy and slick from the rain. There was a curfew here, and it was rigidly imposed.

Barwick ran, and Khia hobbled a few feet behind him, trying to get to the next building so that they could blend with the shadows. No sooner had Khia pressed her back against the building, squeezing closer to Barwick, than two reinforced military vehicles roared by, coloring the black and white world a bright yellow as their headlights illuminated every surface in their path, narrowly missing Khia and the Tin Man.

When the vehicles were out of sight, hundreds of scruffy looking figures scurried like rats from the shadows. Khia was about to make a move, but Barwick held her back.

"Wait."

A few seconds later, a third vehicle silently drove by.

Shots, screams, and thuds that sounded like bodies hitting the ground—the price of getting caught past curfew. What kind of world was this?

"This is the most dangerous," said Barwick. She could see why. The street was wider and pale blue search lights scanned the street, seemingly at random.

Zigzagging to avoid the search lights, Khia followed Barwick, but she was having trouble keeping up. Up to this point, fear had overridden the pain in her heel, but not anymore. She kept moving, but her movements were getting slower and slower, leaving a trail of red blood behind.

Reaching the alley first, Barwick looked back and was horrified that Khia was not directly behind him. He ran back into the street, lifted Khia in his arms, and dashed into the shadows.

Putting her down, he said, "It is my mistake entirely." Because of the monotone aspect of his voice, and the inflexibility of his face, it was not obvious that Barwick was upset. "Aloysius said that he would get you here. I had not realized he would revert to the ancient method prescribed for neophytes. I can only conclude he sought no mishap." His words slowed and sped up again, as he continued on in another vein. "I understand it can be very painful."

Khia nodded. "Yeah, it hurts."

"Many have died from the infection."

"That's really nice to know," she answered sarcastically.

"That was many years ago, but then again, no one has been gilled in hundreds of years."

"Gilled?"

"You've been what we euphemistically call *gilled*. The thin cuts to your heel look like the throat of a fish… but when tended to, the scar will barely be visible."

"If I don't die," replied Khia, smiling slightly and trying to sound more casual than she felt.

"You will not die. I will tend to you."

"That makes me feel so much better." It actually didn't.

"It was imperative that we get you here. This place is not somewhere you can be brought to. It is only a place you can get to."

"Why am I here?"

Focused on a dim incandescent bulb outlining a dark blue door at the end of the ally, it was as if Barwick didn't hear her question. "It is not much farther. We are almost there."

"We have to go there?" asked Khia, recalling another dark alley she and her brother Devon had run into, when they had been pursued by the crazy old bag lady and her screeching grocery cart. If it hadn't been for Dodger and Goula's sudden appearance from out of nowhere, God only knows what would have happened. Half expecting to hear the screechy grocery cart, Khia startled when crackling silver lightning bolts sliced the dark sky like a crack in the universe.

"Would you like me to carry you?" asked Barwick.

"Uh, no thanks, I think I can manage." She hobbled the rest of the way.

When they reached the dark blue door at the end of the ally, Barwick knocked twice.

A small rectangular slot, about eye level, slid open and a beam of yellow light shot out into the street.

After a few words were exchanged in an obscure language, the door swung open and they were greeted by a large caliber machine gun strapped across the chest of a ruthless-looking man wearing dark shades, and his two burly (and well-armed) colleagues... waiting for any give-me-a-reason to pounce.

The man wearing the shades looked at Khia and she saw a double reflection of her face in the frame. He nodded and stepped to the side. Allowing them entrance, he pointed to an open door at the end of the corridor. His two comrades parted to let them pass.

Reaching the room, Barwick turned on the light, which flickered for a moment before turning on. The glaring florescent light revealed a sparse room with a stainless steel table, a couple of chairs, stained walls, and a grimy window with metal bars.

"Let me clean up your wound, so infection does not set in." She saw a tray with folded linen, a glass bowl filled with water, scalpels, and various scary-looking tools that wouldn't go amiss in a torture chamber.

"I will tend to you." He patted the table. "Face down."

Hesitantly, Khia sat on the table and slowly positioned herself face down with her heels up.

"My, my... I wasn't expecting this," he said.

"What?"

"I was expecting three or four but not five cuts to your heel."

Khia grimaced in pain as he cleaned the wounds, digging out the sand that had become deeply embedded.

As he dipped the cloth into the basin, she tried to unclench her jaw... and breathe.

Holding her tighter so she would not move, he reached for the scalpel. It felt like he was peeling off layers of skin and digging deeper… until her blood flowed freely.

Khia saw the glass bowl turning from pink to red. He set the red-stained scalpel down.

"So were you always… ah, a Tin man?" asked Khia, watching him thread a needle.

"I was once a man, but I almost died. The only way to bring me back was to place me in this mechanical invention. There was so little of me left."

"So you were human?" she asked, trying to distract herself from what he was doing.

"I was once flesh and blood just like you. As a young man, I dreamed of being a knight. Must be careful what we wish for…" Barwick talked about how he had gone from a young man with dreams to being mostly mechanical. Although Khia couldn't forget what he was doing to her heel, it didn't seem to hurt as much. Maybe the numbing spray he'd used was starting to work.

She heard his servos. "You are as good as new Khia. You can stand up now."

Khia looked at her heel and saw that the wounds were almost completely healed. Before her very eyes the stitches vanished and the harsh red lines faded into five barely visible scars.

"Your friends," announced Barwick, "they are here."

*Thank God! Norbert and McBride!* She turned around and was completely surprised. "Goula! Dodger!" These two, like Norbert's sword, had an uncanny ability of appearing when you needed them most.

Goula hugged Khia, and then Dodger swirled her in his arm before he set her down.

"Are Norbert and McBride with you? And Catherine and Harold?" asked Khia.

"First things first," said Dodger. "How long has it been?"

"Too long," she answered, thinking how strange it was that she had been just thinking of them.

Placing an arm over Khia's shoulder, Goula said, "You need food and rest. Tomorrow is going to be a very busy day."

"Tonight we've booked the best restaurant in the underground of the Nephalim, but what I'd do for a sausage on a bun!" He winked at her.

Khia smiled.

"Eat, drink, and be merry," Dodger said, "for tomorrow, we may die."

"Dodger!" exclaimed Goula.

But Khia laughed, thrilled to see them again.

CHAPTER 31

# In the Dungeons of the Nephalim

"Don't look down," said Dodger.

Khia followed Dodger across a narrow and flimsy walkway, which had been hastily anchored between two tall buildings. Halfway across, Khia looked down. They must have been five hundred stories high.

The pirate's plank shook precariously. Khia used her arms to maintain her balance. The gusting force of the wind pushed its way around the maze of buildings like a hungry serpent coiling.

"Hurry," said Dodger, "we can't be spotted."

"Dodger," said Goula, "you're adding pressure she doesn't need."

"Oh right," he nodded. "Take your time Khia, but can you try and hurry a little bit?"

It was like she was frozen in time. Stuck. Halfway across.

"Come on sweetie," Goula said, in a reassuring voice. "A few more steps."

Slowly, Khia slid her right foot forward and then her left foot followed.

When Dodger reached out and grabbed hold of her hand, she breathed in relief. Scrambling onto a badly damaged balcony, which creaked under their weight, she tensed.

Gallantly, Dodger bowed. "After you."

They entered the suite of rooms as their covert partisan partners withdrew the gangplank, disappearing into the gloom. Inside the building, the windows were cracked, paint was peeling off the walls, and the floor was littered with broken glass and debris.

Dodger made his way to the door and deactivated the security device. The once great city of the Nephalim was constantly being watched and recorded. There were cameras, guards, and patrols everywhere. The trick, of course, was finding the time in between, when the cameras swiveled, to slip through unnoticed.

Cautiously, opening the door no more than half an inch, Dodger took out a small mirror with an extendable handle to peer out along the corridor.

"Someone's coming," warned Goula.

Dodger looked at Goula. Sure enough, a few seconds later Dodger confirmed. "Hoodies." Ever so quietly he closed the door. The wind whistled through the doorframe, as if wanting to give them away.

Reactivating the security codes, Dodger pressed his back against the wall. Slowly, he withdrew two powerful armor-piercing handguns he had hidden in his coat.

Wordlessly Khia watched and waited, hardly daring to breath.

They heard the Hoodies' footsteps getting closer and closer. It sounded like they were checking each and every door. When they were on the other side of their door, the footsteps stopped. The door handle rattled. Dodger looked at Goula.

She lifted her hand, signaling him to wait.

And the Hoodies moved on.

Seconds passed before Goula nodded to Dodger. Putting his guns away, he once again deactivated the codes, opened the door, and checked the corridor with his mirror.

Out in the corridor they moved swiftly. Reaching the central area, they stopped. There were cameras everywhere. How would they get by? Amazingly the cameras swiveled and pointed in another direction, allowing them to reach a phalanx of elevators without detection. Goula pressed the button on the console. It glowed red. Seconds ticked by like an eternity. Dodger stood at a T-junction, pressed against one wall so he could look down the other corridor with his small silver mirror. "We've got more Hoodies coming," he whispered.

Footsteps were getting closer.

Dodger was reaching for his guns when the red button went out and the metal doors swished open.

"Aren't you coming?" asked Khia.

"No." Goula shook her head as she strapped an electronic device around Khia's wrist. "This will throw off their sensors."

Dodger raised his hand in farewell. "Be fearless."

The sounds of footsteps got closer.

"We've got to go," said Dodger.

"The elevator will stop twice. When it stops the second time, exit."

"Then what?" asked Khia, as the door started to close.

"Trust yourself," smiled Goula. "Remember what I've told you. Look for the patterns; they'll show you the way."

†

Mirrored glass on the inside made the confined space look like it was expanding outwards. Alone, with her reflection multiplied, she felt the elevator whoosh down in its vertical corridor, slow, and then stop. The doors opened for the first time. What she hadn't expected were the three dark masked soldiers who entered, taking up most of the space in the elevator.

*Hoodies,* thought Khia. She held her breath and pressed against the back wall, trying to make herself as small as possible. Fortunately, like Goula had said, they had no awareness that she was there.

Khia felt her stomach lurch as the elevator plunged downwards. The elevator slowed and stopped, and for the second time, the door opened. Khia needed to get out, but they were blocking her way. How was she going to get by the Hoodies? Just at that moment, one stepped out to take a quick look, giving her a little space to squeeze by.

Sliding sideways, she lightly brushed against one. The man cocked his weapon, but saw no one there.

One snickered, "Detecting ghosts again!"

The elevator door closed, leaving her alone in a dark hallway. Rarely visited by those who resided in the city above, few, in fact, knew of its existence. She had reached the dungeons of the Nephalim.

The long and narrow hall that seemed to go on forever in both directions was like a horror movie come to life. Dingy, dim, web-covered lights hung from squeaking, rusty metal chains, and cast an eerie glow. No wonder Norbert didn't like dark underground places. She was feeling the same way. Suspense and tension building with every step she took, Khia checked her weapon. The act brought her little comfort.

This would lead her to the Corridor of Doors. All she had to do was find the right door. The way out. Easy, right?

Fixed to the spot, she didn't know which way to turn. She looked right and then left. *Which way? Which way?* There was no sign to point the way.

She had to make a choice. Only two choices…

Left. She'd go left. *A sinistra.* She smiled to herself as she thought of the little ghost who had helped guide them out of the catacombs.

After passing a lot of doors, she wondered if she was going the wrong way. It was getting harder to breathe; it was like even the air didn't want to stay here. It was as if something invisible was stopping her from moving forward, making each and every step she took feel heavier and harder.

She forced herself to concentrate. She needed to find the door.

Another ten feet or so and she stopped. In front of her was a door that felt different than the rest. She heard screams coming from the other side, sounding like someone was being tortured.

Quickly turning around, Khia retraced her steps and ended up at the exact same spot she had started. She saw her distorted reflection, looking like it was trapped in the tarnished elevator door.

Taking a deep breath, she took her first step in the opposite direction. Walking about five hundred feet, she started to hear snippets of sound flowing out of doors… wanting... waiting for someone to hear. The once great city of the Nephalim had its secrets. It was a keeper of secrets.

So many doors. So many secrets. *Which door?*

"Please," the word floated into the hall. "Help me." The voice sounded young and really scared.

Khia reached out to open the door. Her fingers had barely touched the handle when the door flew open. Beyond, in the darkness, was not a frightened child but a monster—a nameless creature. Malevolent. Hungry eyes. Long sharp teeth.

She froze like a deer caught in headlights. Before she could even try to shut the door, the creature bounded towards her and leapt in the air. So close she could feel its hot breath. She squeezed her eyes shut.

A squeal of throttled pain escaped the creature's lips.

Khia opened her eyes. The creature was being choked by a chain. It was fine and delicate but very strong, forged in some kind of unbreakable metal. The creature was pulled back and the door slammed shut.

Shaken by the experience, Khia took a number of steps back. Her hands were shaking; her heart was pounding. And then she noticed that her back was pressed against another door. She heard the sound of a child crying. The sound tore her apart and chilled her at the same time. The door rattled and black liquid oozed from its frame. She was stepping in something wet and sticky. Quickly she moved along the hall, leaving footprints behind.

Walking, almost running, passing more and more doors... Khia eventually stopped to catch her breath.

*Knock! Knock! Knock!*

Khia jumped.

"Who's there?" said a voice from beyond the red door. "Please let me in." *Knock! Knock! Knock!*

Khia did not want to stick around to know what was beyond that door.

She walked on and on and on… Fire residue and bullet holes marred this section of the hall. Some kind of altercation had been played out here. But she had a strong sense that she was close. She passed six doors and knew the seventh was the one. It was framed by a thin line of gold. The door, riddled in bullet holes, had once been beautiful in its simplicity. Diffused light, from the holes, escaped into the hall.

Her hands shook slightly as she raised her fingertips to lightly touch the old door. At her touch, it glowed. The thin line of gold widened and brightened. This was it. This was the right door. She was sure of it.

It opened… Her eyes adjusted to the light. She saw that there were corridors branching off in various directions. Her first thought was that it would be very easy to get lost. She stepped beyond its threshold and was no longer in the dungeons of the Nephalim.

CHAPTER 32

# Neither Here, Nor There

Here vigour fail'd the tow'ring fantasy:
But yet the will roll'd onward, like a wheel
In even motion, by the Love impell'd,
That moves the sun in heav'n and all the stars.

~*The Divine Comedy, Dante Canto XXXIII*
Translation by HF Cary (1772-1844)

She not only heard but felt the sound reverberating through her as her footsteps echoed on the teal-veined marble floor. She'd made it; she was in the Corridor.

*Nothing,* she thought, *can be as bad as being in the dungeons of the Nephalim.* Now, all she had to do was find the right door—and how hard could that be? In a string of doors to infinity...

*"A little girl who takes the long way to get to her grandmother's."*

"Aloysius," she whipped around, but no one was there.

It creeped her out. The words were his, but it sounded different... like a residual sound.

But it made her think. Was that why she was here? Was she supposed to find her grandmother's world, and reunite with her brother?

As she moved onwards, the teal-veins became lighter and finer... like threads of silver and gold. Pulsing like life-giving blood coursing through arteries, the surface got softer and squishier.

Thinking she'd taken a wrong turn, Khia looked back. There was no path.

She had to remember that the Corridor was a powerful and a dangerous place. It protects itself. The path you thought you were on can change. It can and will get you from here to there—most of the time, but not all of the time. Khia had yet to comprehend the eternal vastness of the Corridor and its infinite possibilities.

Khia found herself within a maze of doors that were scattered about like dead tree trunks in a swamp. Some doors were open… but they should have been closed. She carefully made her way through this eerie landscape of mist and fog, elements spilling from one world into another.

Never take the Corridor lightly or casually. She was supposed to remember that. Hadn't Aloysius warned her of that?

The Corridor could easily lull you… don't forget…

What was she supposed to remember? She had a feeling that she was supposed to remember something.

"Try to remember," Khia mumbled the words aloud.

*"Familiarize yourself with your surroundings and commit them to memory."*

"Norbert!" Khia called out, but he wasn't there.

"Okay," she said aloud, "it's just my mind playing tricks on me." She took a deep breath. "I can do this." But she didn't sound very confident.

"I am in the Corridor… the Corridor of Doors. I am in the Corridor… "

*So easy to let go… let go… just for a minute… an hour… a day… forever.*

"Khhhhiaaaa. Khhhhiaaaa. Khhhhiaaaa." The cries sounded like a rooster announcing the start of a new day. Khia startled.

"Wake up." An insistent voice penetrated her thoughts.

Where was she? She staggered unsteadily to her feet.

"Khia," the voice came from all around her, "it has you."

"Where am I?" Everything looked very strange to her and unfamiliar.

"In the Hall of Eternity." The man's voice was crystal clear. "One can get trapped in a place such as this."

The words, as they broke through Khia's mind, were disjointed. She wavered in and out of her strange reality.

"Aloysius!" she called out, hoping it was him suppressing her memories, but knowing it wasn't.

Khia fell to her knees.

"Damn!"

A slow moving shock wave reverberated through her.

*"You must break the spell!"* The voice penetrated her thoughts like a lost whisper.

Break what? What was she supposed to break?

*"Look deeper… what is it you see?"*

She didn't want to see. It was easier to let go… to forget…

"Khia, wake up!" she heard Nora call.

Khia woke up to the fresh scent of pine and sunlight beaming into her room. She was lying in a comfortable bed, covered with thick handmade quilts. Zip and Zipper were barking outside and she heard Norbert and McBride roughhousing with Devon in the other room.

*It was only a dream. Thank God, it was only a dream.*

Khia jumped out of bed and ran into the other room. She stopped. It was empty.

Jarringly, everything was as she remembered: the sofa with the multi-colored crocheted afghan, the kitchen neat and tidy, and in the corner, a laptop computer displayed its screen-saver—a bistro scene with a table with four wineglasses, filled with rich red wine, and crusty bread.

*They must have gone outside,* thought Khia. Padding towards the screen door, she noticed that it was dark outside… shouldn't it have been morning? Confused, Khia stepped back and stood in the dead center of the cabin.

She felt her heart beating in her chest.

"No." She took a deep breath and then screamed, as realization hit her like the shock of diving into cold water. "NO! This is real! It has to be real!" A horrible feeling came over her. *How can this be real? I was in the Corridor… trapped* in the Corridor.

"But… but I want this to be real," she said in a small voice she barely recognized.

*"Look deeper."*

"Nora," she turned swiftly… but no one was there.

The log cabin was no longer warm and cozy but a burnt-out shell. Everything started to spin around, making her feel dizzy. Around her, the cabin disintegrated into quadrillions of atoms... And Khia was in a dark alley.

She heard the screech of a damaged grocery cart.

"Devon!" she called out. She had to find her brother.

She saw him there… but as she tried to move closer to him, he got farther and farther away.

"DEVON!" screamed Khia. "I'm sorry! I'm so sorry; I should never have left you!" The wind picked up, swirling around and around with litter and dust. Blinking, she tried to clear the dust from her eyes.

It was like she couldn't breathe; she gasped for air and in that blink of time was somewhere else.

With stomach lurching horror, she found herself walking on an immense field of desiccated bones. They snapped under her feet. And then it went from worse… to worst. It was the smell that got to her first. The stench of rotting flesh and blood from severed limbs. Panicking, she screamed and struggled to get out... but as if it was quicksand, she was sucked down... knee-deep in blood and guts… and sinking deeper.

"No, no, no, this can't be happening." She tried to tell herself that this wasn't real; that it was a false reality, a nightmare. If only she tried, maybe she could wake up.

Slowly, she became aware that she wasn't the only one here. As far as she could see, in all directions, there were others—a multitude of others—trapped here too. Some, like her, were knee-deep in sludge, some were still as cranes, and others floated on their backs as if enjoying a leisurely afternoon by the seaside… oblivious, or perhaps seeing something completely different. A few moaned, but most were silent, eyes closed in some kind of a trance. But the most awful were the ones with their eyes wide open, looking like empty souls staring vacantly. Every single one of them was trapped in their own world—a creation of their own minds.

What path had brought them here—by chance or cruel fate—innocently stumbling upon an open door that should have been closed?

With sickening awareness, things started to move around her… sticky, slimy, slithering things that brushed up against her.

"Oh God! Oh my God!" Khia started to hyperventilate. Kicking and screaming, she hoped to wake up from this nightmare… but she only sank deeper.

There had to be a path that led out... but where? She searched frantically around. And there, as if by some miracle, she saw a platform. All she had to do was reach it; it wasn't that far away.

Quelling her panic, she fixed her mind on that single task. She couldn't fight her way through (that just made things worse), so instead she slowly moved her feet, careful not to press down too hard so that she wouldn't feel the tugging at her heels from the bone meal. It was slow and tedious and it took all of her resolve not to freak out. The closer she got, the stronger the pull... each step, threatening to suck her in deeper like the waves within a storm—storms stacked one behind another.

Zigzagging her way, and shifting her body sideways to slip by, she tried to avoid the emaciated limbs that reached out to her.

In waves of mounting horror, she felt that the Corridor didn't want to let her go.

It was like fighting against a strong current pulling her back. She leaned in, and with the last of her strength, she inched forward with outstretched arms. Her fingers clasped the platform, and at last she struggled and clambered on top. Exhausted, she lay on her back gulping in air.

Gradually, her heart rate slowed and she sat up. She wasn't on a platform. She was on a door—a fallen door.

Not more than a few dozen feet from her, a raging torrent of water thundered into a watery world. With amazement, Khia saw how the Corridor adapted itself to the changing conditions. It became wider so that the water could flow more gently.

Khia scrambled onto dry land just before the Corridor narrowed again and the water raged. For miles, she walked along the bank of the raging river. Twice she nearly fell into the strong flowing current.

She had to get to the other side. She just knew that she was on the wrong side of the river. That's when she spotted seven rocks jutting out like the arched spine of a dragon. A way to the other side had presented itself. As long as she didn't slip, she thought, she could make it. She took a running jump and landed on the first slippery stone… and fell. She got up and easily skipped across to the sixth, and fell for the second time on the seventh stone.

*"Only a little farther."* She heard the starting-to-sound-familiar voice that was her companion.

She looked up, not expecting to see anyone, but before her was a stranger, holding a fedora in his hands. "Stitch by stitch we weave our story," he said, his voice gentle. "We so often see only what we want to see. Turn and face your fear, lest you too be entranced by a delusion of your own making."

Khia felt herself drawn by his words. She had to be strong, not get trapped again. She blinked and he was gone. But she wasn't alone. There were souls around her. She saw them. She heard them—some old, some young, some grotesque, some beautiful—chanting their own mantras to unseen gods, and she knew (like you know in a dream) that they were lost... lost in their own visions... lost in their own minds. Some rocked back and forth, and some made bizarre and spastic movements with their arms and hands, endlessly ensnared by whatever they had been taught or learned… their beliefs, truths, or half-truths, which they could not get beyond.

In-between the gaps, Khia found her way back, but she sensed she had been gone for quite some time. Khia looked at him, the man with the fedora.

"Would you like to walk with me?" he asked.

Khia nodded.

"I always ask, but so few accept." He laughed sadly, his face coming within inches of hers, so close that their noses almost touched. "'Tis better you walk with me."

Khia nodded and took his outstretched hand. His hand was cool to the touch and very real. She could feel the blood coursing under his skin.

"'Tis tricky to get out," he said compassionately. "Only a wee ways to go."

"How long have I been here?" she asked, her words slurred and slow, sensing—remembering—that this was not the first time they had spoken.

He looked at her, it seemed, with a bit of sadness on his gentle face. "Funny thing time..." His lips moved, but she could no longer hear what he was saying. He started to fade away from her.

"No. Wait. Please, don't leave me. Don't leave!"

Elusively he slipped away like a fluttering piece of paper in the breeze.

†

Khia took a sharp intake of breath and became aware of the pain in her right knee. She stopped midway.

*"'Tis only a wee ways to go,"* she heard him say.

She'd been genuflecting, making the sign of the cross, her dirty fingers (caked in dried blood) about to touch her lips. She looked down at her knee and saw that she had worn a hole in her jeans, and her knee was bloodied. Her hair was longer, matted, and covered her eyes.

She looked up and saw the man with the fedora waiting for her… as if he had all the time in world. He smiled and looked happy to see her… surprised even.

"You have come back." Once again, he held out his hand to her.

Khia gripped the fellow's hand tightly, not wanting to let go… leaning heavily against him as he half carried, half guided her along the way.

Their steps became like ripples in a pond. The veil about her lifted. It was like passing some invisible threshold.

"Here you be." Fading away, he left her by a pond of calm clear water.

Sometime later Khia awoke, alone. Beside her, folded neatly, were fresh clothes.

The water looked so inviting. Khia slipped off her things and waded into the warm inviting pool.

And she knew, as she peacefully floated in the tranquil pool, that the Corridor had accepted her.

CHAPTER 33

# Pawn

Death's boatman takes no bribe.

~ Horace, (65 BC-8 BC)

On the west side of Africa, just outside of an imaginary two hundred mile demarcation line, a pinched-faced Interpol Officer and his men boarded a freighter named the Iberion. He perused the ship's manifests, and the meticulously penned words written in the Captain's Logs, looking for the tiniest of infractions. His men, positioned like chess pieces on a board, waited for his next move. Finding the excuse he needed, he issued his order and his men scurried like rats through the ship.

Captain Peterson, the captain of the Iberion, remained silent. His papers were in order, but he knew they would find something. This was punishment for being one of the six to help Salix with his grand deception.

The captain, an experienced and authoritative man, was used to giving orders... not taking them. He raised his eyebrows quizzically when he saw two imposing and muscular men, with short-cropped hair, board his ship. The two looked so similar that they could have been twins.

One of them approached and handed the captain a grainy photograph. "Recognize any one?"

The captain shook his head.

A dangerous smile played on the muscular man's face. A subtle nod was the signal for the dramatic escalation in violence that was to be committed that day; he called the other to his side.

The captain of the Iberion hid his growing apprehension, but he stood his ground. This was his ship. They stood on either side of the captain, one a few feet behind his left elbow, the other so close that they almost touched. One leaned in, as if to whisper sweet nothings into his ear. "Look again?"

For the second time, Captain Peterson made his denial.

"One more chance."

Captain Peterson shook his head, thrice denying having known Salix.

But the betrayal was made. The captain had tried to mask his emotions but his involuntary reaction, like an electrical jolt moving up and down his body, gave him away. And what was worse was that he knew that they knew. He tried to step away, but he was boxed in. The control he had believed he possessed evaporated. And a new and very real fear emerged in him. He thought he had understood the risks.

"You've been most helpful." The words were like a sharp knife sinking into soft flesh and slowly twisting.

*Boom. Boom. Boom.*

Captain Peterson was not sure how much time had elapsed. It was as if he were waking from a bad dream. He found himself gripping the cold metal rail, unsure how he had gotten there, and awakened by two rings of a bell. He massaged his stiff hands. Sadly, he looked out to the sea, his mind a roiling turmoil.

By then, the black ship was no more than a black blot on the horizon. The captain felt the wind change—a cold wind from the north. He shivered. He looked up into the heavens; menacing clouds had gathered. He bowed his head and began to pray, something he hadn't done since he was a child. "Our Father who art in Heaven," he prayed for his crew, "Hallowed be thy name," he prayed for those who had helped Salix, "Thy kingdom come…"

*Boom. Boom… BOOM.*

Explosions from deep within rocked the Iberion from bow to stern. The captain of the Iberion looked vacantly out to the sea.

His crew cried out to him, but he didn't hear. His men boarded the lifeboats, but he was lost—lost to them... lost even to himself.

†

Katrina found herself on the shoulder of an endless stretch of a six-lane highway, not sure where she was going. Heavy rigs lumbered past every few seconds, causing a whoosh of wind and the bowing down of overgrown weeds that lined the road.

Katrina had known for a long time that she was a pawn in Ezrulie's game and had thought about running away many times before—but where would she go? She had to be practical.

She'd been fed up with Ezrulie always telling her what to do, when to do it, how to do it... constantly nagging, on and on and on. And then there was crazy Auntie Valerie, who had just shown up out of the blue about six or seven months ago. The two women complemented each other—both off their rockers—but there was something seriously bent with Auntie Val. Sometimes, there was something dead in her eyes that scared her (which was saying a lot because it was an emotion Katrina rarely felt at all; she wasn't even afraid of Cocklebur and Burdock). But it would be stupid not be scared of Auntie Val, because she packed a lot of power and could totally lose it, never knowing what would set her off. One time, tick, tick, tick—nothing. The next? Tick, tick, tick—the big bang.

Unlike Auntie Val, Ezrulie was predictable. Everything Ezrulie did was a means to an end (not to say that it was always easy figuring out what that end was). There were a few things Ezrulie did that didn't make sense, and even a few things that Katrina didn't like and actually found stupid. One thing that bothered Katrina was why she would use her bond with the Sylph to kill an innocent little boy. Yeah, she knew that it was so they could find Khia. But why did they want Khia in the first place? Who was Khia, and for that matter, why did Auntie Val always call *her* Khia? It pissed her off. Auntie Val never called her by her name; it was as if she didn't know who she was. Sometimes she called her Eupheme, mostly she called her Khia, but never ever did she call her by her own name: Katrina.

This frustrating mystery had prompted Katrina to do a little digging. She wanted to find out more about Khia... and Eupheme. After doing a little snooping (which wasn't easy), she had learned that Khia was Valerie's daughter, which would make Khia her cousin. And they were about the same age too. *Cool,* she had thought. One day, she'd like to meet her cousin Khia.

Unable to find any information on Eupheme, Katrina started to believe that she was some fictional character inside Aunt Valerie's head. One day, she asked Ezrulie in a by-the-way sort of way. Mistake. Big mistake. Wow, did Ezrulie ever go ballistic. But Katrina got her answer. Eupheme did in fact exist (or had existed) and it only made her more determined to find out more about her. She had to be very careful though, because Ezrulie would know—Ezrulie had an uncanny ability of knowing things. Katrina smiled to herself. This made her more determined to sneak into Ezrulie's office.

Ezrulie's so called *office* was more of a panic room, and sealed off from the rest of the apartment, it was difficult (but not impossible) to get into. If she didn't want to get caught (and she didn't plan on getting caught), she had to be patient. Trouble was, Ezrulie rarely left the penthouse. Katrina counted the days; for 141 days she waited. Patience. It is a virtue.

So on that rare day, when Katrina was finally alone in the penthouse, she entered the office and logged onto Ezrulie's computer. Her passwords (Katrina rolled her eyes) were so predictable. Searching the files took time. You practically needed a family tree to keep all the names straight in your head—kind of like studying those boring history books with royal lineage: so and so produced an offspring, and so and so had a retarded kid that was destined to be king, and so and so produced the bastard child that was never acknowledged—it seemed to go on and on. Born and died… born and died… it seemed it was just like any family tree (odd names not withstanding), except there were no males in the line… only females. All females.

Katrina's eyes widened. *Oh my God! Ezrulie, Tiamore, and Eupheme were sisters!* Eupheme had died. It wasn't clear when; it could have been a really long time ago or a few months ago. And it wasn't clear how she had died—in battle, murder, or suicide. Katrina shivered.

What had been Ezrulie's role in it? Ezrulie could be so transparent. It was obvious that she hated both her sisters, but what had happened to cause such hatred?

Katrina caught a glimpse of a document that had her name on it, and lost interest in the sisters. She wanted to know more about herself. The file was password protected.

Katrina smiled and typed ••••••••• but it was the wrong password.

*Um,* thought Katrina, and typed •••••• instead. This time the folder opened. But it was empty.

Katrina wanted to hit something, break something, but she didn't. That would only be stupid. Katrina searched a little longer but found no records, no birth certificate—absolutely nothing. She looked up on the monitor and saw Ezrulie with her two bodyguards, Cocklebur and Burdock, driving into the underground parking lot. *That's odd,* thought Katrina. Where was Valerie? Katrina quickly deleted the recent history, logged off, and wiped the computer down. After a quick glance to make sure everything was in its place, she quietly left the office and sat down in the front room playing with her doll. She hated dolls, but it made Ezrulie think she was still a little girl, made her think that she still had control over her. A lesson learned and turned on the teacher. Katrina gave a little smirk.

Traffic whizzed by, and for a moment, Katrina contemplated stepping out. It would be so easy. Who would miss her? She didn't exist.

On the other side of the highway, the glare of bright light from a vehicle carrying panes of glass caught her attention. She liked the way the light bounced off the glass. The vehicle slowed to exit and Katrina decided to follow. It wasn't as if she had a special place to go. Anywhere would do.

Not looking before she crossed, she stepped out onto six lanes of traffic. Cars and large rigs zoomed by. Horns blared, faces in cars looking shocked that anyone would step onto the highway. A trucker, whose rig came within inches of Katrina, yelled, "Are you friggin' crazy?"

Katrina didn't like being called crazy—especially "friggin' crazy". She tapped her thigh, touching the concealed weapon, and thought, *I could use it if I wanted to. I could kill you. But I won't. Not today.* She didn't want to leave a bloody trail; she smiled at the trucker, pressing the knife hard against her skin.

Making it to the other side of the highway, she jumped the ditch and cut through a wasteland to a crumbling sidewalk. She'd lost sight of the vehicle carrying the pretty panes of glass. Katrina looked one way, and then the other.

When she reached the bottom of the street, she saw a homeless guy; she could smell him long before she saw him. He was oblivious to her, his full attention on finding aluminum cans. In his mind, Katrina could hear his mantra as if he'd vocalized it: *5 cents, 5 cents, 5 cents.* Bending down, the stinky old man let out a cry of success and picked up the can, stuffing it in a tattered plastic bag. Katrina stood silently and watched.

He ambled away, never noticing the aluminum cans dropping out of the hole in the bag. He'd most likely find them again tomorrow. Katrina crushed the can with her foot. The light that reflected off the aluminum was like an arrow pointing. They were signs that screamed in her head. *"This way. This Way. THIS WAY!"*

It was a dangerous neighborhood but Katrina wasn't afraid. Having had its heyday generations before, it had fallen on bad times; apathy and a sense of abandonment had seeped into the atmosphere. Katrina could feel it... hear it. Even the police were apprehensive about coming here, especially at night when all the crazies came out. But Katrina was used to crazies.

You never walk alone, not down these streets. Better to have a partner to watch your back and better to act first and ask questions later.

Thinking Katrina was an easy target, a group, brazen and foolish, blocked her way. An overtly confident, tough and foul-mouthed white girl, brazened by a few puffs of a joint that addled her better judgment, started it by trying to push Katrina. They only wanted a little bit of fun, nothing serious, take her money for sure, play with her for a little bit and see how far they could get before the larger more dangerous fish that trawled the streets came to join the fun.

A cold glance from Katrina was like a cold knife that cut into their souls. As if she could hear their thoughts, and before they could count to one, two of the four were on the ground writhing in agony, one with a broken arm, the other with a smashed kneecap. Of the two left standing, one made a move for Katrina's knife, but he was so so slow. A tenth of a second later, it was over.

All gave her a wide berth, and like an angel of death, she passed them by.

Clue by clue, Katrina followed the signs—a light in a storefront window, the flashing red lights of three fire trucks responding to a call, sirens blaring… *this way. This way. THIS WAY.* She stepped over a puddle of water, and in the distance, saw moths flying in concentric circles, attracted to the light over a door. Its soft glow, beckoning. *This way. This way. THIS WAY!*

Katrina turned and walked the other way.

## CHAPTER 34

# Kalise

Neither in nor out, Khia stood within the frame of the opened door. In that moment, she felt somehow trapped... like she could get stuck here. Quickly she stepped out into what once might have been a very large and imposing basilica, with wide arches and pillars supporting its structure. In its time it must have stood proud. Now it was in disrepair. Through a gutting hole in the roof, snow fell lazily from the sky, and lightly blanketed the marble floor. Khia had never seen snow before, and for a moment or two, she lifted her head and let the snowflakes fall on her face.

Suddenly she sensed something.

There, near the back, sitting quietly amongst the old broken pews, she saw ethereal blue light.

"Hello daughter," spoke the light.

"Rainbow Walker? Grey Horse?" Khia's footsteps echoed as she ran towards them.

"Oh it is so good to see you again!" She was about to hug them when she stopped and took a step back. "You are here? Really here? Not some trick being played in my imagination?"

"As real as ethereal can be," laughed Grey Horse.

Their aged physical bodies were far away, lying in their beds as if asleep. Nurse Beverley, their Haitian-born nurse who was on night duty, had entered their room. Her sharp eyes found nothing amiss. Making her way to the window, she looked out from their sixth-floor room and shivered. She recalled the night when the sylph—the creature from hell—had appeared. She closed the drapes. Quietly, she stood over Grey Horse and whispered a silent prayer. Then she turned to Rainbow Walker and gently shifted his comatose body to help relieve the pressure of his bed sores.

"What are you two doing here?" asked Khia.

"Tracking," said Rainbow Walker.

"For what?" asked Khia.

"For you," answered Grey Horse.

"Some journeys," said Rainbow Walker, "can only be taken alone. It is difficult to navigate the in-between places. We are very proud of you, my daughter." He bowed his head to her. "You are shaman, and much much more."

Khia smiled proudly. Rainbow Walker—the powerful and noble father of Nora, one of the most amazing people she had ever met—had called her daughter.

"Come on," said Grey Horse, locking arms with Khia and escorting her out through the front entrance.

Rainbow Walker paused. Curious about something, he looked over his left shoulder. "Hmmm," he said. Bending down, he grasped a handful of snow mixed with dust. The snow melted and the dust fell through his fingers like sand through an hourglass.

A dark shiver flowed through him. He knew that something was coming, and he smiled a smile that only a few non-shamans would understand. His smile widened slowly, as if this was what he had been waiting for all along.

The fog, mist, and snow disappeared… and it was as if Khia had stepped through time itself. They were in a dark forest… surrounded by the contorted shapes of trees, and doors that were all damaged in one way or another.

"Quite the tourist destination," commented Grey Horse dryly.

"What is this place?" asked Khia.

"What once had been," replied Rainbow Walker.

The three traversed the dead forest of trees until they reached the edge of the clearing.

"This is as far as we go," said Grey Horse, and the two ethereal beings disappeared.

†

A gentle undulating plain of lush green grasses seemed to unfold before her. Animals foraged and birds chirped in the trees, but what really caught her attention was the city in the distance. A brilliant multi-tiered city, whose tall buildings looked like multi-colored crystals, hovered in the air like brilliant crowns. It looked like a city suspended in the air, held by magic… powerful magic.

"Uh oh," said Khia, as a large group on horseback cantered into view. Four spherical metal drones flew near her, forcing her back a few steps. The sophisticated machines were in the process of scanning Khia as two riders peeled off from the group and galloped towards her.

Two beautiful ladies, one with short auburn hair and the other with flaming red, approached on horseback. The drones hovered over their shoulders.

"You are in a restricted area," accused one of the ladies rather aggressively, pointing accusingly at her.

"On your knees with your hands behind your head, if you know what's good for you," ordered the other.

Khia placed her hands on her hips, and defiantly stood before them. She'd already been through enough and would not give them any such satisfaction.

A third woman arrived.

She was even more beautiful—if that was even possible. She had long flowing hair and eyes the color of the sky, and was dressed in the finest of riding gear, hand stitched with silver and gold thread.

"I wouldn't talk to her my lady," the young woman with flaming red hair said, as she strategically positioned herself between them. "We'll handle this."

"She could be dangerous," added the other.

"She doesn't look dangerous to me," replied the woman. "Lore and Liz, I love you both, but please stop being so overly protective." Her eyes settled on Khia, assessing her curiously.

"Hello," she said "my name… is Eupheme." She held out her hand in greeting.

"Khia." As their hands touched, Khia felt it tingle with electricity.

"You remind me of someone," the woman said, "yet I know we have never met. You must have come through one of the eastern forest doors. That is, by far, the most difficult way. That is a rare choice these dangerous days. Strange… and the Corridor did not take you?"

The fatigue on Khia's visage told a story that was easy to read.

The woman smiled softly. "You must have had some journey. And you must possess some ability… very rare indeed." The woman's light and gentle laugh seemed to have its own magic. "Welcome to Kalise."

"K-Kalise?" repeated Khia, recognizing the name from Aloysius' stories.

"Yes," answered the woman. "Oh, don't tell me that you got lost and this was accidental."

"No, no, I think this is where I'm supposed to be. I just don't know why."

Eupheme nodded, accepting her answer. "The city before you is my kingdom, a refuge of sorts for wizards, witches, and mages."

The large group on horseback arrived and Khia found herself and her new acquaintances surrounded by a mélange of people, horses, and barking dogs, as well as drones flying chaotically about.

And then Khia saw the majestic bridge... silver and gold in the sunshine. Khia gasped, suddenly realizing what she was seeing. She had been here before in her dreams… the lush green field they were on was the blackened, blasted wasteland or… it would be... and the woman she had seen slumped dead at the tree… was Eupheme.

"It is wise indeed that we arranged to ride on this day, was it not my love?" Eupheme said to the man who jumped off his horse with a swirl of black leather, his sword sparkling in the sunlight and his glorious white wings unfolding.

Eupheme reached out her hand to his, "My love. Meet our new friend. Khia, this is—"

"Norbert!" said Khia, flabbergasted.

Eupheme raised her eyebrows, looking questionably at Norbert.

"Hello." He gave her a warm smile but it was clear that he didn't recognize her. He looked the same, only younger. His eyes were gentler and no scar yet marred his handsome features.

"My guardian angel," said Eupheme. Khia looked at the way Norbert looked at Eupheme, and the way Eupheme looked at Norbert, and knew that he was more than her guardian angel. They were madly, deeply in love.

CHAPTER 35

# The Histories

What you create you must care for.

In Kalise, they light-heartedly referred to the condition as door lag (which is somewhat similar to, but a lot worse, than jet lag). It has to do with the circadian rhythm, which for Khia was set for a twenty-four hour day/night cycle. As every world has a different set of parameters, the physical body can get quite a bit messed up adjusting to not only different time zones but also the local and varied conditions, including variances in air, temperature, and gravity. As a result, Khia slept for almost three days.

Upon awakening, she felt like a new person. She felt renewed and refreshed and as though she had gained a new maturity. Whoever she had been before, a piece of that somewhat naive teenage girl had been left behind in the Corridor. No one goes through the Corridor unaffected.

Khia stood on her balcony, looking out onto the city of Kalise, with its gold and silver bridge in the distance.

†

"Whoa, where do you think you're going?" asked Liz.

"Am I a prisoner here?" asked Khia.

"You are a guest," the red head answered.

"I'm going to explore Kalise," replied Khia, meeting her gaze. "If that's all right with you."

"No, it's not all right with me."

"Join me then."

"I'm coming too," announced Lore, grabbing her coat. The two ladies had taken upon themselves the task of minding Khia.

*Great! My two new babysitters!* Her thoughts turned quickly to how she could ditch them. If she could get away from Norbert and McBride, she could surely get away from these two. But first she'd see what she could learn.

The two were a contrast to each other. Liz was the quieter of the two, but was prepared to take more risks, while Lore admitted to being a little more cautious. They weren't so bad. Both loved adventure and were fiercely loyal to Eupheme. It was Lore who warmed up to her first.

Kalise was a city that was a world unto itself, abound with trees and gardens. Roads and generous walkways spiraled out in all directions. The buildings were made of a rich array of materials. Stone and brick structures from ancient times unwound into buildings that were made of what the locals called *living crystals.* Some were opaque, others translucent, but all were of brilliant hues. It was as if a magic wand had spread pixie dust about, and at almost every turn, there were doors. Khia couldn't help but be enthralled.

"Are we in the Corridor?" asked Khia.

"No. Kalise is not in the Corridor," said Lore. "Kalise is built on what they call a foci point."

"Points where there is a natural convergence between the Corridor and other worlds," explained Liz. "For thousands of years our people have been entrusted with maintaining the integrity of the Corridor of Doors."

"I thought the Corridor protected itself?" asked Khia.

"Yes," replied Lore.

"No," said Liz at the same time.

Liz looked at Lore, and then back to Khia. "It depends how you look at it," she explained. "Like looking at a cup half full or half empty; they're both right."

"What's that?" asked Khia curiously.

"What's what?" asked Lore.

The atmosphere was alive with subtle undercurrents of movement. As Khia started to focus on it, she could see it more clearly and felt it surge through her. She'd noticed it before, but it had taken her a while to figure out how to see it—really see it. It was like it was playing a game with her, fading in and out of existence.

"There," Khia pointed. In the air, a myriad of shivers and ripples flowed in a multitude of directions, emanating from the bridge.

"Wow, you can see that?" There was genuine surprise in Lore's voice.

"Few have that ability," added Liz, with her guard back up. "Who are you?"

"When I was in the Corridor," said Khia, ignoring her question, "there was a place where the doors were open. How do you know when a door should be open or closed?"

"That is not sup—" Liz stopped and looked at Lore.

"You know, what you did was pretty amazing," said Lore, not answering Khia's question. "Do you understand the very difficult thing that you achieved? Since children, we've been going through doors… but were forbidden from using the doors in the forest."

"Why is that?" asked Khia.

"Because it's dangerous," said Lore.

"Some call it a place of in-betweens, or betwixt things; it's really difficult to end up where you want to be."

"Many have become forever lost."

"At its simplest, the Corridor exists as a conduit between worlds. But I supposed you already know that."

Khia nodded.

"Some people believe it was created by the First Born. Like a lot of things, no one really knows… it could be that it has always been."

"How does it work?"

"Physics," replied Liz.

"Magic," replied Lore at the same time.

Khia raised her eyebrows as Liz and Lore started to explain the physics and the magic of the Corridor.

"Forces and fields," said Liz. "It's like a rather large and long vibrating string. Where it touches a three-dimensional plane, doors come into existence."

"Think of it as a big turning hula-hoop," said Lore.

"Of course, there could be many hula-hoops," added Liz. "The ground is our three-dimensional world, and—"

"Or—" jumped in Lore.

"The hula-hoop can touch the ground in many places and on many planes. Therefore it is both a wave and a particle," explained Liz.

Khia looked confused.

"It's a spacey-timey thing," said Liz.

A long and awkward silence ensured, eventually broken by Liz. "Yeah, I'm a lot of fun at parties too."

"You should tell her about The Book while you're at it," offered Lore lightly, "since you're doing such a bang-up job explaining the physics."

Liz leapt in with both feet. "The Book confirms that the Corridor was created by the First Born—"

"The First Born," Lore added, "were a super race that existed a very long time ago. They created the Corridor. The proof is in The Book."

"But there's no proof that The Book ever existed."

"And without the Book there is no proof of the First Born."

"The Book?" asked Khia.

"Doesn't exist," said Lore.

"Does too," countered Liz. "There are myths and documented sightings too. Every now and then it is said to show up. It can never be copied or destroyed."

Khia held back her temptation to tell them what she knew. She had seen The Book and had a pretty good idea where it was.

"And," Lore said, finishing for Liz, "it preserves information."

Khia's spine tingled, "What does that mean?"

"According to legend," said Lore, "the First Born were left with an ethical dilemma. They could not abandon us."

Khia listened with interest, as Liz and Lore gave her the brief history of Kalise.

"You wanted to see Kalise," said Lore. "Can you ride? Best way to see Kalise."

"Yes and yes," answered Khia.

†

Less than an hour later, in the late morning of their second sun, the three riders approached and crossed the bridge that shone silver in the light. Khia froze.

It was, for Khia, like time stood still.

*Khia was standing high upon the bridge that shone golden in the fading sunset. A small breeze caused the earth to swirl and she saw the horde, like a black tide. She saw a blackened, blasted wasteland. The scale of destruction was horrific—the final battle, epic and cataclysmic. On the bridge, fine cracks emerged and stretched from one end to the other. The fault lines deepened and the fissures fanned out like the branches of a tree.*

*Nothing was alive; there was no heartbeat. The remains of the fallen were scattered upon the arid land like leaves. It was eerily quiet. And slumped by a tree, old and gnarled by time, was Eupheme…*

"Are you okay?" asked Lore.

Khia looked at her two companions. "Uh, yeah," she lied.

"Where are you from?" asked Liz curiously.

Khia smiled, "A beautiful world. It's called Earth."

"Never heard of it," said Lore.

CHAPTER 36

# What Lies Beyond

Questions I do ask myself. Like what would I find on a witch's shelf?
I haven't seen it… yet, perhaps one day I shall.
On a crimson blue cloudless daylights' eve. Or better yet on some dark and stormy night.
Things that caught this woman's eye.
Vials and things that come in pairs.
Things that sparkle and perhaps do shine.
A treasure's trove that few behold.
I may yet stare by light of day or dark of night at
these things laid bare on this witch's shelf.

Minutes before its first sun's sunrise, the sky was streaked in pinks and mauves—the start of a new day. It was peaceful and quiet. Khia felt like she was the only one awake. As her steps took her towards the center of Kalise, she was starting to feel like it was the beginning of the end.

Reaching the amphitheater, she found it empty except for a middle-aged, somewhat disheveled woman sweeping the stone steps. Puffs of dust and dirt, lifted by her coarse bristled broom, were taken up by the wind. In the distance, she heard what sounded like approaching thunder.

"Hello," said Khia.

The woman stopped her sweeping and leaned on her broom.

The woman looked so familiar. "Do I know you?" asked Khia.

"Perhaps the better question to ask," the woman answered, "is if I know you."

Convinced that the woman was a bit touched, Khia wanted to walk by, but the woman blocked her path with her broom. "There are, after all, many heres and theres, but only one now," she looked at Khia intently. "Or is there? The here, the now, or the here and now? Which is the one that you seek?"

"The here and now," repeated Khia, but her words came out sounding more betwixt and between a statement and a question, as she tried to make sense of the woman's words.

"That is the right answer," said the woman kindly. "My name is Crydermann." A deep, knowing smile played on the woman's face, as if she were recalling a memory… or perhaps anticipating something yet to come.

Khia blurted out, "You're a witch aren't you?"

"Have you met witches before?" asked Crydermann, her eyes sparkling brightly, and Khia realized that there was nothing touched about her.

"Uh, no," replied Khia, "I don't think so."

"The broom gave it away didn't it," said Crydermann, looking at it. "Oh well, it does have its uses. Now, the more important thing for you and me, as our time—yes time—is running out, is to get you from *here...*" she turned and pointed down towards the center of the amphitheater, "... to *there.*"

Khia looked to where she pointed, but there was nothing there—just an empty stage.

Crydermann held out her hand. The moment Khia touched her hand, it felt like they had not only met before but were actually close friends.

Escorting her down the freshly swept steps, Crydermann spoke words like a spell,

*Voices in the wind.*

*Be here. Be now.*

*Ask. Listen.*

*Show us now.*

*What it is there is to tell?*

Everything turned still and silent, as if she'd stopped time itself.

Khia wrenched her hand from Crydermann. "What did you do?"

On the far side of the dais, what looked like a picture frame appeared. It shimmered a burnish silver and revealed a dark door that filled its frame.

"What lies… beyond that door," said Crydermann to Khia, "… it is for you to find."

Palpable fear rose up in Khia. Crydermann was well aware of how Khia felt, for she could feel it too.

"More answers are promised, but even more questions there will be," said Crydermann, as she absentmindedly fished for something in her pocket. Withdrawing a black key, she placed it in Khia's hands. "Don't be afraid."

*Yeah, easy for her to say; she isn't the one going through the door.*

With every step she took towards the door, it seemed to get bigger, as if it had been waiting for her to swallow her whole. Apprehension grew.

Khia hesitated and glanced back at Crydermann. She didn't have to do this. She could turn and walk away… *run* away.

Before the door's cold blackness, Khia slipped the key into its lock.

*Click.*

The door unlocked.

From behind, Khia felt a hand on her shoulder.

She jumped. Her first thought was that it was Norbert (because he always had the ability to sneak up behind her), but when she turned, it was Eupheme.

"Now what kind of a Doorkeeper would I be if I didn't know what was happening in my own kingdom? Dark passages should not be walked alone."

Without words being exchanged, Crydermann knew she was to stay and guard the door.

Khia and Eupheme faced the open door. It revealed a dim stairway with thirteen stone steps going down.

With each step downward, the sounds grew louder and louder—clinks, clangs, and clanks… and the whooshing sound of air that screamed in violent protest.

At the bottom of the stairs, there was red and orange light that revealed dark brackish smoke, which flowed above and around them. It felt like entering a dragon's lair. A powerful-looking man with sweat-stained muscles stood before them, blocking their way. He wore a thick leather apron and heavy boots, and held steel tongs and a heavy hammer. He squinted at them, shrugged once, and stepped aside… allowing them passage.

It soon became apparent, from the acrid smell of arsenic-laced sand, the heat from the fiery furnaces, and the clang of silvery hammers on hot steel, that they were in a foundry. In the glowing light, lines of metalsmiths, stained with soot and sweat, worked. Hammers rose up and crashed down. Forceful blows released sparks and scales of bright slag that skittered across the floor to rest a time before cooling.

"Welcome to Hell," a workman shouted out pleasantly to Khia and Eupheme. He paused for just a moment in the pounding of the white-blue hot steel that he held against an anvil, in the process of turning it over and over, shaping it into a sword. With a nod of his head, he indicated the direction they were to take.

"Are we really in Hell?" asked Khia.

"No such place," replied Eupheme.

In the gloom, the two of them neared their destination.

They walked towards an empty table and a pile of dirty rags sprawled across a chair. As they got closer, Khia realized that, whatever it was, it was alive... or (more accurately) barely alive. A truly frightful sight, it was what was left of an old and withered man.

The fear within Khia intensified. She didn't have a good feeling about this.

"Wake up," Eupheme said loudly into his ear.

He jerked. "Why do you wake me?" he mumbled, his eyes unfocused. He lashed out with his arm, as if swatting away mosquitoes, but struck nothing.

With difficulty, he sat back up and looked at them till his unsteady and glassy gaze settled on Khia.

"You're here," he said.

He looked beyond frightening. Khia held back her shudders of revulsion. The skin on his face was wrinkled, by lines and scars, and where his mouth should have been was something mechanical. Khia heard an intake of his breath, a wheezing and clunking sound, and realized that the metal was embedded into skin and bone, keeping him alive, more or less... forcing air into his lungs and in turn expelling the tainted air from deep within him, in an endless looping cycle.

"A drink," he demanded.

Eupheme reached for her flask, placed it on the table, and slid it towards him. He took a sip of the fluid and choked. He coughed and spluttered, and wiped his mouth with his sleeve.

Sliding off his chair, he lost his balance. Eupheme kindly reached out to steady him. He lashed out at her; he wanted no womanly help. Khia looked into his bloodshot eyes. He didn't need or want coddling. He was beyond such kindnesses.

"Remember, dear one," Eupheme said gently.

That caused him to pause, his eyes narrowing darkly. And then he laughed, sounding like a dog yelping.

"Who are you?" asked Khia.

"Do you really want to know?" His voice was a hoarse whisper.

Khia nodded.

"So be it." This time, his voice was full of unspoken condescension.

He took a few unsteady steps towards Khia. With a fixed stare, he held out his arms. He was bent and gnarled like an ancient tree. He slowly lifted his left sleeve, revealing his withered arm, which was bent awkwardly where his bones had been broken and badly reset. There were brackish spots where his flesh had not healed. His skin was crisscrossed with scars and burns. Not only age had taken its incessant toll. If you could read the script, his arms recounted an ancient history. And then she saw it. The color was faded by time and barely discernible, but it was there: a tattoo of a red bear, standing on its hind legs, that had once roared defiantly towards the heavens.

Khia recoiled… but she didn't look away.

"Red Bear."

CHAPTER 37

# The Return of Red Bear

"Hey buddy. BUDDY! Wake up!"

"Spray him with the hose, Russell. How come they always sleep under my front porch?"

"Aw damn doesn't he reek. Christ, you'd think they'd stop selling the poisonous stuff to them."

"Is he dead?"

Russell prodded him with his boot, "Nah… he's still alive."

"Get up!"

Struggling to his feet, the figure staggered along his twisted path.

†

"Red Bear. RED BEAR."

"Hrrgg, Leave me… leave me be."

He thought he had hit bottom, but he hadn't even come close. How far he had fallen!

Once he had been young, strong, powerful… and now? Now only snippets of echoes traced his memory.

"Pick him up."

Slung over a hard shoulder like a sack of rotting produce.

"She'll be pleased," said Cocklebur, for they had been hunting this one for a very long time.

"Don't know why she would still want this one. He's past his date. Should have sent us to put him out of his misery," grumbled Burdock.

"Since when are you into mercy killing?" Cocklebur laughed coarsely, finding humor in the situation.

"I'm not," replied Burdock darkly.

"She'll work on him."

"What's left to work on?" responded Burdock.

"She'll find something," Cocklebur's eyes glistened in anticipation. "She always does."

†

Red Bear started mumbling, "Never do we know what things we will unleash when we set things loose."

Khia looked at Eupheme questioningly.

"I feel sorry for you." He pointed his crooked finger, but Khia wasn't sure if it was pointed at Eupheme or at her.

He laughed, but it was a bitter, sad sound. "About as sorry as I feel for myself."

"I didn't think you could feel," responded Khia. She was angry. Why had her path led her here? To him. She was repulsed—she had heard of the things he had done. Nora had shared the tales of his evil and cruelty, which had spawned countless generations of hatred. Why would Eupheme offer him sanctuary?

His eyes went vacant again and he stared at nothing at all.

†

"Wakey-wakey," the female voice yelled into his good ear.

Red Bear's eyes slit open. He groaned from the intense glare of lights and the nausea that flooded through him.

With what little strength he had left, he tried to get to his feet but only managed to fall to his knees.

He tried to remember that he was an old warrior. This gave him some strength, but not enough to face what he knew he had to face. Doused by a sea of misery, it held him down like a multitude of lost souls. His eyes watered.

"You know what I want," she asked.

He remained silent.

She struck him, like she had many times before, and he sank under her heavy blows.

Lying on the cold stone floor, curled up in the fetal position, he received another hard kick that caused another rib to crack.

†

"I can feel. You'd be surprised how much I can feel."

Khia shrugged her shoulders.

"She kept me alive by a thread." His eyes were cloudy orbs. "She wanted what I had created: The Red Bear Clan." His voice was raspy. "She wanted our secrets... magic uncovered. Some things, no matter how hard you try, you never forget." He stared at Khia. "I give the thread to you." His body was racked by a fit of coughing. Not able to keep his head upright, he slumped.

Khia looked doubtfully at Eupheme.

†

For a few more seconds, he neither moved nor said anything. He sucked in air like last breaths and found comfort on the cold floor.

†

Red Bear lifted his head and whispered, "Some can bend forces and fields around themselves. But for a few," he looked at Eupheme with what could have been a smile but was also a scary expression that deepened the web of scars on his face, "the universe will bend itself."

He paused briefly and then continued in a loud, booming voice that startled Khia. "BUT YOU?" He eyed her for a moment, before nodding. "You are going to meet him. Soon."

"Who?" asked Khia.

"Your father."

"What do you mean my father? My father is dead!"

But he was gone again, unable to explain.

"Shit!" Khia screamed in frustration.

†

Burdock and Cocklebur dragged him down the corridor to his prison. Blood streaked the floor.

†

"How long I lay in my dark cage," he said, after some time had passed. "I received a gift. A gift… from her."

Although he didn't move, it was as if he had inched closer to Khia, and whispered in her ear so that only she could hear. "There is more at play."

"What?" asked Khia, trying to piece together his jumbled words.

"She was an angel." He sighed. "An angel of light."

The seconds ticked by. He hadn't moved or breathed in what seemed like minutes. Khia was starting to think he wasn't coming back this time. Maybe he was dead. She leaned closer to him.

"I was on his wall," said Red Bear.

Khia startled back.

"A beam of light… a tiny *sliver* of light. At first I thought he had placed it there to torture me… if they took it away, I would be left with nothing. Long I stared at the light. I followed its curve on its path. I yearned… to feel… its warmth."

†

He could hear whispers in the hallway, and his name being called.

*"Red Bear?"*

†

"She sent me a message." Tears fell from his eyes. "Here too, she keeps her secrets. Her whispers, I could hear. She hates him. Look into the light. She told me… look into the light." He laughed.

If he had not been so old and weak, and the table had not been between them, he would have lunged at Khia in his zeal. *"It is in the light!"*

Khia's breath caught. Fear and wonder surfaced.

"And the closer I looked, the more I saw." His eyes shone, as if he had witnessed the glory of creation.

"It was she who ripped the page from The Book… she who hid it in the light… "

A long silence followed.

He looked at Khia and smiled. Beyond the physical abomination, she saw the warrior within, and his smile wasn't quite as grotesque. He had atoned for all of his sins in more ways than were imaginable. She felt his remorse… for the things he had done. The universe had long ago forgiven him, but he had yet to forgive himself.

He raised his trembling hand. The light dimmed, accentuating the light from the furnaces that spilling onto the arsenic-laced sanded floor… and a strange, unreal quiet seemed to take the place over.

Khia leaned forward and blinked to make sure that what she was seeing was really what she was seeing. Floating in midair was a sliver of light… swirling, twirling, twisting... and then it curved around itself. The light expanded and it was as if, for a fleeting moment, she could see through it like a window. She saw an art gallery. Red Bear on his wall. As the light curved along the corridor, she saw a crumpled piece of paper—a page ripped from The Book.

The paper unfolded, and like butterfly wings, fluttered in the light. She saw colors: aqua and teal... orange wedges of shimmering energy, coming in and out of multiple-dimensional space and time. Khia reached out, but it skirted playfully out of reach.

"You are linked with the Corridor." She heard Red Bear's far-away words drift towards her as the parchment of light fluttered playfully closer. Khia could see the writing, unfamiliar symbols and geometric patterns… and then it wrapped itself around her forearm.

"Oh my!" Khia heard Eupheme declare.

It burned her skin, and she watched as the image on the paper transferred onto the inside of her right forearm. The image, indelibly placed upon her, was a brilliant tattoo. A tattoo of the most complex kind, layers upon layers in which one could seemingly get lost, like a maze of dead ends, with blind alleys and one (and only one) way to the source. The page lifted in the air and turned over, but before it could imprint itself onto Khia's other arm, it disappeared.

"He is coming," Red Bear pronounced. "That is the key that will open the door. Beware that it is the door he seeks."

"He is here." Red Bear collapsed as if he'd turned into rags.

"Khia!" spoke Eupheme urgently, grabbing her hand.

They fled. Leaving Red Bear, they passed furnaces and metalsmiths, taking the last few steps three and four at a time, and exploded out onto the amphitheater where Crydermann waited anxiously.

Charged with color and violent sounds, Crydermann looked relieved to see them and quickly locked the door and slipped the key into her pocket.

Loud explosions shook the ground. *Boom. Boom. Boom.*

Kalise was under attack.

"Khia, you have to leave," said Eupheme. "This is not your place, or your time."

A sad silent look passed between them. It was as if Eupheme knew. They hugged and Eupheme was gone.

CHAPTER 38

# On One's Honor

Like one, that on a lonesome road
Doth walk in fear and dread,
And having once turned round walks on,
And turns no more his head;
Because he knows, a frightful fiend
Doth close behind him tread.

~ Samuel Taylor Coleridge, *The Rime of the Ancient Mariner*

No concrete proof, nothing tangible on the radar screen, nothing on the horizon, and yet a pall of dread hung around his neck. Salix could feel the approaching maelstrom.

Pensively, he took the last drag from his cigarette and threw away the stub, which was caught by the wind and in turn taken by the sea.

"North," said Salix, his decision made.

"Poppy, are you sure?" asked Melalaia.

†

Through swells so deep that the crew—young and seasoned alike—were green with sickness, everything Salix tried, learned from pirates and navel men who had sailed the deep ocean waters, was for naught. Salix slowed the Abraxis.

"We must keep going," Salix's daughter pleaded with her father. "We can't stop." She too felt the nameless thing that stalked them.

"Face the fate," said Salix despondently. "We do no more."

†

A black ship closed the gap between them. Ropes were cast and the two ships were lashed together. Mercenaries toting automatic weapons swarmed onto the Abraxis, forcing the crew onto their knees, their hands behind their heads.

The last to board the Abraxis were two large men so similar that they could have been twins.

"We're in international waters!" cried Melalaia. "You have no jurisdiction here."

She was met with a vicious backhand that threw her to the deck. Blood trickled from her cracked lip.

"What jurisdiction do we need?" he said, looking down on her. "We follow a higher order."

Melalaia watched in disbelief as that man's brother walked towards her father, pointed the gun at him, and without any hesitation pulled the trigger. Twice.

"Noooooooo!" screamed Melalaia. As the two shots rang out, it was as if time slowed. The thump of Salix's body, landing hard on the surface of the deck, brought it back up to speed.

Melalaia tried to scramble to her feet, intent on reaching her father, but was threatened by an automatic weapon, aimed at her left temple. She froze and did the hardest thing possible—nothing. She didn't move. She didn't say a word.

"Mighty Captain Salix," sneered the one who had *not* pulled the trigger.

In agonizing pain, Salix tried to stand, but he could only crawl to a railing, holding onto the lowest rung, both his knees shattered.

He laughed. "Still trying? You possess an unnatural talent for elusiveness. But it appears your luck has run out." He said the words slowly, enjoying every word. He leaned over and rummaged through Salix's shirt pocket, taking the pack of cigarettes. Placing two cigarettes in his mouth, he lit them both. Two tips glowed red. He held one out, but as Salix went to grab it, he withdrew it from the injured man's reach. He laughed, and then offered the cigarette to Salix once more.

Hesitantly, Salix took the cigarette, took a deep drag, and started to cough. Unhurriedly, the large man standing over him inhaled smoke deep into his own lungs and slowly exhaled. From a distance, they could have been mistaken for two long lost friends reminiscing of years gone by.

"You should have died in your God-forsaken homeland. Strange," he mused, "that you survived. Everything taken from you and you make a life for yourself," he said, in such a matter of fact way that he could have been discussing the weather and not his fate. Then his voice changed. "That fine weave, the one that has protected you for so long... has frayed." He snapped the burnt wooden match, which he still held in his hand, into two pieces.

Like a man in front of the firing squad, Salix took another drag from his cigarette.

"You know who I am?" the large man asked.

Salix's eyes betrayed him.

He laughed. "Of course you do." By way of a proper introduction, he said, "Burdock." He nodded towards the other man. "And my brother, Cocklebur." He smiled, showing his perfect white teeth.

Fear for his daughter, fear for his crew, and fear for his ship had given Salix away. He looked down at his shattered knees; blood flowed on the deck. Fortunately, the adrenaline coursing through his body had shut down the pain receptors in his brain. Unfortunately, he felt lightheaded and was having trouble staying focused.

"I do apologize," Burdock said, flicking his cigarette away. "Unlike my brother, I like to ask questions first. You never know what kind of an answer you'll get." He leaned a bit closer. "Where is Norbert?"

Salix didn't answer.

"Fair enough, old man." Burdock cocked his revolver, pressed it against Salix's forehead, and then suddenly started to laugh. "Oh, that would be too easy."

Cocklebur grabbed Melalaia roughly by her hair and dragged her to her feet.

"I'll ask you one more time," said Burdock. "Where is Norbert?"

Salix watched as Cocklebur's fingers found Melalaia's slender neck.

If he talked or not, the outcome would be the same: They would kill his daughter and they would kill him.

"No know where is Norbert," choked Salix. He would not betray his friends.

"I believe you."

As Cocklebur squeezed his fingers around Melalaia's neck, cutting off her air supply, and Burdock aimed his weapon at Salix's temple, an angry figure emerged, exploding out of the ship's hold. With a large cleaver in his hand, Honoré—the Acadian chef, who over a period of twenty-two years was hired and fired by Salix at least six times—bowled over two surprised mercenaries, running towards Burdock and screaming, "Roast in hell!"

Burdock squeezed the trigger, releasing the bullet that sped through the air, hitting Honoré right between the eyes. Chef Honoré hadn't even crashed to the floor before he had the weapon pointed back at Salix and had started to squeeze the trigger…

"Careful my brother," Cocklebur's voice calmly drifted towards him.

Burdock stilled his action.

"You cannot kill him now… or his blood," Cocklebur said, as he released his stranglehold on Melalaia. She crashed to the ground, gasping for air as she crawled away from him.

Burdock hesitated.

"The sacrifice has mended the weave," said Cocklebur.

Burdock grudgingly put away his weapon. Leaning forward, he kissed Salix's cheek and whispered, "Saved by the bell, yet again."

And they left… just like that. The ropes cut, the two vessels separated and the gap between them widened until the black nameless ship veered south and disappeared from view.

But they had left a gift. Explosions deep within the ship caused the Abraxis to shake and shudder.

Thick black smoke streamed out of the holds. She was taking on water and starting to list towards her starboard side. "The lifeboats!" Melalaia screamed to the crew. "Prepare the lifeboats!"

Melalaia ran to her father, who was dragging himself along the deck, in great pain, leaving behind him two bands of blood. "Poppy, what are you doing?"

He pushed his distraught daughter away. "First! *She* is first."

Melalaia understood. Captain Salix would not abandon his ship.

Salix turned his face away.

Tears streamed down Melalaia's face. She felt her father's torment.

CHAPTER 39

# Calling Card

If there is no beginning, then there can be no such thing as an end... just as the difference between any number, say 0 and 1, is both finite and infinite...

Khia and Crydermann skirted the edge of the amphitheater.

Kalise was under siege. From this vantage point, Khia saw the great expanse of the city. Great explosions had carved paths of devastation. Fire and smoke billowed from buildings, and glass from shattered windows was falling from the skyscrapers like hail.

"We can't go that way!" yelled Khia. "It's blocked!"

Crydermann veered around and led them down another way, but that way too was blocked.

Crydermann grabbed Khia's hand.

"Where are we going?" shouted Khia.

"A short cut," said Crydermann as she fished in her pocket and removed a key, leading Khia to another door.

"I can help. I can help stop this," said Khia, not wanting to go through the door.

Turning, Crydermann looked at Khia. "You cannot be here. This is not your time." She looked at Khia's forearm, where the new tattoo had been etched into her skin. "Khia, what will be... has to be."

So Kalise would fall, because it had already fallen—several hundred years before.

Tears sprang into Khia's eyes as she looked upon the city. Eupheme's people were forming lines to defend it. Soldiers, men and women in their silver and gold armor, were headed towards the hidden fields, marching in a matrix of columns and rows and disappearing into the fog; others made their way to the flying ships that were taking off at regular intervals.

"You need to get back to your own time," Crydermann said to her with some urgency.

Khia followed Crydermann through the door that opened onto the bridge. It shone golden in the light.

Khia froze. It was like she was back in her dream, except this was real—happening in real time. She watched as a crack formed on the bridge and expanded outwards. She felt the bridge creak and groan and lose a little of its luster.

An imposing figure in a dark robe collided with Khia, bouncing her back to reality.

"Sorry," he said dismissively, hardly looking at Khia. He stepped to the side, intent on walking around her, but Khia made the same move and the two blocked each other's path. Placing his hands on her shoulders, without a word, he moved her to the side and proceeded on his way.

"Aloysius!" called Khia.

He kept going. Perhaps he hadn't heard. About to call his name again, she watched as he took a few more steps, slowed, and then stopped.

Wizards, he had told her, were supposed to pay attention to details. He turned slowly. His cold youthful eyes settled on Khia. "How is it you know my name?" A look of more than just curiosity crossed his face.

"Khia, come on! We have to go!" Crydermann desperately tried to pull her away.

Despite the great urgency and mayhem happening around them, it was as if everything got put on hold... waiting in suspense.

Khia met the wizard's gaze without flinching… for she had spent too much time ensnared in his tricks and traps.

"Who are you? How is it you know my name?" he repeated. "Have we met before?" The rapid-fire questions didn't give her enough time to answer.

Khia smiled. He didn't know her.

It was, of course, not exactly the same Aloysius that she knew… well it was, but it wasn't. This Aloysius was much younger, more angry, and less controlled. She saw it in his eyes; the wizard that stood before her had a very long and difficult path ahead of him before they would meet again—before he would tell her his story.

He stepped back. Now truly a surprised look came into his eyes.

Seconds of silence passed before Crydermann spoke urgently. "Khia needs to get back to her own time."

"Khia," Aloysius said her name very slowly.

"There's no time," Crydermann said. "She—"

"Be quiet, witch!" he snapped at her. Then he looked back at Khia. "What idiot sent you here?"

An inadvertent, quirky smile played on Khia's lips.

"Answer me!"

Before she could answer, his eyes opened wide as the realization struck him. "Oh no!" He placed a hand over his mouth, as if in pain. "It was me. Now why would I send you here?"

"Perhaps this," Khia said, and showed him the tattoo on her arm.

"Oh my!" He shook his head. "That's quite the calling card." There was an unmistakable hint of awe in his voice.

"Did I… by chance... cut your heel?" He asked this in a way that suggested he hoped that he hadn't… but knew that he had.

Khia nodded.

"Three cuts?" He held up three fingers.

She splayed out her hand

"Five! Ohh... I must have really wanted you here." The look on the wizard's face was one of puzzlement.

He shook his head. "You have to get out of here," he announced. "Now."

"What do you think *I've* been trying to help her do?" replied Crydermann.

"Captain!" called Aloysius to a soldier who was crossing the bridge.

"Yes sir?" He stopped in front of them.

"This girl needs to get to the plains below."

"Right away, sir."

"Priority."

"Yes, sir."

On impulse, Khia hugged Aloysius. Taken aback, he reacted awkwardly... not knowing quite what to do.

"Until we meet again," Aloysius said, not quite sure why he was grinning but knowing that it came from deep within him.

"Take her to the Tin Man," Crydermann said with finality, taking a step back. "He'll escort you." She reached out her hand and stroked Khia's cheek. "You remind me so much of your grandmother."

"You're not coming with me?" asked Khia, from the foot of the steps.

Crydermann picked a tiny thread from her dress and examined it, as if it had been cut. "I am needed elsewhere."

Unexpectedly sad to see Crydermann go, Khia boarded the craft. A soldier pointed to an empty seat, which meant that someone else had been left behind.

With a resounding thump, the door closed. Moments later, she was strapped in and the craft accelerated. Khia felt herself roughly thrust backwards into her seat. Rising vertically above the city, they burst through the turbulent sky. Below, it looked as though an ocean wave of darkening proportion was poised to roll over the city of Kalise.

Reaching the highest point in its vertical ascent, a strange silence came over the ship. In the cabin, Khia heard concerned voices. Then there was a loud explosion. The ship jerked roughly to the left. Her stomach lurched.

Violently, the craft decompressed and there was a rush of heat and then cold. Wildly out of control, twisting in the air, they fell from their dizzying height and crashed.

CHAPTER 40

# Mathyssen

But it is even so; the fallen angel becomes a malignant devil. Yet even that enemy of God and man had friends and associates in his desolation; I am quite alone.

~ *Frankenstein* by Mary Shelley

"My Lord," she bowed to Asmodeous, who appeared before her in holographic form. It was so real that he could have been in the room with her. He was beautiful, tall and dark, and the holder of near absolute power.

"All is as you have planned. On this day history will be rewritten."

"Would you dare betray me?" His eyes flashed at her accusingly.

"My Lord..." She felt uneasy and cleared her throat. "I am your loyal servant."

"There is another," he said.

"I assure you, I am alone," replied Mathyssen.

Looking beyond her as if she wasn't there, Asmodeous pointed out her error, his voice echoing deeply and profoundly in the large chamber. "ALOYSIUS."

Mathyssen spun around. She had sensed no one there. And yet, he had known. He had known... even though Aloysius was but a whisper in the room. How had Aloysius acquired that kind of power? The ability to conceal. For the first time, she wondered if (all those many years ago) she had been wrong. Swivet had told her she was making a mistake by dismissing Aloysius as a stupid sniveling boy with little ability. She remembered the day because of the rarity of the event—so few had the courage, or the audacity, to challenge her.

"Come out of the shadows," demanded Asmodeous, whose very voice drew others to him like pens to paper.

Mathyssen raised her arms and cast light into the darkest recess of the vast chamber, where she detected a small disturbance in the pattern of the air. In no time, her knife left her hand.

Aloysius stepped forward. With only a slight movement of his hand, the dagger lost its velocity, fell to the ground, and came to rest at his feet. The walls, in front of which he had been standing, burst into searing flame.

"Well done," Asmodeous applauded. He was amused, as if it were a very fine sport indeed.

"I am sorry, my Lord," said Mathyssen, kneeling before his image.

"Mathyssen, you know what you must do," said Asmodeous.

"Yes," she replied submissively.

Aloysius arched his eyebrows. He tried to discern what kind of spell Asmodeous had woven around Mathyssen.

Closing the gap between them, Aloysius almost reached Mathyssen before he was roughly restrained by two mechanically powered creatures. His arms were seized and his hands held painfully behind his back.

"That will stop any of the tricks you have up your sleeves," Asmodeous laughed. It was a novelty to see someone try to defy him. It had been such a long time.

"I've been waiting for you," Asmodeous spoke to Aloysius, "and I do hate to be kept waiting—almost as much as I hate secrets."

Aloysius remained silent. He was having difficulty focusing, trying to remember why he had chosen to risk coming here. He knew Asmodeous was powerful, but knowing and being tested were two very different things.

"I would hazard a guess that you have a fine appreciation for things," said Asmodeous.

Aloysius wondered where Asmodeous was going with this.

"After all, don't we all have an appreciation for the finer things in life? Good wine, fine food, beautiful women?" He looked at Mathyssen. "And of course, what would life be without art?"

In a grand and dramatic display, Asmodeous unfolded his dark wings. As he turned, the hologram swirled with black and silver streams of color, expanding outwards. He wrapped Aloysius and Mathyssen in his great wings, and they suddenly found themselves before him, in his Hall of Horrors.

"Surprise!"

Mathyssen looked just as surprised as Aloysius.

"Do you like my artwork?" he asked.

Thousands and thousands of frames lined his walls. One by one, his artwork was illuminated. Within the frames were not paintings by the masters, but wretched living beings, tortured figures—some barely recognizable—of males, females, and creatures that one's imagination could not conjure up in an eon, all trapped in frames for Asmodeous' pleasure.

"Join me Aloysius."

"No," Aloysius said firmly.

Asmodeous made his pronouncement. "Then your presence shall grace these halls. But first, I want you to see. Mathyssen!" he yelled. "Unlock me from my vault."

Calling upon deep strong magic, Mathyssen began her incantation. Magic that had fluctuated in smooth and regular oscillations from the very beginning of time converged in this single moment, when the boundaries between worlds were at their thinnest. A thin line of silver appeared, widening into a narrow rectangle. Aloysius knew immediately what it was that she was conjuring.

Constrained by Asmodeous' servants, Aloysius continued to struggle. He needed to stop Mathyssen before it was too late. "Mathyssen!" he shouted. "You can't!" But she didn't hear.

Aloysius began a counter spell. Words chipped away not at the door that she was bringing into existence, which would release Asmodeous, but at the carefully crafted veil of lies and deceit that Asmodeous had woven about her. Over time, and with great pleasure and patience, Asmodeous had imperceptibly gotten inside Mathyssen's mind. He played upon her vulnerabilities—always in her dreams, haunting them, his voice, deep and alluring. She'd never realized that he'd taken possession of her.

Aloysius heard a slight stumble in her words and redoubled his efforts.

With a final crack, the door materialized. Slowly it began to open.

Asmodeous' insatiable eyes settled on Mathyssen. "You have done well. You shall be rewarded." Mathyssen was of tall stature, but looked small next to him.

Asmodeous walked through. In the light of Kalise, he stood more beautiful and more powerful than ever before.

Freedom.

Walking to the great windows that lined the room, he spread his black wings to their greatest width. And he rejoiced. Glass cracked around him. He was free! His planning was impeccable. On the plains below, partially hidden under a blanket of cloud, a thin, jagged black line was forming. The city was ablaze. What he had long envisioned had come to its fruition. He—their new sovereign—had arrived. He would control Kalise.

Two down and one more to go.

†

Aloysius' eyes met Mathyssen. The fabric frayed, snapped, and recoiled… and the weave around her was dispelled.

Mathyssen wavered. As if coming out of a disturbed sleep, she was unsure what was taking place around her. A plethora of emotions crossed Mathyssen's face, and then a look of realization as to what she had unleashed… and shame.

Asmodeous was busy admiring the culmination of his long awaited plans, basking in his glory, and enjoying his freedom and the fall of Kalise, when their combined wrath fell upon him. Mathyssen and Aloysius worked together and with successive magical attacks pulled him spiraling back towards them.

"We can't stop him! Even with our combined power, he's too strong," lamented Mathyssen. "One of us needs to get out of here alive. Our deaths or entrapment will not solve anything. Aloysius! Go. Get out. I will destroy the door!"

But Aloysius ran towards a wall, intent on releasing at least some of the tortured souls within Asmodeous' artwork.

"You fool! There is no time!" screamed Mathyssen.

Asmodeous rose up in anger.

"Aloysius!" she called in desperation. "I can't… hold him… much longer!"

Dark wings—made black by a choice Asmodeous had made long ago—unfurled and beat powerfully against the air that seemed to want to hold him against his will. His face red with fury, he gathered up his great power.

Mathyssen struck back. "Aloysius!" she called once more.

In a loud strong voice, Aloysius invoked a spell that ricocheted down the hall. Great flashes pierced the dark recesses, reflected like a million mirrors shattering. From far away, the vibrations were heard and felt. Living shapes that had been trapped in their individual frames fell to the ground. Not looking back, Aloysius ran and dove through the door.

It vanished from sight.

Not sure if Aloysius had made it through the portal, Mathyssen braced herself for what was to come. She hoped it would be quick.

CHAPTER 41

# Mother's Day

When it comes your time to die, be not like those whose hearts are so filled with fear of death that they weep and beg for a little more time… Sing your death song and die like a hero-warrior going home.

~ Chief Tecumseh, 1768-1813

Floating above the crash site, Khia looked down and saw her body sprawled awkwardly, but still securely strapped into the aircraft. It was strange—strange to see herself like this: her head tilted to one side, her face pale and mask-like, and bright red blood gushing from a nasty looking wound on her thigh.

If she was dead, wasn't she supposed to go into the light or something? But just like a ghost not wanting to let go, Khia remained close to her physical body.

She didn't want to be dead.

She kept staring at herself. Seconds ticked by—how many, she didn't know… then she saw her physical body shudder and her chest slowly start to rise... then it fell and rose again.

She was alive! Unconscious, but alive. So what was happening to her? Why was she having an out-of-body experience? Why couldn't she return to her body, if she wasn't dead? Her head felt fuzzy; it was so hard to think. She tried to trace her thoughts back to what had happened.

She had been in Kalise… The battle… the battle had begun; Kalise would fall... and Aloysius... Aloysius was… she had been on an airship… there had been an accident…

Hearing moans and pleas for help, Khia's ethereal self became more aware of her surroundings, and the destruction around her. It was like she was in the dead center of an apocalyptic film. Crushed metal and debris was everywhere. The ship had fallen from the sky. Large sheaths of metal cladding had been ripped from the airship's sides, but the malleable metal, like protective ribs, had absorbed much of the impact, shielding its living cargo.

Khia looked at the blood pooling. If someone didn't stop the bleeding, she would die.

Help was in fact on its way. With fascination, she watched as tiny lightweight mechanical creatures emerged from crevices of the ship: medical bots. Compact mechanical creatures, with a complex quantum-muon programming that prompted them to save biological life, swarmed the area. Moving over the ship's mangled remains, they spread out. Prioritizing their work, some extinguished fires while others began the task of assessing and assisting the living. Efficiently they went about their business: helping the survivors, counting heartbeats, measuring blood pressures, inserting sterilized needles into flesh while chirping in a high-frequency language, communicating to each other.

One of the mechanical bots reached Khia's unconscious body. Her ethereal self watched in some fascination as it skittered over her. She felt a ticklish sensation as it checked her vitals. It pricked her arm and injected her with something. Khia felt a strong pull to return to her physical body. And that's when she saw the light.

A figure wrapped in golden light, as beautiful as an angel, descended from above and floated towards her.

Then a cold chill washed over her.

This was no angel. What had looked like a golden halo was in fact the residual energy from a portal that had been forced opened and had cast its iridescent glow.

"Mother!"

More than anything in the world, Khia wanted to go to her mother, hug her, and tell her how much she missed her... tell her how much she loved her. She wanted to go back to a place where her mother had been loving, caring, and… sane.

But no matter how much she wished it, she knew, looking into her mother's cold, lifeless eyes, that there was no going back to how things used to be. Her mother was crazy and intended to harm her.

"Mother please," Khia begged as she inched her way back. "You don't have to do this."

Dread enveloped Khia. She didn't want to fight her own mother, but what choice did she have? She didn't want to die.

She glanced back at her physical body, to check that she was in fact still alive. The mechanical bot had successfully stopped the bleeding, a liquid salvo had been sprayed over the wound, and it started to stitch her leg with what looked like a silver needle and golden thread.

Khia knew it wasn't the time to be sentimental, but she had to try. "Mother, do you remember Devon?"

Her mother paused, as if searching for memories buried deep within her. "Devon." Her eyes glassed over as she stared at Khia. "He is lost to me. He's coming… he is coming for you. You're going to need to fight him and… and I won't let you."

Who was she talking about? What did she mean? Red Bear's words came to mind: "*You are going to meet him soon.*" But he had been talking about her father. Hadn't he?

Did her mother still possess a mote of sanity? Seizing on a thread, Khia took a few tentative steps towards her.

Or not. She recognized her mother's expression and quickly retreated a few steps. Her mother's strong maternal urge may have been to protect her daughter, but it was warped and fixated on killing her instead.

Casually, Valerie withdrew two metal pins from her hair. Her long blonde hair unraveled and fell about her shoulders. Long sinuous ropes and dark twisted shapes of mist swirled around her like a black aura.

Khia felt the coldness. Black forms materialized. Seven vultures fixed their red eyes on her.

Khia's eyes widened. So... she *had* seen her mother in Rome, and as for the vultures, they had evolved since the last time she had fought them. They were bigger, more threatening, and now had feather tips that were razor sharp.

"It would have been so much easier for you, if I had killed you then," her mother said indifferently, as the vultures took to the air.

A tightening gyre of vultures caused Khia's heart to beat faster. Her mind raced, trying to think of ways she could defend herself. The vultures swooped upon her.

Khia twisted in the air and kicked and punched, swerved and dodged. She felt her arm burn as one of the vulture's wings grazed her skin. Dodging beaks, talons, and razor-sharp feathers, Khia needed a weapon. Anxiously, she searched for something she could use—anything to defend herself. She spotted a large metal rod. It was from the craft, and near to her physical body. Running and rolling towards it, she drew it up like a sword from a stone. The rod became ethereal as she drew it towards herself. Vultures crumpled under her blows, but they only turned into dark vapor, reformed, and then returned.

Valerie screamed in fury. She seemed to grow in stature and energy crackled about her. She raised her hand, and with deadly accuracy, threw one of her razor sharp hairpins at Khia.

For a split second, it was as if Khia were back in the cave with Nora… and she could hear Nora's words aloud: "*A true warrior if ever I saw one.*"

The air around her felt thick and heavy. Her entire focus was on the sharp blade coming fast towards her. And then it seemed to slow… and then everything sped back up to normal time. Quicker than she thought possible, Khia bent her upper torso sideways and the blade narrowly missed her. Turning, everything became reversed. The sharp object moved passed her, and in one fluid motion, Khia extended her hand and gripped the hairpin, drawing it from the air.

Khia hesitated. Sadness overwhelmed her. What was she doing? She looked at her mother's weapon, uniquely crafted, sharp, and deadly. The metal grew hot in her hand and she could feel its hatred.

The weapon, like Norbert's sword, turned into liquid metal and returned to its mistress's hand.

She resisted the pull of her ethereal self wanting to return to her physical body. She needed to fight, but how could she fight this alone? Her pendant started to glow.

*"Khiaaaa. Khiaaaa. Khiaaaa."*

Out of nowhere, the black bird flew over Khia, its dark wings spanning the sky. Then she heard the rumbling growl of Timothea's other totem animal and knew that, this time, the black bird had brought its mate.

Khia instinctively crouched down as a whirl of flowing silver leapt up and over her. The silver wolf jumped towards the largest of the vultures, snatching it from the air. With its strong jaw it broke the vulture's neck. Khia heard the sickening snap. It had had no time to turn into black vapor. It was dead. And now there were six.

The sense of overwhelming hope engulfed Khia. With renewed strength, she fought on. She wasn't alone. Her makeshift weapon, so light in her hands, seemed to fight for her. She maimed another one of her mother's birds, but was unable to kill as it turned into black vapor.

The vultures launched themselves at the silver wolf and the screeching black bird, leaving mother and daughter alone.

"Just you and me." Valerie made a subtle motion with her hand, and the space between them grew colder. "Just as it should be." The ground cracked and fissures fanned out.

Khia felt like she was on a growing sheet of ice, but she resolved herself. She rose up, ready to face and fight her mother. If it was to be her death, so be it. Nora had said that she was a warrior, and like a warrior, she would not go meekly. She felt surprisingly calm, aware of everything around her: the silver wolf, the black bird, the vultures that circled above… and the narrowing gap between her and her mother.

Instinctively, Khia was able to still the coldness, combating it with warmth, dissipating it and melding the surface smooth again.

Like a finely choreographed dance, Khia and Valerie circled each other. Her mother attacked and Khia evaded, round and round blows from both of them were blocked and parried with ever-increasing speed and fury. Finally, one of Valerie's moves found one of Khia's vulnerabilities and she was sent sprawling backwards, spinning to the ground into an anomalous heap. Momentarily winded, Khia looked over at her physical self. Her physical body convulsed. The tiny medical bot, not knowing what was happening, started to reassess her.

Khia staggered to her feet, and then wavered.

The medical bot injected something into her body with a needle. Feeling woozy, Khia struggled not to go back into her physical body. She watched as the bot staunched the flow of blood, trying to figure out what was happening.

Khia opened her mouth to try to speak, but no words came out. Exhausted, she fell to one knee and bowed her head.

"Who's going to save you now?" Valerie sneered.

## CHAPTER 42

# It is Time

In the chilled frosted air
a warrior walks
on a faraway shore.

"We are," replied Rainbow Walker.

Khia lifted her head.

"Rainbow Walker! Grey Horse!" cried Khia with relief.

"Sorry we're late, kiddo," said Grey Horse. "It took us a little longer than we would have liked to break into this place."

"But we're here now and that's what counts." Assessing the situation, Rainbow Walker's eyes glistened. His tone changed as he peered into the fog. "Grey Horse. Take Khia to the Tin Man. Go."

Grey Horse looked at him questioningly.

"And do not return," said Rainbow Walker. "Do you understand?"

"Yes," grumbled Grey Horse, "but I don't have to like it."

Rainbow Walker stepped into the fog. Silently, Khia and Grey Horse watched as his ethereal body merged with the fog and he disappeared.

"Ohhhhhhh..." Khia felt her ethereal self being pulled back into her physical body. It happened quickly, like she was caught in a whirlpool and dragged down.

"Ow," she moaned. Pain flooded through her. Everything hurt. She swatted the medical bot away from her. Righting itself, it skittered away. Willing her body into action, Khia unclamped her restraining device and clamored over obstructions and debris towards Grey Horse, who waited at the edge of the craft to lead her away.

Grey Horse, in ethereal form, was young and strong with two good legs. Hobbling in pain, she followed as best she could.

Khia heard her mother scream.

The silver wolf howled and the black bird screeched. The black bird, in a magnificent display, flew above the vultures and seized one behind the neck, driving it to the ground. The wolf leapt into the air and closed its maw around another.

"We must move faster," said Grey Horse, and he transformed from a man into his namesake. Khia pulled herself onto his back and they galloped across the plain, making their way across the surreal terrain to where, she hoped, Barwick would be waiting.

Setting dust clouds free with each strike of his hoofs, they thundered along until they entered the dead forest. They weaved in and out, over and under huge desolate, gnarled trees and limbs that reached out towards them.

Swarming like wasps out of the hundreds of doors that littered the landscape were creatures and beasts from other realms, marching towards Kalise.

This way and that, Grey Horse picked a tangled path to a clearing that led to the door that would take her home. A figure waited, shining like a beacon. Khia's hope rose, but in that split second of inattention, she cried out in pain. A wake of vultures swooped down and one wing, like a sharp knife, had drawn blood.

So quickly that she had no time to react, Grey Horse stumbled and she was flung from his back. Landing hard, she crashed to the ground. Rolling, she avoided the horse's hoofs as he reared up and stomped on a vulture.

In a swirling silver light, the Tin Man appeared at her side and offered Khia his hand. "My Lady." His voice, despite the servos and electrically generated speech pattern, sounded noble. "Your portal awaits."

Khia grasped his hand. Together they walked into the light.

†

The thick fog made it sound like Valerie's voice was coming from all around. "How endearing. You've come to save Khia," she taunted. "But beware your back old man."

Rainbow Walker made no direct reply but started his warrior's chant, *"Hawn gnebig, aabnang, we baashid."*

What looked like fog took form as the Great White Bear. Rainbow Walker greeted his totem animal as it rose up to its immense height and roared.

Screaming, Valerie threw one of her poisonous hairpins. Straight and true, it flew and pierced the shoulder of the Great Bear, remaining there like a jeweled broach. The great Bear growled in fury, as a trickle of blood seeped from the wound.

†

A silent figure plied a darkened hallway. She had to be careful; she had no magic of her own—just her wit and cunning. She would make Ezrulie proud. She wouldn't fail—not this time. She knew all too well the price of failure.

Entering the nursing home had been easy, almost too easy, which had made her ever more vigilant. For this occasion, she had so wanted to wear her nun's habit (for she was so fond of it and it had served her well), but such a garment was suited to other places. A nurse's attire, she had decided, would be much more appropriate. And it would have to be white... she so loved white. It was so pure and clean.

This night she would provide a mercy. She prided herself on being quiet and quick. Her victims rarely suffered; few of them ever even knew as she sent them into eternal sleep.

Her white shoes silent, she walked the sixth floor corridor nearing room 616B.

†

Rainbow Walker had fought many battles and little fazed him. He'd seen much and took little for granted. But this was different; it was Valerie,

Khia's mother, and this saddened him to no end. His ethereal self whirled about like a swirl of light, avoiding the projectiles aimed at him.

And, then all went quiet… as if time had stilled.

Catching one of the projectiles, Rainbow Walker looked at it closely. Razor sharp; finely crafted. Near the tip there was a tiny reservoir (barely visible to the human eye) where he detected the unmistakable aroma of poison.

*"Be kaa,"* he said aloud.

Obeying his command, the air and the wind rose up.

†

She looked down at the old man lying motionless in bed.

*Beep. Beep. Beep.*

So sallow and waxy.

Leaning over, she casually switched off the machines that played out a rhythmic beat.

Without rushing, she opened a small satchel and withdrew a needle and a vial. Slowly, she filled the needle with a dark fluid. She smiled as she stuck the needle into his thin atrophied arm and hit a vein. She pressed the plunger until its contents flowed into the comatose figure. She waited and watched as his chest rose… and fell… rose… and fell…

A hint of a smile played on her lips. A little memento to mark the occasion, she thought. She took the knife that she kept concealed… and that was her undoing.

†

Ethereal Rainbow Walker fell to one knee. A look that at first was surprise was quickly replaced with resigned humor, and he laughed.

"No more time my friend," he spoke to his totem animal. "But one last chance to be fearless."

He felt the bonds releasing him: the bond from the ethereal world and the bond with his totem animal, the Great White Bear.

He squared himself to face her.

†

Back in the rainy gray world of the Nephalim, with the thunder rumbling and the lightning flashing, Khia found herself clasping her pendant tightly. It felt so cold to her touch.

And then she felt the black stone move... of its own volition.

†

Ethereal Rainbow Walker ripped his pendant from its cord. It was identical to the one Khia held in her hand. It too had been a gift from Timothea—one he had carried with him for a lifetime.

Stumbling, the pendant fell from his grasp. The black stone, held by a bear claw clasp, moved of its own volition and jumped free. The black stone circled Rainbow Walker and rolled out in expanding circles.

Valerie watched as if mesmerized. And then the stone rolled to a stop near the fading Great White Bear.

The Great White Bear looked at it curiously.

Aware of what this could do, Valerie screamed, "No!" Then she turned and ran.

The Great White Bear, Rainbow Walker's totem animal, rose up with an angry roar… and brought his paw down square upon the black stone.

There was a loud crack and the world that they were in exploded into a huge vortex.

†

She never heard it coming, but the last thing she felt was the large hand on her neck. She felt the squeeze… and then the snap.

The silence in the room spoke to him… as did the darkness—the ethereal glow gone.

In vigil, Grey Horse bowed his head; he would miss his friend. "Dream well, warrior."

With quiet determination, he wheeled himself out of the room and into the dark corridor of the sixth floor. He did not look back.

Unnoticed, Grey Horse passed Nurse Beverly. Strange that her Haitian genes, normally acutely aware of her surroundings, were unaware of his passing. Whistling a soft lullaby, she got up to check on her patients. She didn't hear the sound of the elevator doors swish open, nor see the grainy image on the monitors of the sad and tired old Indian by the name of Grey Horse, in his wheelchair, leaving by the front door.

At the same time that a silver and gold sports car pulled up in the circle like a swirl of light, Nurse Beverly was walking down the dimly lit corridor approaching room 616B. And that's where she found him. Rainbow Walker was dead.

Bowing her head in silent prayer, she spotted white nursing shoes sticking out from under Grey Horse's empty bed… and there she found the contorted body of Sister Clair.

In the circle, at the front entrance, a lithe feminine figure stepped out of the silver and gold car and calmly walked towards Grey Horse. Effortlessly, she picked up the one-legged man in her arms and carried him to her car, placing him gently in the passenger seat. With no words exchanged, they drove away in a blur of silver and gold.

Left behind was the wheelchair. Ever so slowly, it gained velocity as it rolled down the ramp towards the curb, where it toppled over—its wheel turning round and round and round… like the Wheel of Time.

# Epilogue

A stream of water followed Khia from the world of the Nephalim onto the desert floor.

She looked back. Barwick stood behind her at the portal door. Behind him, the night sky crackled and lightning flashed across the sky.

"Thank you," said Khia.

"Most assuredly," he answered. His eyes, ever so slightly dilated, focused on her. "It has been a pleasure to serve you Khia Aleyne Ashworth."

She jumped from the portal and landed on the desert sand.

Swiveling back and forth, he raised his arm, and like a compass, pointed her to the east with a slight six degree adjustment. "It is in that direction that you must go. No more than a few miles."

"Barwick," Khia said.

"Yes?" His head tilted ever so slightly to the side.

"You are a true knight."

His silver eyes unblinkingly looked at her, and then he bowed.

She heard the gyros underneath his metal skin, whirring, making slight adjustments. "Until we meet again."

Khia stood silent and still. She waited until the stream of water trickled to a stop and the portal faded away.

Silently, she walked down the hill, pushing down loads of sand in front of her. She felt sad and excited all at the same time. Sad to leave, yet excited to be back. So much had happened. She couldn't wait to tell Norbert. And then she wondered how long she'd been away. She had spent thirteen days in Kalise and had no clear sense of how much time she'd been in the Corridor.

As she kept her eye on the direction of the sun, she spotted something in the distance. It looked, at first, like a small black dot. But as it drew closer and closer… it got bigger and bigger and seemed to transform into a black cloaked figure on horseback, riding through the last vestiges of the storm, sand kicking from the hoofs of his charger as the space between them grew smaller.

Khia shivered.

Flapping in the wind, his black garment appeared as menacing as a pirate's flag on an approaching ship on the open sea.

As his figure cast its shadow on the sand… she took her stance.

Gripping her knife, Khia started to count… one, two, three… She assessed the closing distance between them… four, five... She could see his muscular physique.

At six she could see his eyes as he bore down on her.

At seven…

Here ends

seVens † sIXes

Printed in Canada